PALAWAN STORY

■ A NOVEL

by

Caroline Vu

Deux Voiliers Publishing, Aylmer, Quebec

First Edition

Published in Canada by Deux Voiliers Publishing, Aylmer, Quebec.

www.deuxvoilierspublishing.com

Library and Archives Canada Cataloguing in Publication

Vu, Caroline, 1959-, author
        Palawan story : a novel / by Caroline Vu.

Issued in print and electronic formats.
        ISBN 978-1-928049-01-2 (pbk.).--ISBN 978-1-928049-02-9
        (epub).--
        ISBN 978-1-928049-05-0 (kindle)

        I. Title.

PS8643.U2P34 2014   C813'.6   C2014-902819-9
                                             C2014-902820-2

Cover Design - Ian Thomas Shaw

Cover Photograph – Ivan Tankushev

Red Tuque Books distributes Palawan Story in Canada. Please place your Canadian independent bookstore and library orders with RTB at www.redtuquebooks.ca

FOR ALL THOSE LUCKY ENOUGH
TO SET FOOT IN PALAWAN,
THIS IS YOUR STORY.

PROLOGUE

The beach behind the old man's house stretched far. A half moon shed light on a bobbing boat. Already it looked unsafe. For an instant my mind hesitated. But in the excitement of the moment, my feet kept running. When the captain beckoned impatiently to me, I had no choice but to splash through the shallows and be pulled over the railing. The trip was already paid for. I didn't even know how to swim.

I sat squeezed between strangers at the end of the boat. My bag served as a bumpy pillow. Pressed against my breasts, my straw hat protected me from the wind. Someone's tuneless singing drove me mad. But since the words sounded familiar, they somehow gave comfort. "Go to sleep. Your dreams are still normal. Go to sleep, your dreams are still normal. . . ."

Sadness overwhelmed me but no tears flowed to mark the event. I felt exhausted, yet sleep refused to come. I strained my eyes searching for a familiar silhouette on the beach. But she had already left.

"What happened on the boat?" they ask. "What really happened?" They always press me to remember. I would like to tell them fanciful stories but my mouth aches from dryness. I am thirsty. We are all thirsty. It is past midnight and I feel tired. Yet they clamour for more stories. "We drifted for days on the boat," I say.

"That's it? That can't be all!" they insist. And maybe that wasn't all . . .

Vietnam

One

Nobody knew how the war started, but we all saw how it finished on television. Nobody remembered when the war began, but we all watched it fizzle out on April 30, 1975. When the last helicopter took our fear and hope into the clouds, we knew the war was over. Saigon had fallen to Communist hands. This event took no one by surprise.

"And any generals worthy of two stars already walk the streets of America!" I blurted out excitedly.

"Hey, Kim, who told you such nonsense?" Mother demanded, cutting my talk in midsentence. It was a hot, windless day and my mother's stern looks added sweat to my already dripping forehead. Watching frantic people dashing for the last American helicopter out of Saigon made us feverish. We jostled each other to better catch the scene unfolding on television. The chop-chopping sound of the helicopters electrified our feet. We felt like running too. We yearned to join this human mass with their cloth sacks *and straw hats* in hand. Imagine people not forgetting their hats in their flight to freedom. And these weren't just any hats. They were the stiff, conical ones taking up all the space denied those still left behind. My mother owned one of those hats years ago, but these days she preferred tossing her hair in the wind. "Freer that way," she said. Besides, she hardly needed protection from the sun. Her skin already glowed in darkness—not the ugly, wrinkled darkness of peasant women, but a brilliant, diluted-jasmine-tea colour to go with her perfectly white teeth.

My father! Could that strange-looking figure on television be my father? My mother's lack of reaction erased my hopes. Yet I recognized my father. He fought for the last spot on that last helicopter out of Saigon. He pushed an older woman to the side and used her fallen knees as stepping-stones. At the last second, he threw his suitcase away to unburden himself of the weight. Then, for a few minutes, he dangled in the air with only his hands grasping the helicopter's ledge. The wind dislodged his few remaining strands of hair. They flopped over his left eye, leaving him partially blind. His mouth gaped, letting forth inaudible sounds. When we thought he'd surely fall, he succeeded in climbing up. The door opened for him, a big American hand reached out from inside, and in an instant he disappeared from view. The last person to be rescued turned out to be my father. And I saw that close-up on television. Yet my mother acted as if this man's acrobatic feat deserved no more than a "tsk, tsk."

"Did you see our father on television?" I asked Mai and Thu, my two younger sisters. "Are you crazy?" Mai barked, while Thu simply shrugged her shoulders. I should've known they wouldn't remember him. They have forgotten the shape of his body, the angle of his eyes, the texture of his hair. But I remembered the hunched back, the crossed eyes, and the wispy hair that used to shield his balding head. How many other hunchbacks could also claim baldness and crossed eyes! Yes, that nimble hunchback on television fathered me.

"Must be your malaria acting up again," Mai said.

"What malaria? I don't have malaria!" I argued.

"You do too! Grandmother said you got it as a baby. The mosquito bit you, made your head spin and put all these crazy thoughts in your brain. That's why you're always seeing weird things!" Mai cried.

"My head is not spinning! And I did see Father on television!" I protested.

"Be quiet, you two! Who gave you permission to talk about your father?" demanded my mother.

My father had disappeared two years ago without warning. We never noticed his absence until dinnertime. Neither my maternal grandmother nor my mother could remember what he did that day. When he failed to return for supper, we thought it uncharacteristic of him. So we waited and waited.

2

But my mother lacked the patience for a long, drawn-out wait. After four days without news, she put his bowl and chopsticks away. "Your father has left us," she said simply. Left us for what? Another woman? The Revolutionary Army? Did the Communists kill him? Did they kidnap him? My mother never went into details. She simply gave his clothes away to the neighbours. Only my youngest sister, Thu, reacted to this act of charity.

"Why are you giving his clothes away if he is not dead?" Thu wailed. She must have cried for an hour or more. I remember the terror I felt upon hearing Thu's question. Her words gave shape to a fear still vague in my heart. But I also worried about my mother's reaction to Thu's outburst. This second fear seemed more immediate, more real. I could smell it in my fetid breath. Nobody in this household ever questioned my mother. Nobody ever accused her. And I knew Thu had broken an unspoken rule with her wailing.

Many unspoken laws ruled our lives. The most important of these was to mind our own business—don't ask and don't tell. We felt compelled to leave our unhappiness in its rightful place, buried in our heart. To disturb adults with our childish sufferings meant wasting their precious time. I knew these rules too well, but unfortunately, little Thu lacked expertise in this game.

When Thu's crying would not stop, my mother ordered me to shut her up. I obligingly took my youngest sister in my arms, rocking her back and forth. But the more I tried talking sense to her, the louder she screamed. My other sister, Mai, suggested we give her our mother's usual treatment instead. That would be a slap in the face. It always worked. But I resisted and Thu finally fell asleep in my lap.

We understood from then on that we could no longer talk about our father. His absence never wrinkled my mother's flawless complexion. She never bothered calling the police. When people asked about my father, my mother simply said, "He went to Saigon for a better job." Most of the time I swallowed whole my mother's line, "Your father left us." But sometimes I imagined him captured by the Communist army or dying a heroic soldier in a battle somewhere. To these ideas, my mother asked, "Who told you such nonsense?"

The hunchback was my father's curse but also his lifejacket. Fortunately his deformity spared him the draft and the sorrows of battlefield. Yet in my longing for my father, I could at least accord him the honour of a fallen soldier. In my mother's busy world, my father had already ceased to exist. Four days after his departure, he became a nobody in her eyes.

"Who told you such nonsense?" my mother always demanded. Actually it wasn't a question—more like a warning for us to stop our foolish talk. My mother never expected an answer to her query. She expected silence instead. "Kim, who told you that nonsense about important generals already walking the streets of America?" Mother asked again. That nonsense came from my teacher, I almost replied, but stopped in time. One unwanted remark seemed enough. No need to take a chance with another one. Yet despite my silence, or rather because of it, my mother grunted, obviously not pleased with my behaviour. "Stop repeating nonsense heard elsewhere," she warned through clenched teeth. And to make sure I thoroughly understood her orders, she threw in a raised left eyebrow for emphasis. My mother specialized in raising only one eyebrow while the other stayed still as a dead worm on her forehead. But controlling her eye muscles wasn't my mother's favourite sport. She preferred controlling our every word and act with one swift blow of the hand. I feared not the pain of a slap across the face. I just hated being treated as a punching bag in front of others.

"Life will be hell under the Communists! Kids will denounce parents! Brothers will spy on sisters! Aieyyaahhh!" moaned my grandmother. And whenever she pouted to moan, a line of betel juice would roll down the side of her chin, ending as brown spots on her blouse. With her crooked hand, she pointed accusingly at us kids. Actually she pointed more to my troublemaker sister Mai than to me. "American goods will disappear from the market. Soon, we'll be out of Ivory soap! Just wait and see!" Grandmother continued. Before anybody could add more, Aunty Hung wasted no time hushing us up. This woman I called Aunty shared none of my ancestors. She only shared our street and my mother's tea. Living next to my mother, Aunty Hung learned some of her tricks. She could hit me just as hard and as swiftly as my own mother.

With her big toe, Aunty Hung lunged at the colour television. She switched it off and in that one pedal movement, put an end to our cravings for helicopters, freedom, and America. She cleared her throat as she swung

4

back and forth on her hammock. A toothpick hung from her lips as she spoke. "No one badmouths the Communist Regime in this house, understand?" Aunty Hung warned, indicating the bare walls of her living room. Less than a month ago these walls sported *The Godfather* and *Love Story* posters. Lately, they showed only dirt marks no one had seen before. As if by magic, all traces of America had disappeared from her shop. In better times, this shop sold recopied tapes of American music and attracted excited young people to our street. The music also covered up noise from a gambling den in the back. These days, only traditional Vietnamese music blared from her store. The high-pitched sounds of old-fashioned opera replaced the pounding of "Like a Rolling Stone." "Yet even then you aren't safe," Aunty Hung often complained to my mother. Traditional operas inevitably sang of unrequited love. "And love in all its forms must sound like endless chatter to Communist ears," sighed Aunty Hung's husband. What in fact did the Viet Cong like? Did they listen to music? Who knows? The unknown kept people awake at night. After all these years fighting them, then losing the battle to them, we still couldn't picture the enemy. And in our imagined fear, it seemed better to leave them faceless. "Fear of winds, fear of shadows . . ." My grandmother liked painting our apprehension in poetic terms.

Yes, we all feared the new Regime. Of course, we all wanted to disappear into the crowd and be forgotten. But some of us disappeared better than others. Aunty Hung became an expert at this game of erasing her past. To further blend with our compatriots from the north, Aunty Hung had a complete change of wardrobe. Overnight she went from tight shirts and slacks, revealing a curvy body, to loose-fitting black pyjamas. Her Viet Cong outfits may have fooled some but not me. Even without the lipstick, I noticed her thick lips still pouted in the right direction when talking to men. And the gap in her front teeth still drove them to distraction. Naturally, Aunty Hung's bulky gold chains and jade earrings disappeared. To hide the sagging holes left by too-heavy jewellery, she pasted mud on her earlobes. Sagging earlobes, a sign of worth in the old days, became a mark of guilt under the Communists. Nowadays, even cheap, weightless plastic jewellery finds a hiding place underground.

If Aunty Hung's look changed overnight, her talk changed even more drastically. The ease with which she added "comrade" to everyone's name never ceased to amaze me. *Please Comrade, thank you Comrade, may I, Comrade . . . ?* Her new Viet Cong talk drove me crazy. Not so long ago, we only heard "Hey you!" from her. What's the problem with her, I wondered. Did she become an instant Communist like those instant noodle soups she used to eat for lunch? But since her husband owned the only working colour television on our street, we knew better than to cross her.

Vietnam

Two

Despite my grandmother's dreaded predictions, life under the new Communist Regime went on as before. Besides the forced neighbourhood meetings held for us to pretend-spy on each other, our activities continued unchanged. Our narrow street of candy stores, popular restaurants and stationery shops stayed as animated as ever. Not one property got confiscated, not one store forcibly closed. The gambling den next door disappeared, of course. "The gambling den, it never existed, do you understand?" I was repeatedly told. "And the colour television, we never owned that either, is it clear?" Aunty Hung made me rehearse this interrogation over and over until I remembered it right. But no one ever asked me about her strange business. In fact, none of our friends tasted the bitter pill of re-education camps.

Yet the fear of those dreaded camps remained palpable. After all, we belonged to that undeserving group of small merchants whose main ambition, besides staying alive in times of war, was to make more money. Owners of little shops, our family and neighbours were far from the exploited peasants the Regime made into martyrs. In school, my new teachers labelled us "counter-revolutionaries with bourgeois aspirations." No matter how hard we tried, we couldn't escape that "counter-revolutionary" label. The teachers shoved it so deep down our throats, we

7

could only swallow it farther in. Spitting it out seemed impossible.

But aside from the revolutionary vocabulary forced on us in school, life flowed on as usual. I heard that in Mao's China, we would've ended up in labour camps long ago. But here in Hue, the Regime somehow tolerated us. Here where bullet-ridden walls still lamented the horrors of Tet '68, the Regime let us be. "Why they let us be? 'Cause they're too afraid to dig up old graves, that's why!" This catchphrase of my grandmother's always mystified me. If I so much as asked what happened during Tet '68, my grandmother would immediately dismiss me. "Can't you remember? New Year's Eve, Communists came. Boom! Boom! Boom! Lots of deaths. We saw it on television. You were there!" Grandmother always stopped after "You were there." No matter how many times I asked her about Tet '68, her answer would remain the same. So with time, my own vague recollection of the 1968 conflict became nothing more than "New Year's Eve, Communists came. Boom! Boom! Boom! Lots of deaths. We saw it on television."

Because of her thinning grey hair on a C-curved back, my grandmother thought herself exempt from any kind of Communist punishment. She also felt a strange kind of joy every time she could insult the new Regime in public. So emboldened by old age, she went on firing her unfiltered thoughts at anyone willing to listen. "Don't you 'comrade' me, boys, can't you see how old I am?" Grandmother once scolded some young, confused Viet Cong wandering in our neighbourhood. "Those Communists, they're just a bunch of ignorant kids," she told my mother afterward, upon which my mother swiftly moved her chair indoors. "Those commies never saw a toilet bowl before! Don't know what to do with it when they see one! Keep fish in it and when the fish disappear, blame it on us Capitalist Devils!" Grandmother continued, undaunted by my mother's frowns.

The image of fish in toilet bowls tickled my fancy. I wondered if those fish actually existed or did they swim only in my grandmother's exaggerations. Grandmother loved twisting the truth to scare us, to transform our sleepless nights into nights of wonder. For many years, she told me that baby girls came out of armpits while baby boys came out of bellybuttons. "If you want a baby sister, you better go check your mother's armpits for signs of swelling!" Grandmother used to tell me. When I became old enough to realize babies didn't come from armpits or bellybuttons, she said, "Babies come out of your asshole instead—so you'd better wash that place well or else you'll have two-headed worms wriggling out of there too." And to conclude her story, Grandmother told me about the worm she once had coming out of her bottom. "Thick and long, it looked like noodle! My mother had to grab it with the tips of her chopsticks, roll it around four times before she could pull it out. But the vigorous worm wouldn't give up. It twisted and turned, trying to climb the side of the potty. Ha ha! It wanted to go back inside my asshole," Grandmother said, giggling. I stopped eating noodles for a month after that. My grandmother's strange childhood stories frightened me, yet they fascinated me.

My grandmother's exaggerations had the aura of a nostalgic tale. My exaggerations, on the other hand, always remained stupid talk, "stupid nonsense," as my mother would say. But even if I heard "Who told you that stupid nonsense?" a dozen times a day, I could not stop repeating the fantastic tales that Grandmother knitted for us kids.

Exaggeration or not, this toilet story of my grandmother's seemed too funny to keep to myself. I laughed so much imagining some poor goldfish brought home in a plastic bag, innocently poured into a toilet bowl and flushed accidentally down the pipes. Or maybe it wasn't a goldfish. Maybe a fat black carp, to be served for dinner, swam to its death down the toilet! Imagine toilets plugged by live fishes! I loved twisting and turning this story in my head. The next day when my trusted old professor came by for my daily lessons, I didn't think twice about repeating the tale to him. But he didn't laugh—he only grimaced.

"Kim, who told you this?" Professor Son asked, spitting out the last of his cigarette.

"My grandmother," I said, lowering my voice. Despite my foolish ways, I knew better than to be caught making fun of the Communists.

"Of course," Professor Son sneered, showing a row of yellowed teeth.

"Do you think the toilet bowl story is true, Professor?"

"Maybe," he said. "Or maybe not. It doesn't matter. Many people have never heard of toilet bowls—not just Communists. There're lots of unfortunate people right here in this neighbourhood," Professor Son reminded me. "They are people making a living out of their shit because that's all they have. Yes, selling their shit to farmers who use it to fatten up our tomatoes. Why should anything be wasted? Why should anything go down the toilet?" asked the professor in a stern tone. Obviously, he found no humour in fish swimming down the toilet.

"I see, Professor . . ."

"Stop repeating your grandmother's nonsense," warned Professor Son.

"Yes, Professor."

"Did you do the French homework I gave you last week?"

"Of course, Professor Son . . ."

"Let me see it. And stop grinning!"

Fish in toilet bowls, like tapeworms so long you'd have to curl them around your chopsticks to pull out of your asshole. This colourful nonsense from my grandmother held no truth. I should've known better. And since her nonsense filled our empty evenings, it became a source of constant worry for my mother.

"She'll get us all into prison with her crazy talk!" Mother mumbled this every evening as we sat down for dinner at our usual table in the restaurant that she owned.

Sitting down for dinner and wishing good appetite to everyone became a chore. In the old days, only adults sat down to eat. We kids could run around the street with our bowls of rice and vegetables. We often mingled with the girls next door to exchange food. Since my mother's cooking surpassed all others' on our street, we often gave more than we took in return. The other kids loved picking at our bowls. But we didn't mind, for we enjoyed bragging about our mother's talents. One day the kids ganged up on Thu, my youngest sister, to see what smelled so good. Thu tried hiding the bowl behind her back. The older kids laughed at her naive gesture and started tickling her. In the tumult, Thu spilled the food, dropped her bowl and broke it in half. Some of the kids mocked her clumsiness—others bent down to retrieve the pieces of fried tofu on the grass. When Thu ran home crying, my mother screamed, "Shut up!" so loud we could hear it from across the street. That got Mai, my other sister, incensed. She handed me her bowl of rice and ran after the other girls, despite my attempt to hold her back. "I'll beat you all to pieces!" Mai screamed. But she soon realized they outnumbered her four to one. One push from Mai meant four punches in return. Mai fell on a rock, ripping her white satin pants near the crotch. A trickle of blood ran down her left leg, leaving a crimson trail on her pants. Mai endured the pain without tears. She never cried at home. Unlike Thu, Mai and I both knew crying would only earn a "Shut up!" from our mother. When my mother saw Mai's torn and bloodied pants, she gave us both slaps on the face. "You're the older sister. Your job is to see this kind of thing doesn't happen!" Mother lectured me. She forbade us to eat on the streets from that day on.

How I missed eating by the curbside, watching local boys play ball. It seemed so much cooler in the shade of the frangipani tree than under the red tile roof of our restaurant. We stayed indoors, even when the temperature reached a scorching 35 degrees Celsius. If my father were still around, he would have made exceptions for us once in a while. He would not be so rigid. But my mother lived by rules so strict even my grandmother shuddered at the thought of breaking them.

My mother never cared for frivolity. She hated laziness. If she wasted no time on our useless emotions, she also showed no tolerance for her own weakness. I never heard her complain in the kitchen of her restaurant. She could cook all day in that dark and stuffy place and not utter a sigh. She never flinched, even when splattered with hot oil or scalded by boiling broth. She often stank of fish sauce and old garlic. Food residue always spotted her blouses and crushed coriander forever filled the space under her fingernails. Yet she looked beautiful. Her small, straight nose, round eyes, and dimples shone through the grease and sweat. While my ordinariness triggered no memory recall, my mother's face lingered on. Diners remembered her striking features years after glimpsing her in the kitchen. They also found unforgettable the force of her spices and condiments.

Vietnam

Three

The changes to our city, although symbolic, stood out. Coca-Cola ads once competed with Nestlé's for our attention in the Central Market. We now saw huge posters of a long-dead Uncle Ho urging us to sacrifice for the nation. Cars soon disappeared to make way for bicycles. In the markets, second-quality local goods replaced much-missed American ones. "No more Ivory soap," my mother finally admitted defeat after circling the market three times. No more perfumed soaps, but somehow, fat cigars appeared for sale everywhere. Strange jars of tiny pebbles soaked in black ink also popped up out of nowhere. "Foodstuff or medicine?" we asked each other. The writing on the jars gave us no explanation. A strange alphabet dished out instructions no one understood. Russian, my teachers said, but what did it mean? Since no one could read Russian, those jars stayed a mystery for me. Pictures of fish on the labels only added to the enigma of the black jars.

Dubious Russian goods served as a prelude to the real thing. Pure-blooded Soviets also came in the flesh. They replaced their departed American colleagues. The first bunch of Russian visitors to Hue caused quite a stir. Many of us kids hung around the Citadel hoping to catch a glimpse of these new overweight and pasty-faced invaders. They often travelled in groups with huge metal suitcases. These new white men kept to themselves most of the time. They spoke a harsh language that, at high volume, sang like a quarrel. Unlike the Americans during the war, these men offered nothing to poor street kids, not even a smile. So in return nobody greeted them with the victory sign. Even the shoeshine boys withheld their "Hello, Mister!" At the market, these men attracted curious glances from shoppers. We all itched to ask about their black jars with the fish labels, but timidity kept us from approaching these "poor Americans." With time, fascination for the Soviets wore off. We couldn't understand how such grim-looking people could inspire the Viet Cong to win the war against the real Americans.

Naturally, my grandmother developed a strong aversion to the Russians. She would cross the street whenever she spotted one coming our way at the market. More than once, she tried pointing her finger accusingly at them. I had to grab her hand to stop her menacing gesture. My grandmother didn't always behave like this with foreigners. She used to smile at French ladies and wave at Americans before the Revolution. These days only bitterness radiated from her.

"Americans were good at building roads during the war," Grandmother told me. "But these Communist fools, they're only good at confusing people by changing road names!"

Despite her crazy talk, my grandmother's remarks sometimes made sense. Under the Communists, pretty-sounding streets and those with dynastic connections did get chopped off the city map. In their place sprouted Revolution Street, General Uprising Boulevard and The South Has Risen Road. Saigon became Ho Chi Minh City. But for my mother, Saigon remained Saigon. Her husband had moved to Saigon for a job. He never set foot in Ho Chi Minh City.

If most institutions got a change of name under the new Regime, my dear old school still stayed Quoc Hoc School. For who dared change the name of this prestigious place that had once produced not only Ho Chi Minh, but also General Vo Nguyen Giap? "General who?" asked my grandmother, as if she'd never heard of this man, winner of two wars. "He beat both the French *and* the Americans," I tried explaining. But Grandmother loved playing deaf and dumb. She refused to hear what she didn't want to. In her mind, no Communist was a good Communist.

In school, we could not escape Uncle Ho's stares. Reprints of his old class photos hung on all the walls. "Uncle Ho studied here! You too can help the nation by studying hard!" We saw this in every classroom. So study hard I did, excelling in all my performances, even in the after-school street cleaning my Uncle Ho Youth Group assigned me. But no, I didn't convert. My grandmother's mean tongue kept me from believing what the teachers taught in school. Like most of my friends, I joined the Communist youth group only for the library access accorded to its members. We put up with political lectures and street cleaning daily, just to get a book once a month. Yes, I enjoyed nothing better than reading a heavy volume in the quiet of the night. Often that volume only told the story of cells transforming into tadpoles. But tales of life fascinated me, so I devoured them under my blanket with much pleasure.

In school, I kept quiet about my father. I couldn't have a father flying off to America, and at the same time be a good Communist. When asked about my father, I would repeat my mother's lies. "He went down south for a better job" automatically flew out of my mouth. Of course, I feared being caught with these lies. The Communists had televisions too. They too must have seen my father hopping into an American helicopter on the last day of the war. Running off with the enemy—this must rate quite high on the counter-revolutionary scale! If my mother feared Communist punishment for Grandmother's loud mouth, I too worried about a traitor father. To make up for my father's counter-revolutionary ways, I pretended to be more Communist than the Communists. In school, I worked harder than all my classmates. My essays on the virtues of collective farms often garnered top marks. My poems to Uncle Ho didn't bring tears to my teacher's eyes as I would've wished, but they were always the first ones to be read. My research papers on Comrade Lenin frequently earned me the smiles I so longed for. My teachers noticed this change in me. I had been a reluctant student, secretly mocking them at first. With time, I became totally engaged in their game.

If I kept quiet about my father in school, I couldn't do the same at home. Since my mother rarely talked to me, I pestered Grandmother for answers. But my grandmother offered little consolation. "Study hard and forget him for now," she said. "Maybe one day when you become important, he'll come to you asking for favours. Men are always like that," she concluded. Whenever I looked at my sisters and mother, I saw only calm. From the blank stare they gave me, I knew my father had stopped haunting their memory. But for me the haunting persisted. I could not forget him. I missed him so much. I also resented his absence. What did we do to deserve a father deserting us in front of the camera? I imagined throwing temper tantrums at him. I imagined him rushing to my call of distress, his crossed eyes even more crossed in their confusion, his solitary clump of hair glued even more tightly to his left temple by the sweat of fear. "Shhh, don't scream so loud," he would say. "I can't help it!" I would retort. "Why are you so upset?" he would ask. Then he would vanish before hearing my reply.

Those exercises in imagination served little purpose. My exaggerated indignation faded after a few minutes. Emptiness invariably followed my dramatics, an emptiness that my mother never attempted to fill. She knew we shared a love of books and stories, my father and I. Yet barely a month after his departure, she managed to sell all my father's books to second-hand bookstores. When I later spotted these books in the stores, my pulse quickened. I thought my father had returned. Perhaps he needed money, I told myself. I ran home as fast as I could. But the false hope vanished the minute I reached home. No laughter, no excited talk—the talk of a family reunited—flew from our opened windows. The house emitted no light. My parents' room remained empty. In the kitchen, I found my mother busy cooking as usual. My mother had sold Father's books on a whim, not for the money, but for the need to declutter her life. My father's absence hung in the air. Without his books in their usual places, the void became unbearable. I loved smelling his books, hoping to catch the lingering nicotine odour of his breath. I loved touching their pages, hoping to feel the oily traces left by my father's fingers. I loved leafing through them, hoping to find a secret note, a clue to his disappearance. Daily, I inspected my father's books, searching for that secret note. The books stayed mute after weeks of inspection, but the hope of a revelation kept me going. I was sure they would talk one day. When I came home to the empty bookcase, I gasped for air—I felt as if I breathed with only one lung.

Vietnam

Four

When my grandmother refused to get out of bed, I had to assume her chores. "Too much back and joint pain," she complained to my mother. Doing my grandmother's chores meant going to the Dong Ba Market at dawn before the start of school. The early hours didn't bother me, but the stinky smell of old fish bowels thrown into the Perfume River below turned my stomach. The odour of week-old garbage macerating on slippery floors made me curse my fate as a first-born. I could smell the rotten fish as soon as I turned off our street. No, the Perfume River emanated no perfume.

The leper boy on his cardboard box also bothered me. He begged at the market from dawn to dusk. You couldn't avoid him. He went from stand to stand begging, calling on people's charity. If that didn't work, he would play on their fears. He would reach out to touch them with his bandaged, bloodied hands. This always did the trick. Shoppers invariably threw him some coins to shoo him away. I first noticed him when I was five or six years old. That day, I accompanied Grandmother to the market. I helped her carry a bag of turnips and garlic. As I turned around to retrieve some fallen garlic, I noticed a dirty boy dragging his legless body on a cardboard box. His greasy long hair covered most of his eyes. His naked torso showed the irregularity of ribs. He approached me from the side, raising his left hand to ask for a turnip. "Don't let him touch you or you'll lose your legs too," my grandmother screamed. To get rid of the leper boy, she threw him a coin.

16

Then she gave me a hard knock on the skull for being careless with her garlic. This scene left me perplexed for a long time. Despite repeated scolding from Grandmother, I refused to return to the market after that episode.

Yet with the arrival of the autumn moon festival, I yearned to go back. In my excitement and anticipation of the festival, I had forgotten the leper boy on his cardboard box. "Short people have short memories!" Grandmother always said. At the autumn festival, Grandmother and I admired the stalls of persimmons so beautifully arranged. We bought sweet lotus cakes and a paper lantern in the shape of a butterfly for Mai and me. Then we went to look for a hand fan to replace my grandmother's old one. I spotted the leper boy behind a stand selling straw sandals. The boy seemed so focused on the sandals, he didn't see the coins being thrown his way. Then a loud "Get out!" brought him back to reality. He reluctantly left the sandal shop, dragging his torn and taped Sunkist cardboard with deliberate slowness. With the leper out of sight, I approached the sandal stand. The sandals fascinated me, for I never saw sandals like this before, just like my plastic ones, but made of cord and twine instead.

I almost slipped them on my feet, when my grandmother suddenly yelled "No! What bad luck to be playing with those things. They are burial sandals for dead children!" she screamed. "If you touch them long enough, you'll end up wearing them for real! It is like choosing your own coffin— you just don't do it. You certainly don't try it on for size!" my grandmother exclaimed.

"But how should I know there are two types of shoes, one for the dead and one for the living!" I protested.

"There's even a third kind, for mourners," screamed Grandmother. "While I'm still alive you're not going near those either, understand? Now shut up and stop crying," she ordered.

I came home that day confused and scared. The thought of touching strange things and being touched by strange-looking people terrified me. In my mind, lepers and death, *my* death, became interchangeable. Unfortunately, no one in the family shared my lepers = death nonsense.

As I got older, so did the leper boy. When he outgrew his old Sunkist cardboard box, he got a bigger one. With time, the new box also lost its brightness and shape. The pictured oranges faded into blobs and the word "Sunkist" became unrecognizable. The younger leper boy had regarded me with curiosity. Later, with stubble growing on his chin, he stared at me with squinty eyes. To other shoppers, he nodded. To me, he only gave cold glares. If he could, he would have jumped up to kick me with his rotting thighs. I was scared, very scared.

My fear of the leper boy turned shopping into a dreaded chore. Yet I did my duties every morning without a word of complaint. For my midday rest, I came home as fast as my rusty bicycle would carry me, to feed not myself, but my grandmother. As usual, my mother seemed too busy feeding others to worry about her own mother. Rice porridge in chicken broth with a hint of ginger gave pleasure to my grandmother's toothless palate. "Don't forget the ginger, otherwise I can't digest properly!" Grandmother forever reminded me. But my memory never tricked me. I always remembered.

In her better moods, my grandmother would ask me to recite one or two lines from *The Story of Kieu,* which I did with a smile. I had no problem remembering this never-ending poem. Even if I didn't understand all the verses, I liked the sound they made coming out of my mouth. When I recited, my grandmother always listened with a grin. Sometimes she would close her eyes, but I knew she resisted sleep, for she never snored during those times.

I enjoyed reciting verses from *The Story of Kieu* for my grandmother. Giving her a bath in bed was another matter. Since she didn't want my mother seeing her naked, she chose me for the task. Although I'd seen my grandmother's nakedness many times, I could never get used to the sight of wrinkled flesh framing a wispy, white-haired triangle. During those times, Grandmother would turn her face away from me, so I imagined she too felt embarrassed. When I finished, she would hum some verses from *The Story of Kieu,* not to break the awkward silence but to give proof of her keen mind. And to prove it even further, she would order me to clean her room after I'd cleaned her.

"Try to do a better job with the floor than you did with my armpits! I still feel soap in there—it's itching like hell. Of course, itching won't kill me. But if I feel slippery soap on the floor, that will certainly send me head first to the ground and feet first out the door! You don't get it? Where's your brain? You only carry dead people feet first out the door!" My grandmother may have been bent over, but her tongue still sliced like a week-old knife.

In the evening, with school over and my communal street cleaning done, I came home to more chores. Being the oldest child, I had endless duties to my family—I cared for my grandmother, my younger sisters and my house. Since my mother only worried about her restaurant, she never noticed the lack of laughter at home. I did my best with the housework but my best never seemed enough. The house smelled of dirt and sadness. If only my father were still here to help! But he had already left for America— I saw it on television. No use dreaming about his return, I told myself repeatedly.

By this time, nobody asked about my father anymore. They all took as truth my mother's line, "He went down to Saigon for a better job." Or maybe they didn't believe a word of it. It didn't matter anymore. Lately, people had started disappearing by the dozens in our neighbourhood, so my father's story ceased intriguing neighbours and friends. Only the new disappearances tickled their curiosity. Yet we knew better than to ask why, how or where at neighbourhood meetings. Sometimes whole families vanished, other times only the father or oldest boy disappeared. Apprehension followed us like a shadow with each disappearance. Rumours of deaths at sea kept our feet planted on the ground. But we also heard of successful escapes and new lives lived beyond regrets. At such times, we yearned to fly too. That is the problem with rumours. They scare you but they also make you dream.

If things followed a downward slope at home, they took a different path at school. All my efforts earned gold stars. Promotions came my way easily. Within a year I had jumped from level one to level three in my Uncle Ho Youth Group. My teachers only gave this distinction to the best. I became a model for young socialists. "She'll get ahead in the Party one day," I heard my teachers say, discussing my case. "And her mother owns private property! Goes to show you we're not fanatics like the Chinese! Or that crazy Cambodian, Pol Pot!" one of the teachers remarked with a satisfied chuckle. But they couldn't fool me. I had learned my history lessons well enough to know that only northerners received real Party promotions. My three stars sounded impressive but earned me no advantages besides the library access I already had. Even my mother, who knew nothing of revolutionary history, showed little interest in my promotion.

But then again, my mother reserved her interest only for my faults. My achievements left no impression on her. "Why do you always walk with slouched shoulders? Can't you brush your hair right? Why are you late for Grandmother's meal?" How I longed for a smile once in a while. But my mother smiled only to satisfied customers at the restaurant. To us kids, she gave a gift of money once a year during the New Year festival of Tet. That's also the time she wished us good luck in school, and in return, we wished her longevity. A yearly exchange of goodwill left us craving more. I wondered if other families followed this same path to tenderness.

My mother only said, "Humph," when I showed her the newspaper article mentioning my promotion. "Promotions" in a system she mistrusted meant nothing to her. Even Aunty Hung, who once ran a gambling den, got promoted! We heard all about it at our last communal meeting. This woman next door, who once force-fed us American music, had become the official Communist neighbourhood guard dog. She no longer had to report to anyone—we had to report to her now.

Vietnam

Five

My mother's nudging woke me in the middle of the night. She gestured to me to get dressed, then eat a bowl of cold soup. She kept the light off to avoid waking the rest of the family. The wall clock struck eleven. My thirty minutes of sleep left me too tired to protest or even question her judgment. Bewildered, I forced myself out of bed and swallowed the soup.

Although she had tried hiding it these past few weeks, I had noticed my mother jumpier than ever before. Her hands trembled so much that the kitchen knife became a formidable weapon. I feared for her fingertips as she chopped onions. My mother also stumbled over words, forgetting the names of her own dishes. Once, a bowl of hot soup fell from her grip, splashing her pants and scalding her feet. Absentmindedly, she stepped on the broken porcelain with her flip-flops and complained of pain only after a puddle of blood formed on the floor.

In her "normal" state, my mother would urge me to eat more of the dishes cooked just for us. "For family only, not clients," she would say to diners lured to our table by the scent of miniature prawns fried in chilies. But the tiny prawns seemed more alluring in smell than in taste. In better days, we had fat shrimps jumping up and down in her hot skillet, not the stacks of shells that stuck to the bottom of the pan. Yet my mother never gave up cooking, and guests still filled her restaurant even if the food market offered few goods. Since paper money carried little value, many paid her in

21

favours. Bars of scentless soap and spare light bulbs became our weekly income. "I'll clean the street for you this week, I'll go to the meeting on your behalf," they would say. All this for the nostalgic scent of a meal.

Before I understood my fate, I found myself furtively heading for the back road with my mother. Torn old clothes covered our bodies. Our faces also received the dirty treatment to better hide us in the night. As we approached the city limits, the night turned darker, more silent. Houses gave way to bushes and children's cries faded from earshot. This was not the soothing calm of rural roads. It rang more like the imposed quiet of curfew. More like those eerie hours of stillness before shooting starts. This deceptive absence of noise I knew only too well. It was what I remembered most about the war.

The darkness disoriented me. Only my mother's occasional whispers gave direction to my wanderings. Turn right, turn left, straight ahead. For the longest time, these few words from my mother kept me company.

Reaching the outskirts of the city, we turned for a last look at long-suffering Hue, our hometown—poetic, tragic like all the songs written about it. From this distance, I could see the spire of St. Redempteur Church on the left while the bridge over the Perfume River loomed sulkily to my right. In our city of low buildings, these two landmarks stayed visible from all angles. "Orient yourself according to these structures," my grandmother once taught me, as together we mapped out the road home from school many years ago. Those two beloved points of reference never failed me. Thanks to them, I never got lost in all my years of running errands for my mother. But on this night, I *was* lost, hopelessly lost.

A sense of dread overtook me. I had heard stories of neighbours leaving the country in the middle of the night, but never did I imagine being in such a venture myself. Why didn't my mother warn me? Why couldn't she say something? I would have packed my own things. I would have said goodbye to friends . . . Of course she kept everything secret exactly for this reason. Nobody could know of our hasty departure.

"There are eyes and ears everywhere," Mother used to say. And the eyes of my Uncle Ho Youth Group must see farther than anyone else's. Eyes —didn't she say something about her twitching eye? Of course she did! "I have a twitch in my right eye," she'd been saying for a whole week. Why didn't I figure it out sooner? In my mother's complicated world of beliefs, a right-eye twitch stood for good luck, fortune coming, while a left-eye twitch meant the opposite. So all week she had tried to tell us, "Good luck has found us—time to change our destiny," but I heard only grumbling. The week flew by without my catching her meaning. We were leaving this country of ours forever. Without fanfare, without long farewells, I could understand that. But when secret goodbyes remained unspoken, that seemed sad.

I suddenly thought of my two younger sisters. Who will take care of Mai and Thu? Grandmother? She couldn't look after herself, much less worry about two young girls. And who will bring Grandmother her porridge? Aunty Hung next door? No, she would report our departure to the Commissioner, and send the rest of our family to re-education camps first. Socialist duties before neighbourly duties, as my grandmother would say.

All these thoughts raced through my mind when my mother finally whispered a few words to me. "If we get stopped on the road, say nothing. Leave the talking to me. We are going to Hoi An for Sunday afternoon market. To sell incense, understand? The incense is in your bag."

Besides the turn-right, turn-left thing, my mother did not speak to me again that night, as we hiked in silence the mountainous stretch that separated our city from Hoi An. When I got out of breath, Mother would let me rest a few minutes only, before tapping my shoulder to hurry me on again. Lost and confused, I surrendered wholly to my mother. We drank when she decided to drink. We turned left when she gave the signal. We turned right when she said so. How she found her way in the darkness, I didn't know. She acted as if she'd done this trip many times before. When? I wondered vaguely but did not ask. I just had to trust her. Only the surrounding odour gave me a sense of direction. Although I could neither see nor hear it, I could smell the fishiness of the Perfume River. I knew we followed in the fish's path.

When my left sandal snapped, my mother replaced it with a new one from her bag. The rigid new plastic cut into the side of my big toe. When the hurt in my foot forced me to limp, my mother tied a washcloth around my toe. But the washcloth didn't ease the pain—it only made my steps less steady. I felt my skin burning under the new sandal, and my dripping sweat further eroded the flesh. But I couldn't stop for fear of losing my mother. Already she walked far ahead of me. The rustling of her pants already sounded faint.

We finally reached Lang Co as the sun rose. I had learned in school about this leper colony by the beach. But I never thought to experience it in person! For a brief minute, I thought of the dirty leper boy in his Sunkist box. Goosebumps soon popped up all over my body. Yet from a distance, Lang Co seemed the typical village represented in my school books. A clutch of straw huts lined two quiet streets. Two little white dogs slept under a wooden bench. Palms alternated with banana trees for shade. I almost expected to see water buffaloes cooling in the mud. But common sense told me no such beast dwelt by the beach. And what a beautiful beach I saw! Fine white sand stroked by deep blue water, waves foaming at its edge. In the heat, I felt an urge to jump in the ocean, but of course I didn't. I didn't know how to swim. More importantly, I didn't want to catch the lepers' sickness in the water. After only a moment of rest, I itched to resume our journey. Despite the blisters on my foot, I wanted to leave this village as soon as possible.

"We spend the day resting here. Boat will be here tonight or tomorrow," Mother said.

"But I thought you said Hoi An?" I asked, not just confused but also terrified at the thought of spending the day in a leper village.

"No, that was in case we got questioned on roads. Hoi An is too far. Also too dangerous, many soldiers there. Safer here. Because of lepers, no policemen come to bother us here."

"But where can we rest here?" I continued.

"I have friends who can lodge us," Mother replied, already annoyed at my questioning. Since when do you know lepers? I wanted to ask. But my mother's raised left eyebrow told me to shut up.

An elderly man with bulging bloodshot eyes met us at the village entrance. His bald head and long white beard reminded me of Uncle Ho. This sign of familiarity eased somewhat my anxiety. On first inspection, he seemed to have all his limbs intact. Although I tried not to stare at him, I couldn't keep my eyes from his claw-like hands. I forced myself to calm down, to be reasonable. But for the rest of that day, I dreaded catching leprosy more than the risky journey ahead of us.

This fear of lepers was my own nonsense. Unfortunately, my mother tolerated none of this crazy idea. But still . . . Did she have to bring me to a leper village on the eve of our most important trip? Lepers = death came back to haunt me. In my confused state, I heard again my grandmother's strange warning: "No! Do not touch! Do not choose your own funeral garments! Do not pick your own coffin!"

"Good to see you. Been a long time," Mother said to the toothless Uncle Ho lookalike.

"1968, wasn't it?" he asked.

"Before that—1965. Spent '68 hiding in Hue . . ."

"Ah, yes. I remember. Very cute baby. And?"

"She is fine now," Mother answered vaguely.

"Lots of Hue refugees came here during the Tet '68 massacre. I thought you came too . . ."

"No. But we took the same road yesterday," continued my mother in this strange conversation I no longer followed. What happened in '65? What exactly happened in '68? Which cute baby are you talking about? How do you know this old leper? I had a hundred questions for my mother, but no sound came out of me. Her raised left eyebrow remained intact throughout this talk. I knew I must keep quiet.

Old Uncle Ho lookalike led us inside his straw hut and showed us a tattered mat on a dirt floor. Besides two plastic stools and a small wooden crate functioning as a table, no other furniture cluttered this dark corner of the world. My mother immediately lay down to rest her dusty body. Only then did I notice the trace of blood on my mother's feet. She too bled from raw blisters. Despite my tiredness, I initially refused to lie down. Fearing contact with leprosy, I stood for hours near the door. Then I sat on the edge of the stool staring stupidly at a wall clock. But sleep soon overcame my stubbornness. I ended up sleeping next to my mother while the old man stood guard. When I awoke, darkness already surrounded the hut. A flickering candle inside a drinking glass cast moving shadows on the walls and gave the room a ghostly feel. The elderly man continued his conversation with my mother.

"Good, good, only a half moon tonight," he whispered.

"Just enough to see but not enough to be seen," added my mother. Seeing me awake, they both changed topics.

"Snoring, that's bad for a boat trip, will keep everyone up," the man joked, rolling his bloodshot eyes upward. To this comment, my mother only smiled quietly. The man then handed us two sets of clothes. They were dark brown blouses over loose-fitting black pants.

"Don't forget to rub them on the dirt floor first," he told us. "This makes them softer to the skin and less conspicuous to curious eyes. They're humble enough to pass as fishermen's clothing in case you get caught," he went on.

"Yet presentable enough to get by in the West in case we do escape," my mother quickly added.

"My niece made these clothes. A goodbye present for you. She's a great seamstress," he didn't fail to mention.

"I know, she's very good with embroidery too," answered my mother.

The old man turned his head toward the windows so my mother and I could change into our new clothes.

"Don't forget the hats," he added, pointing to two conical hats on the floor. "Will be good for catching fish on the boat," he said as my mother nodded in silence.

The old man then offered us bowls of hot soup, which I tried eating without touching the utensils. By refusing to share a leper's spoon, I burned my tongue in more than one spot. After supper, we waited in darkness for a sign of some sort, before making the furtive dash to the vast empty beach behind the man's house. That sign came at about one o'clock in the morning, in the shape of a flashing light, meant only for our strained eyes, as others slept without suspicion. I knew it was time to leave the leper's shelter. I felt relieved but also scared.

From a short distance, I could make out the bobbing of our boat anchored not far from shore. No bigger than four by seven metres, already the boat looked unsafe and rickety in the calm water. Amongst those seated, I recognized with surprise the unmistakably sweet-and-sour voice of Aunty Hung, our next-door neighbour back in Hue. She sat there with her husband

and their brood of six already-whimpering kids.

"Go to sleep, go to sleep, your dreams are still normal . . . ." she sang to them.

No, I wasn't dreaming. Aunty Hung herself stood in front of me. Imagine the Eye and Ear of the Communist Party fleeing on the same boat as us! In the darkness, I could barely make out three other families plus a tall, large man, whom I assumed to be the captain. Seeing us, he angrily pointed his finger at my mother, muttering, "One! Only one, I told you!" To this, Mother replied, "I know!" She then grabbed my right hand and dragged me to the boat. At that moment I realized she would not accompany me on this trip. The two conical hats, the two sets of clothing—that deceiving ploy had succeeded in luring me to the beach. But I wanted to stop the charade.

Wasn't there enough space for my mother? Did she lack money for her own fare? These trips cost a livelihood, I heard. A bar of gold per person, it seemed. For whatever reason, my mother had chosen me. I would be the first to face the sea. If I made it alive, I would send for the rest of my family later. My mother didn't say it as such but I understood her intention. If the Communists had eyes and ears everywhere, we also cultivated our own system of invisible telephones. These whispering phones daily blew into our imagination incredible stories of midnight escapes and faraway lands. Over the years, I'd seen enough of my friends disappear overnight to know they didn't all labour in Communist re-education camps. Despite the lack of official news, the hush and silence around their departures, we knew what usually happened to these people. They ended up in a paradise on earth called America. That's if they didn't drown at sea first. The drowning, we heard about that too . . . Paradise or no Paradise, I felt unable to leave my family behind. I felt unready to assume the load asked of me. But how could I back out? After all, I couldn't run back to the leper's hut. Why leave now? I wanted to ask. Life is not that bad here, the war is over and we still have our restaurant, I tried explaining. And what about my promotion? So many things I wished to mention to change my mother's mind. But she refused any last-minute bartering. The captain signalled me impatiently with his hand. I had no choice but to embark on this pre-arranged, pre-paid trip. And I didn't even know how to swim.

"I'll catch a later boat with your sisters. We'll see each other in America," whispered my mother. "Aunty Hung has agreed to take care of you. So be good and listen to her. She's your new mother now. She'll bring you to America. America—that's where my cousin Lan lives. Lan will take you in. She's a good relative. Her address is written on the back of her photo. It's in this bag. So look her up," my mother went on. "I took care of everything for you! You'll be fine. Just be brave," concluded my mother.

I wanted to scream, "Who are these people? Where am I going? Why am I going alone?" But only "How are you getting back?" came out of my mouth. I asked this question because the journey back to Hue seemed imaginable. But not the boat trip to nowhere. Its paths floated like a thousand loose strings about to be knitted into a labyrinth in my head.

"I'll take bus back to Hue, easier that way. Nothing to hide now!" my mother answered.

With those words, she handed me a brown burlap bag that would become my treasure chest for many years. I said goodbye to the mother I had known for fifteen years, feeling all at once scared, angry, sad and betrayed. Shamelessly betrayed, as she carelessly handed me over to a neighbour I trusted least. Yet despite the fear and sorrow, despite the feeling of rejection and anger, I had no tears to shed on that boat as I left my mother behind to embark on the most adventurous journey of my life. I tried waving at her but her wind-swept hair no longer graced the beach. In the confusion, I thought I saw my father dangling from a nearby helicopter. I called to him but the sounds of the motorboat drowned my hoarse voice.

The Philippines

One

We roamed around the South China Sea in an endless silence. We thought we would never see land again but dehydration kept us from voicing our fear. Our bobbing boat full of thirsty children turned round and round on itself. One day a big Norwegian freight ship appeared on the horizon. Tall blonde men waved at us from their decks. To our outstretched arms, they threw down cans of Coca-Cola. Then they promptly transferred us to Palawan, a small beach town weighted down by high temperatures, high waves and high winds. In Palawan, a local official led us to a place called the "refugee camp." Two dark-skinned men barking orders in a strange Vietnamese accent guarded the entrance to this huge space. Barbed wire surrounded the camp like a military outpost. Once inside, we knew it wouldn't be easy to get out.

I received a bamboo mat to be shared with Aunty Hung's three oldest girls. Hut number 231, row 23, section N, South Side became our new address. Inside the straw hut, on bare earth, lay sleeping mats for four families. Seeing the other families, Aunty Hung lost no time rearranging our space. She wanted nothing to do with their sad faces and snivelling noses. Once the invisible borders were drawn, we settled in our secluded corner of the hut. And we slept a most melancholic night.

I knew Aunty Hung's kids back home, but had never exchanged anything more than casual greetings. Only Titi, the oldest girl, got my

29

attention. She often came to me for help with schoolwork. But aside from those occasions, I hardly gave her any notice either. Yet things changed at the camp. Proximity brought us closer together. After a few weeks sleeping side by side, we became familiar with the shape of each other's toes and heels. We recognized the comfort of our knees settling against someone else's bottom. We also knew each other's dreams. In that small space, we became friends, spending many sleepless nights speculating on our future while others slept. We told each other stories of hope and wishes to be fulfilled. We imagined a life of abundance, magically covered in snow. Yes, the America of our desires would be as snowed-in as the Christmas scenes we used to see on television. "Where Father Christmas is real so I get lots of toys!" squealed Titi.

"With lots of books to read and no lepers," I added.

"And no more Communists!" screamed the three-year-old sister. We all laughed at this outburst, as we knew she hadn't a clue what a Communist was. "Yes, I do know!" she insisted, and we laughed even harder.

The little girl's innocence reminded me of Thu, my youngest sister, whose childish ways always got on my mother's nerves. "What do you know about communism?" Mother demanded when Thu naively voiced her opinion one day. "Well, Grandmother said they are . . ." Thu responded, but Mother interrupted her with a forceful "Shut up and stop repeating your grandmother's nonsense, understand?" Remembering Thu's words filled me with longing for a time that wasn't better, only more real.

Life at the camp, on the other hand, flew on a lopsided cloud of make-believe. We lived wishful days and dreamy nights. To the group's wish list, we added our own fantasies, one sentence at a time. This imaginary world we constructed did its job, if only partially. It didn't completely shield us from the unpleasantness of the camp but it did filter out some of its uglier elements. We saw the rows of straw huts as a mirage. We compared it to identical images infinitely bouncing off parallel mirrors. The reflection of a reflection fascinated us. We saw the barbed wire as a game. How close can you get to it without ripping your clothes? We saw the swarm of mosquitoes on garbage as a math lesson. Number of mosquitoes on garbage A plus number of mosquitoes on garbage B equals how much? Titi could never figure this one out. Of all the games we played, the Waiting Game got under our skin the most. We gave ourselves one thousand days to reach our goal of America. Getting there before the fixed date would make us all winners. So we counted the hours and waited. The days seemed to drag on forever under the hot tropical sun. Yet the humid nights offered little relief for our impatience. We wondered if time would ever tick again.

Life at the camp also meant weekly lineups for food handouts. After a couple of weeks my stomach started reacting badly to the daily diet of rice and canned peas. No, I liked the canned peas at first, as their newness added excitement to my taste buds. But with time, the novelty of those peas wore off—I soon got tired of eating them. Just smelling the sickly sweet odour made me nauseous. Oh, how I missed my mother's cooking! Simply thinking about her coriander fingers brought cravings to my mouth.

Yes, I missed home badly. Even the political lectures and street cleaning seemed pleasant to my homesick memory. My mother's stern words and beatings no longer bothered me. All that mattered was the memory of her meals: colourful, fragrant, and most importantly, tasty. If I missed my mother's cooking, I missed my grandmother's nonsense stories even more. In my boredom, I would pass the days repeating Grandmother's tapeworm tales to Aunty Hung's kids. At first they would shriek with a mixture of disgust and delight. Eventually they lost interest. After a while, only the youngest girl reacted to my story. Still, we found it comforting to have her laughter grace the nights.

At the camp, we no longer feared punishment from the Party. We could talk freely. I could ask a thousand questions about my father without worrying about Communist eyes and ears. Did my father really escape on the last helicopter out of Saigon? Did an American arm really save him? Did he end up in America? I assaulted Aunty Hung with all my doubts. But like my mother, she had no reassurances for me.

"I thought he went to Saigon for a better job," Aunty Hung remarked innocently. My mother cooked that story up for our neighbours. It couldn't be true. Aunty Hung of all people should know better than that. She seemed too clever for that kind of deceit.

"What's my father like, Aunty Hung?" I inquired.

"You forgot already?"

"It's been a long time. Please remind me, Aunty Hung . . ."

"You know, bald, hunched back, short with crossed eyes. Very ugly. But a nice man," she said.

"Yes, but what did he like to eat? What made him laugh?" I insisted.

"Who knows? Your father, you should know better than me!" she cried in disbelief. Aunty Hung wanted to shut me up, but I couldn't put an end to my questioning.

"Could he hang on to a helicopter ledge?" I asked again.

"Don't think so. He's not the brave type. But people can do tricks when desperate."

"Aunty Hung, did you know my mother has leper friends?" I continued.

"So what? Lepers are humans too!"

"But my grandmother hated lepers . . ."

"OK. Nobody likes lepers, but your grandmother's thing for the lepers goes back a long way. It's a complicated story. You're too young to understand it."

"What's complicated, Aunty Hung?"

"Your grandmother and the lepers and all that story! Maybe I'll tell you when you're older. OK?"

"But . . ."

"Enough now! Go get some water at the fountain! I have to cook."

Aunty Hung's verbal stinginess left me craving for more. Her one-line revelation of my family's secret bothered me. Yet, no matter how hard I tried, she never indulged me with more tales. Her tight lips reminded me of Grandmother's compact version of Tet '68. "Bang! Bang! Bang! Lots of deaths! We saw it on television!" Yes, we saw it on TV, but what really happened?

"Aunty Hung, what happened in '68?" I asked my caretaker one day.

"You mean Tet '68, during the New Year's festival? You were there! Can't you remember?" Aunty Hung screamed.

"No, I was too young to remember, Aunty Hung. Please tell me," I pleaded.

"Well it's long and complicated. I don't know the whole story. Only know what I see with my eyes and what I hear on television. You must know the Communists invaded on New Year's Eve, don't you? Well, they attacked many cities. Worst battle occurred in our hometown, Hue. It lasted more than a month. Communists shot rockets everywhere. They went from house to house looking for American sympathizers. They also took away any educated-looking men. My brother-in-law worked as a policeman. He knew he would be in trouble with the Communists. When they banged on our door, he ran out to the backyard. He hid under a bush. He thought he found safety in the darkness. Then he heard a strange sound coming from above. He looked up the sky and saw a huge piece of metal coming down his way. I heard his scream but couldn't go check. Rocks from the sky fell everywhere around me. Burning debris and shrapnel covered our yard. I only went to get his body two days later. Killed by an exploding car door, can you imagine? What a stupid way to die! Blood still leaked from his skull when I found him. His eyes still open wide, as if looking at the sky, as if checking for falling objects. The Communists occupied the city for weeks. Americans responded with bombs. Between the bombs and the rockets, Hue became a place of ruins. Houses on our street burned for days, because we lacked water to put out the fire. Electricity was also cut. Homeless people took refuge in the cathedral. The Communists soon hauled them out. Communists hated these people who pray to the man on a cross. What's his name? Yeah, Jesus. They took them out and shot them all. I heard 300 people died outside the church. After the battle, people found mass graves around Hue. I saw that on television. No I don't want to remember anymore."

The Philippines

Two

"What will happen to us now, Aunty Hung?" I asked my new caretaker repeatedly.

"We wait."

"Wait for what, Aunty Hung?" I once asked stupidly.

"Wait for America, what else?! Why, you are stupid like an ox!"

So wait we did. Days became weeks that stretched into months. While waiting, I somehow lost track of time. Somewhere on my imaginary calendar, Mondays and Tuesdays ceased to exist. Only the weather mattered. Sun or rain? I inquired repeatedly. Sun meant unbearable heat, while rain meant mud in our hut, which I liked even less for the leeches that came with it. I preferred windy, cloudy days. On those days, the breezes brought with them the salty fragrance of the ocean to remind us of the beach within our smelling range. We saw that beautiful beach getting off our boat. But the camp's barbed wire prevented us from returning to the sea.

Waiting didn't mean doing nothing. When Aunty Hung grew tired of doing her chores, she pushed them on me. "You're big enough, you do it now," she said. I didn't mind going to the fountain three times a day for our water. Carrying buckets of water nearly broke my back, but at least I knew

34

water flowed from the faucet. Waiting in line for my turn at the fountain seemed long, but impatience never showed its face. No, what I disliked most was the impossible search for the branches and twigs that would fuel our fire. The firewood officially given us hardly sufficed to cook half a meal. We had no choice but to supplement it with twigs and fallen bark. With so few trees left, it became harder to find branches around the camp. I had to fight with other kids for the few twigs to cook our food. This made my wood-gathering task nastier than expected. Unlike me, some of these street kids lived from day to day. They knew how to fend for themselves, since no one else did for them. Life at the camp paled in comparison to their former Saigon existence. Sleeping in cemeteries, eating leftover garbage, stealing from blind beggars—I heard those stories.

The more I saw those street gangs, the more afraid I became. They were a dirty, smelly bunch who spoke coarsely if at all. They had scars on their faces big enough to be visible from a distance. And their black teeth looked so rotten you'd wonder how they ate. Some even had pieces of fingers missing—no doubt the result of fights. No, it couldn't be leprosy. The rest of their limbs seemed too intact for lepers. Yes, this bunch of hoodlums terrified me, but I had no choice but to go on scurrying every day —for how else would we eat?

One day after the customary "We wait," Aunty Hung added these worrisome words: "I heard if you have family in America sponsoring you, you'll leave camp fast. If not, you can wait forever. Sometimes they send you back to Vietnam. When they're sick of seeing your face."

"Do we have sponsors in America, Aunty Hung?" I asked anxiously.

"Of course! My younger brother's studying there," Aunty Hung replied proudly. "He's the one who sent me American tapes. Good music! 'Let It Be,' remember?" she asked.

"But what about me?" I wanted to know. "Your brother doesn't even know I exist," I told her.

"Don't worry, I tell them you're my adopted daughter," Aunty Hung said casually. "Where I go, you go too. OK?" When I raised my doubt, she hushed me up. "We got here fine, no?" she screamed. "I kept promise to your mother, no?" she raged on.

To this, I could only say, "Yes, Aunty."

"Your mother packed your birth certificate in bag?" asked Aunty Hung.

"I don't know but I will go look," I said.

"If you find it, destroy it," ordered Aunty Hung. "Why? Because I don't want proof you belong to other people. Stop asking stupid questions!" she exclaimed.

"Yes, Aunty . . ."

"And don't forget your Aunt Lan's address. She's your mother's cousin in California. Can't you remember? What a stupid ox! There's a picture of her somewhere in your bag. The address is on the back. Your mother said so. I need to know where she lives so I bring you there. I hope her address is good—otherwise we're both in trouble! Should've checked with your mother before. But too busy to worry about everything!"

So all those weekly communal meetings reporting to Aunty Hung served no lofty socialist goal. Pretending to criticize my mother for her less-than-perfect street cleaning, Aunty Hung in fact plotted my escape from Vietnam. I wondered if they talked in code. "I've a twitch in my left eye bothering me . . ."

"Isn't that funny? I've a bad twitch in my left eye too!"

"Comrade Hung, can we put off the street-cleaning project till my twitch goes away?"

"Of course, of course Comrade Tam . . ."

I knew Aunty Hung excelled at this game of deceit. That my mother played it too surprised me a bit. But did she have a choice? Not really. And now I had to participate. Time to destroy my birth certificate, pretend to be someone else. But first, I'd have to open my bag.

My bag, my precious brown burlap bag—I had tried opening it a dozen times, but each and every time, became too emotional to go on with my task. So I just left it there in a corner of our hut. Now I had no choice but to look inside. In it, my mother had neatly packed a set of winter clothes and a set of summer ones. As I looked further, I found my identification card, a couple of pens and my precious diary, begun many years ago when my father left us. The diary, leather-bound and imported from Hong Kong, was a gift from Aunty Hung in exchange for hours spent tutoring her

36

daughter, Titi. (Only in first-year grammar school, and already she needed someone to do her homework!)

The bag also contained my middle school diploma mentioning my excellent academic performance. My heart jumped a bit when I found a photo of our family taken years ago when we still posed as a family. My father's bald head looked more naked than I remembered it. While my father smiled for the camera, we all squirmed on his knees in our starched new pants. On the back of that photo my father had written "Tet 1972 with Kim, Mai, Thu." Aunty Hung muttering, "Well, did you find it?" prevented me from drifting into a nostalgic daydream. Hastily I continued my search. At the bottom of the bag, inside a black plastic pouch, I found a sealed envelope. In it my mother had hidden an American fifty-dollar bill and a snapshot of Aunt Lan, looking beautiful for the camera. On the back of that photo, I saw the magic words that would give wings to my dreams: "Nguyen Xuan Lan, 16 Spring Street, California, USA."

Excited to have found Aunt Lan's photo and address, I rushed to show it to Aunty Hung. "Don't get worked up! I'll ask around if anybody knows this place!" she said. I spent the rest of that afternoon writing and rewriting "California, USA" on the wet soil in front of our hut.

Aunty Hung came looking for me the next day with pouting lips. "This address is no good! We need city name or we never find her. California's a state, not a city! California thirty times size of Vietnam. California has hundreds of cities! How I find someone with only street name? I should've known your mother's story is unreliable! She tricked me! Stupid old me! Why I trusted her? She tricked me! Now what I do with you? Now what I do with you?!" Aunty Hung went on and on, but I stopped listening after the first minute.

I didn't dare talk back, but in my head I wanted to scream, "You dumb cow! It was only a mistake! My mother forgot to write the city down, that's all. Perhaps she thought California a city. How could she know? Why do you accuse her of being deceitful?" Aunty Hung's questioning of my mother's intentions offended me. I had to defend my mother's good name—I wanted to save our faces. Yet I had to ask myself, What if Aunty Hung spoke the truth? What if my mother had lied to both of us about a cousin in California? If she could fool me with the two conical hats and two sets of clothing, she could easily fool me with the photo and fake address. My mother wanted me on that boat at all costs, and I blindly took her lies for truths. Perhaps I too wanted to believe in a future called America. But now, where would I go from here?

Because of my mother's false words, I became a burden to Aunty Hung. She got stuck with me like a man stuck with a clumsy wife after a bout of bad negotiation. I felt so ashamed. My mother's lack of care for me became open news for everyone to comment on. All our neighbours looked at me with pity. "Poor girl! Poor woman! Bad situation!" they exclaimed. I wanted to cry but tears would only fuel Aunty Hung's exaggerated sense of self-pity. "What I do with you now? What I do with you now?" She mumbled this all day like a prayer. I knew I had no one else in the world to trust. This made me extremely anxious and unbelievably lonely. Yet I managed to keep an obedient smiling face. Being at Aunty Hung's complete mercy, I had to act like the maid that I would inevitably become.

The Philippines

Three

For a week after the episode with Aunty Hung, I couldn't sleep. My stomach problems deteriorated. I spent hours in the latrine excreting a brown liquid that squirted down, then splashed back on my bum. Diarrhea occurred every day, everywhere in our refugee camp. "You could die of it before any doctor will see you," Aunty Hung said. But my diarrhea seemed different. I had bloody stool while running a fever.

The French doctor at the camp took a quick look at my sweating forehead and sunken eyes. Without taking his eyes from the chart, he gave a swift "Yes" to the nurse. I had passed the first test.

The doctor then gesticulated with his hands, trying to communicate with me. To his surprise, I reported my sickness in a perfect French picked up from private lessons forced upon me. When the doctor gave me a smile, I knew I had passed the second test.

For the first time in my life, I appreciated Mother's strict hand. All those French and English lessons paid off after all. Actually I enjoyed the language lessons. I liked speaking in foreign tongues. I liked it when I could say, "*Sapristi!*" in front of my mother and she'd go on cutting onions as if nothing had happened. Getting away with bad words in my mother's presence gave me a sense of power. Translating for Aunty Hung at her music store also made me feel important. I received a candy every time a client smiled with satisfaction. But things could get tricky at times. Certain terms remained stubbornly American. Expressions like "let it be" became nonsense in Vietnamese. "Let it be what?" the customers all wanted to know. When I failed in my translation, Aunty Hung would skillfully steer the conversation away from American music. Afterward she would call me a stupid ox.

My stomach cramped. Its gurgle echoed across the quiet clinic. I felt my intestines rupturing inside me. The doctor lifted my shirt and pulled down my pants. He put his sweaty palms on my naked abdomen. He palpated me everywhere. His big white-man hands lingered on the left side of my pelvic area. Then to my surprise, he lowered his left ear and pressed it to my belly. As he listened to my rumblings, I felt his warm breath on my skin. It gave me goose bumps. My diarrhea almost leaked out of me, but I succeeded in keeping in the stinky liquid.

"No rebound tenderness. Peristaltic sounds normal," the doctor said to the nurse by his side. Then he pulled down my shirt and used it to wipe the traces of sweat left by his hands. He never touched me again.

"Typhoid fever," announced Dr. Jacques. "Michel Jacques, Médecins Sans Frontières," said the sticker on his white coat. "It can be very serious. Last month I lost a family to it, so I am not taking any more chances. You'll stay at the dispensary until the fever and diarrhea stop."

The doctor set up a cot for me at the dispensary so I could be checked regularly by the local nurse. Having my temperature checked twice a day by a pretty-looking woman reassured me. All of a sudden, my health mattered to someone. Aunty Hung had only shrugged when I told her about the diarrhea. "What you want me to do?" she retorted. She pointed to my dirty fingers, as if saying, "There's your problem, wash them and you'll be fine." But where would I find soap in this place? The absence of soap left its traces on my body. A gooey, stinky, black film covered my skin, but also hid the imperfections of a teenaged face. Months without soap—no wonder I itched all over.

At the clinic, things worked differently. A clean cement floor and a working fan greeted me at the door. I immediately noticed a large sink with soap and running water. So of course I gave myself a sponge bath that very night, before settling down to the luxury of my own cot. Rolling up my clothes to clean my arms and legs posed no trouble. Reaching for the armpits and groins seemed a bit harder, but I managed. All those months washing my grandmother in bed had taught me a few tricks.

We were four spending the days and nights at the dispensary. Next to me slept a quiet infant, looking like a giant dried plum with its exaggerated skin folds. At the back of the clinic lay two elderly women coughing and spitting non-stop into their bronze spittoons.

Since I had learned about tuberculosis in my science classes, I dreaded the presence of these two coughing women. I tried avoiding contact with them as much as possible, disrespectfully turning my back to them virtually all the time. The grandmothers, too busy coughing, didn't mind my un-Confucius-like behaviour. So our "hospital" room, devoid of small talk, became a place of solitude.

Medication flowed from a plastic bag into the vein of my left arm. To rest my sick intestines, the doctor ordered a strict no-food diet. Imagine no food, when my stomach growled with so much hunger! Despite the liquid dripping into my veins, my body dried out. My tongue felt sore from the absence of saliva. At night, I could have cried from hunger but no tears rolled down my cheeks. My fever also remained uncontrollable. My forehead still burned under layers of cold washcloths. I felt a dizzying pain just turning it a bit. The sight of a mere lighted bulb sufficed to send the pain right into my irises. I had no choice but to lie absolutely still with eyes tightly closed.

"Where did you learn your French?" asked Dr. Jacques one day. I opened my eyes to see him staring intently at me. His bluish-green eyes caught me off guard. I'd never seen such colour before. I could have studied them for hours without losing interest. Dr. Jacques wore his thick grey hair in a ponytail. A big beauty mark sprouting hairs on the left side of his nose also left an impression on me. Dr Jacques seemed special. I wondered why he even wanted to talk to me.

"I learned it in school before the Revolution. Afterward my mother hired a retired teacher to give us private lessons at home."

"Aren't private lessons frowned upon by the Communists?"

"Yes. But it was all hidden. My mother ran a popular restaurant, so it didn't look suspicious having people come and go at our place."

"Your mother sounds like a clever woman!" commented Dr. Jacques.

"Yes, very clever. And a great cook too," I said. "Food—that was how she paid my teacher. Free meals in exchange for language lessons given in the back of the kitchen. Even Communist soldiers from the north developed a taste for my mother's food. After they tried her cooking, they didn't have the heart to close her restaurant. Somehow, certain private properties became less evil than others," I told the doctor. He smiled at this.

"Who taught you that?" he asked.

"My mother," I replied.

"Of course. Where is your mother now?"

"She is still in Vietnam."

"Where is your father?" Dr. Jacques also wanted to know.

"He left us years ago without a word," I said. But on the last day of the war, I saw him on television. When we saw the end of the war on television, I also witnessed the end of my childhood fantasy. My father didn't die the heroic soldier I imagined he had. Instead he pushed an old woman out of the way to get on the last helicopter out of Saigon. Could Dr. Jacques understand this act of cowardice? Perhaps not, so I asked him about the causes of my typhoid fever.

"Well, you get it through contaminated water or food. So make sure you boil your water well," Dr. Jacques replied.

"Undercooked food can cause this disease?"

"If the water is not thoroughly boiled, yes. The water here is not clean."

"I've been eating undercooked rice ever since I got here," I told him.

"Well, now you know what to do! Cook your rice longer next time."

"It's hard, Dr. Jacques. We don't have enough firewood to cook properly."

"They don't give it to you?"

"Yes, but very little. It's not enough. I have to look for twigs and branches every day. Some days I don't find any . . ."

"*Conneries*," he muttered to himself, then turned to me, asking, "What do they give you to eat?"

42

"Bags of rice and canned peas, day after day. Twice a month we get chicken wings. But it is hard to cook them properly too, so we eat half-raw chicken," I replied.

To this, Dr. Jacques cried, "*Putain!*"

Putain, conneries—I didn't understand these words, but from the way he said them, I guessed they were swear words. Since I liked the sound of *conneries*, I made a point of remembering it for the next occasion that demanded a bad word. Like my mother, Aunty Hung knew nothing of foreign languages. It would be good saying *conneries* to her face the next time she complained about my mother tricking her.

"Dr. Jacques, does malaria make you see crazy things?"

"Not really, why?"

"My grandmother said I was bitten by a malaria fly as a kid and that's why I have weird thoughts . . ."

"Well, malarial infections can give episodic bouts of fever. At high fever some people do hallucinate. I mean, they start to see or hear things that don't exist."

"I see."

"Why do you ask?"

"Sometimes I see or hear things nobody else does," I replied.

"Well, could be the malarial fever. But it's probably just your fertile imagination!"

My conversation with the doctor suddenly came to a halt. One of the coughing grandmothers went into a retching fit, followed by breathlessness. By the time Dr. Jacques reached her bed, she had regained her colour. She signalled to me to come closer. I did with much caution.

"Little One, tell him I coughed blood yesterday . . ." she said, gesturing for me to translate her words to the doctor.

"Dr. Jacques, the lady here says she coughed blood yesterday."

"I know. The nurse saw her spittoon this morning. Tell her I am treating her for atypical pneumonia."

"Is it tuberculosis?" I wondered.

"No. Just a complicated name for a disease I can't put my finger on."

"I can't translate atypical pneumonia into Vietnamese, Dr. Jacques."

"You'll manage."

"What did he say, Little One?" asked the blood-spitting grandmother between coughing fits.

"He said you have typical coughing disease, so everything will be fine," I answered in a tone that must have been convincing, otherwise she wouldn't have rewarded me with one of her rare one-tooth smiles. From that day on, she coughed so much less and smiled so much more, she was discharged by the end of the week.

"Too bad because I wanted to stay longer," she told me. "Food so much better here," she insisted. But I only shrugged. I couldn't repeat this to Dr. Jacques.

"Got to spit blood too," muttered the remaining grandmother. But despite her effort, no blood came. She only exuded the quiet of half-sleep to match the sick infant's silence. One night, they both stopped breathing, leaving me the next day to face two bodies with eyes rolled upward. The sight of those open eyes paralyzed me. I almost urinated in bed. Thank God the nurse came in time to close their eyes. Imagine, sharing a room with two open-eyed corpses! I wondered what my grandmother would say to this. Was this bad luck or what?!

Whatever healing power my words exerted on the first blood-spitting grandmother, they failed on me, for, two weeks later, I still suffered from bloody diarrhea. Dr. Jacques worried about my slow progress. He frowned every morning, coming to check my temperature. But with living conditions so much cleaner at the dispensary, I didn't mind staying a bit longer. New patients arrived to replace departed ones. These were talkative young mothers with their crying babies. They loved their new surroundings so I spared them the truth. Spared them the spooky stories of hospital beds and the ghostly tales of those who had died the day before.

Cleanliness must've brought me back to life, for slowly but surely, my condition improved. My diarrhea diminished, then stopped by the end of the third week.

"You can leave today," Dr. Jacques said. "But not before telling the woman in cot number six to stop with the water bottle and go on with her

breastfeeding," he ordered. So all bad things, as all good things, must come
to an end.

The Philippines
Four

My first menstrual period came unannounced one day. This added further humiliation to my only pair of underwear. I had to go to Aunty Hung for special requests. "More problems," she said, before handing me two clean underwear and a few pads. "They are washable pads," she mentioned, "my *own* washables. You can borrow them as long as you give them back *washed and clean* next week." So like it or not, my ties to Aunty Hung deepened with each day—sharing her neighbourhood, sharing her boat, sharing her hut and now sharing her menstrual pads.

Washing the bloodstained pads at the fountain became a source of embarrassment for me. Even if I went at twilight, I still felt exposed. I felt everyone's gazes on me. No wonder Aunty Hung stopped going there.

"You do good job, you wash my dirty pads too," she said to me one day. "And because you're just a kid, nobody would bother noticing," she continued. But people did notice my sudden entrance into womanhood. Well, perhaps not everyone, but the street kids who would beat me for a piece of firewood did take note.

The ugliest and meanest of those kids was a boy called Minh. Shorter than me and probably not much older, he had crooked black teeth and a crossed eye that looked beyond you even while looking at you. This trick of his always scared me. It felt as if someone approached me from behind. And if I turned around to look, he'd grab my piece of firewood and disappear before I could scream, "A dog gave birth to you! A damned dog gave birth to you!" I knew screaming got me nowhere—no one would come to my defense. I'd only get scolded for making noises and swearing. Besides, I could never outdo those kids in bad words. But the frustration of stupidly losing my day's labour fed my mind with gutter phrases.

Minh ceased torturing me when he saw me washing bloodstained pads. He actually smiled at me when our paths crossed one day. "Fuck your mother!" I almost screamed to his face. But his crooked smile stopped my words in mid-sentence.

"Want a surprise? Meet me behind the clinic tonight," he said, reaching out to take my hands. I could only nod for fear of displeasing him. His firm grasp on my arm told me I had no choice but to agree. Disobeying him could mean more trouble. Only Titi knew of this meeting. "Come look for me if I don't return by bedtime," I told her. In her fear and amazement, she nodded her head.

"Where you from?" Minh asked as he motioned for me to sit next to him.

"Hue," I said.

"Yeah, I heard of it—Tet '68. Me, I'm from My Lai—ever heard of it?"

"No."

"You how old?"

"Sixteen," I lied, to give myself some advantage.

"Me, seventeen. Or more, I don't know. Can't remember. No birth certificate. Your family here?"

"No, my mother is still in Hue. I'm here with a neighbour."

"Too bad!" Minh exclaimed, but not in a mean way.

"Your family is here?"

"No, no family. Ran away from orphanage."

"Really? Must be scary having no adults around."

"No, not scary. I'm used to it. Do what I want. Nobody shouts at me."

"So how did you get here?"

"Took boat of course."

"I know. But don't you have to pay? I heard people paid a gold bar each for the trip."

"No, I don't pay. Captain's my friend. I bring him customers for boat."

"I see. Anything bad happen on your trip? I heard lots of bad things," I continued, being friendly.

"Nothing really bad. You?"

"I don't know."

"Don't know! You asleep or what?" Minh said mockingly.

"Maybe that's it. Maybe I slept through it all. I just can't remember," I replied with a shy laugh.

"Can't remember? No!"

"Really, I can't remember the boat trip. Only remember tall, blonde men throwing us cans of Coca-Cola."

"OK, whatever. Want to see surprise now?" asked Minh.

"Yes, what is it?"

"Beautiful fan for lady," Minh replied. From his shirt pocket, he brought out a fan whose details I couldn't quite see in the dark but whose scent I couldn't mistake. Sandalwood. I'd smelled it before—years ago in pre-revolutionary times. This was expensive stuff no street kid could afford. Knowing that he probably stole it added a touch of danger to our encounter.

"Smells nice," I said nervously.

"Yeah, takes stink away. For you."

"Why?" I asked, surprised.

"You lady now. I like you," Minh laughed.

"Thank you," I said, afraid of offending him if I refused the gift.

"One more thing . . ."

"Yes?"

"Touch me here . . ." Minh ordered. Before I could react, he pressed my right hand down on a hard lump between his legs. With his hand on top of mine, he forced me to rub back and forth while screaming, "Quicker! Quicker!" After a few minutes, he let out a sharp cry as a liquid spurted from his lump. He told me to stop. He had had enough. So had I.

"More surprises tomorrow!" Minh promised as we got up to return to our huts.

I knew these acts were wrong. But the forbidden game intrigued me. My textbook on cells and tadpoles had never prepared me for this. So I returned often to our secret meeting place. I wanted to see how far the game would lead, but it never went any further than on that first night. As I rubbed the lump between his legs, Minh's body would become tense. He would breathe fast. Sometimes he forced me to squeeze so hard, I thought the lump would surely fall off. But it didn't. The more I choked it, the more it came to life in my hand. It became so hot it felt like a lump of coal. When Minh had had enough, he would let out a cry. Then he would remove my hand from his lump and we would go on talking. Once he tried cupping my breasts with his hands. He never dared repeat it after I punched his stomach. I also hated being splashed by his liquid. With time I learned to avoid getting sticky hands. Our forbidden acts became a bit mechanical after the third week. Eventually I lost my curiosity. I visited Minh only to see the fancy stuff he showed me. He didn't always give them to me, but I liked the stories that went with each object—to whom it belonged, how he'd gotten it.

"The nice-smelling fan belonged to bargirl who dropped it in the street," Minh said. "Gift from her male client, but since she couldn't appreciate it, she lost it. What's a bargirl? That's someone who sat in bars drinking beer with American soldiers during war. Sometimes they danced with Americans and sometimes they did other things too. Don't you know anything? Why are you so stupid?" Minh scolded me.

The Philippines

Five

Stepping out of our hut one day, I found four piles of twigs and cut branches neatly stacked to form the letter M. Somehow I expected this from Minh. "Like a love letter," Titi whispered excitedly in my ear. Although the firewood pleased me, my heart didn't palpitate with joy. This was no love letter, more like a contract. That night, Minh came late to our meeting. I thought he wouldn't show. For a brief moment, I even sighed with disappointment. I'd spent the whole afternoon brushing my hair, hoping he could at least feel the hair even if he couldn't see it in the dark. Despite his ugliness, Minh still tickled my curiosity. Our midnight meetings, although perverse, satisfied my need for compliments. With Minh around, the waiting game became more tolerable. I liked the gifts he brought me. I enjoyed the stories he told me. His tales, like those of Aunty Hung's, soon became a part of my Palawan collection.

"What's the orphanage like?" I asked Minh that night, as my hand slowly searched for the lump between his legs. This act had become automatic by then—he didn't have to ask for it anymore. And finding it through his loose shorts no longer posed a problem. I knew where to look.

"You want to hear my orphan story, Kim? Nothing good to say. My parents died in war. I went to orphanage in '68. Was eight years old. Maybe older, not sure. Nuns at orphanage were mean. They were monsters in dresses. Beat us up all the time. They had whips. They searched inside our underpants to see if we stole stuff. One nun liked to search inside my pants. I was oldest boy there. So I get hard when she touched me. When I get hard, she whipped me. She said, 'You're a beast!' She searched me all the time. And she whipped me all the time. At night I looked through keyhole to see her undress. She knew I looked. But she didn't turn off light. I was oldest boy so I did all heavy work. I took care of younger kids. I lifted large tables. I carried big rice bags. I cleaned all bathrooms.

"Every month nuns drove us to the beach. We went in a big bus. We had lunch on sand. We played ball for one hour. Then we sang songs. In evening, I helped nuns carry two orphans to captain's hut. Orphans didn't want to go. They kicked and cried. I had to tie them down with rope. They were stupid orphans. Always careless. Always breaking things. Or always crying for no reason. Nuns were tired of them. Nuns wanted to get rid of them. Nuns told captain, 'Take these children to America. Give them a better life.' Then nuns said, 'God watching you, God watching over the children.' You know, captain's afraid of God. So he takes two orphans each trip. Nuns didn't have to pay. That's how orphans travelled free. They're for good luck. After orphans went with captain on boat, we returned to bus. Nuns drove back to orphanage. On roads, no soldiers asked, 'Where you going?' They trusted nuns and kids. At orphanage, there are two less orphans to worry about.

"I knew nuns would never let me go. I'm too good for them. They need me. But I'm tired of heavy work. I'm tired of orphanage. I want to go to America. I have things to do in America. One day I ran away from orphanage. I slept on streets. I begged near pagodas. Sometimes I stole money from rich ladies. Just snatch their purse and run. Easy stuff! They couldn't run after me in high-heeled shoes! Stealing from markets was harder . . . Shopkeepers all knew each other. They helped each other. They all gang up to beat me.

"I met young girls on streets. Also poor like me. They were starving. I took them to captain. He kept them for a few nights and gave them some food. He also gave me food during those nights. Next day he asked me to bring different girls. Younger girls. And I did. So captain became my friend. One day captain said, 'We go to America next month!' I was so excited! I came to his hut every day. He taught me about boats. It wasn't easy to learn.

When I became better, he said, 'We're ready!' We had bad weather on boat. Two days of bad rain and two days of heavy winds. Boat went up and down, up and down. People vomited everywhere. I helped captain to steer boat. Then I cleaned vomit mess. I worked hard. Captain liked me. After rain, we had good weather. So captain lent me his picture book of naked woman. I read it with him. It was good! That's what I remember most about boat trip. Picture book of naked woman. Red hair. Big breasts with pink nipples. Nuns didn't have breasts like this.

"Want to see gift now? It's a Seiko watch. Ever seen one? Don't stop rubbing. Another thing, Kim. Want to kiss me down there? OK! Calm down! No need to scream, 'Fuck your mother!' God! You talk worse than me!"

Rubbing Minh could be tiring. Sometimes it took so long my hands ached badly. But I liked the feeling of his warm breath down my shirt. This cross-eyed orphan stood out from the crowd. Despite his small body, he exuded cockiness. Talking to him made me realize how little of the real world I knew. As my fear of him dissipated, so did my disgust for him. I began to admire his courage living alone. I liked his carefreeness. I tried picturing myself as an orphan or street kid, but couldn't. I had parents, after all. Cowardly, deceiving parents, but parents nonetheless. And despite everything, I missed them.

Minh liked me. He wanted to see me every night. Sometimes when I rubbed him twice, he would give me two presents on the same night. Sometimes he gave me none, but I didn't mind. Imagine the meanest street kid sharing a secret with me! This gave me protection from other bullies. For once I felt powerful.

One day I asked Minh why he wanted to go to America. At first he refused to answer my question. He looked at me as if to say, "Why you so stupid? We all want to go to America!" Then he shook his head and turned away from me. He whispered something that sounded like "Charlie Company. . . ." His words became nonsense rambling. I had to hug him tight to catch his story.

"My village is My Lai. I stayed there with my parents, grandmother and little sisters. American soldiers came often to My Lai village. They gave candies to kids. We liked them. They said, 'Hello!' We said, 'OK, Mister!

Gums, Mister?' They threw us some gums and laughed. Then they waved, 'Bye! Bye!' We wanted them to come back. We were always waiting for them to come back.

"One day Americans did come back. March '68. Springtime. Two months after Tet '68. I was eating breakfast with Grandmother and Little Sisters Number Two and Three. My parents were out in field. I heard loud noises outside. Bang! Bang! Bang! Then Americans came in our house. There were four of them. They all wore dark glasses. They all chewed gums. They pointed guns at us. Little Sister Number Two was so scared she hid in rice bag. But her cries gave her away.

"Americans took us all outside. They screamed, 'Any Viet Congs here? We kill anybody hiding Viet Congs!' But there's no Viet Congs in our village! 'No VCs here! We're not Communists! We don't like Communists!' Grandmother shouted. One American soldier spit his gum on her chest and hit her face with gun. She fell down. She choked on her broken tooth. Americans laughed.

"Then Americans took everyone into field. My young sisters only four and five years old. They can't walk fast. American took them both on his back. He gave them candies to stop the cries. I was afraid. Didn't know what's going on. On road to field, I saw many dead bodies. One kid was searching for his mother. 'Mother! Mother!' he cried. Then American soldier came and shot him too. Another American put flames to people's houses. He burned our rice storage. In field, there was big pit. Very deep. We were forced to stand in front of pit. Many people there. The neighbours, my aunts, my uncles, my cousins. But my parents were not there. Then Americans shot us. We fell in pit. I heard screams. Then I fainted.

"When I woke, it was quiet. No more Bang! Bang! Bang! Dead bodies on top of me. But I'm still alive. My uncle's body on top of me. When he died he fell on me and pushed me down pit, so I wasn't hit. His spirit protected me from bullets. I tried climbing out of pit. Very hard. A lot of heavy bodies on me. A lot of blood. Very slippery. Hard to breathe. No air, only smell of blood. I moved dead arms one by one to get out. But arms were stiff. Hard to move. Like they all wanted to strangle me. After a long time I got out. Very tired. My legs hurt. So much pain in my head. I couldn't believe what I saw. Blood everywhere. My two little sisters were shot in head. My aunts and cousins all dead. I walked to our house. Grandmother dead from choking on her tooth. I walked back to field. Tried looking for Father and Mother amongst the dead. I turned dead bodies around to check for their faces. Some faces had no more tongue. Some bodies had no more hands. It was horrible.

"I finally found Mother and Father in field. Shot in the head. Throats also slit. There were words written on their chests. Words written in blood. I didn't understand those words. Later at orphanage, nuns taught me alphabet. I learned to read. Then I remember the words on my parents' chests. It was 'Charlie Company.' I asked nuns, 'What's Charlie Company?' They answered, 'Must be a name, American name.' I think about Charlie Company all the time. So I'll go to America to look for Charlie Company. Want to ask him why he killed my parents. Why he killed so many people— 200 or 300 dead. We're not Communists. We're on American side. After I get my answer, I'll kill him. I'll slit his throat. Then I write 'Minh' on his chest. His blood will be ink. I still hear my sisters' cries. I dream of dead bodies all the time. My village is waiting for revenge. Ghosts scream to me every night. I have to do it. I have to find Charlie Company in America.

"I remember walking for long time. Roads were empty. Very quiet since everybody's dead. Then I saw helicopters coming from sky. American helicopters. I was scared. I ran away. But I had pain in legs. Couldn't run fast. Then I tripped on rocks. Fell down. I tried hiding in grass. But it's too late. Americans already saw me. American soldiers ran to me. One picked me up. Gave me candy. But I spit it out. Didn't want their poison. They brought me to hospital. Then they waved, 'Bye! Bye!' At hospital I told my story. But nobody believed me.

"'Americans don't kill villagers,' Vietnamese doctors said. After hospital, I went to orphanage. I asked nuns at orphanage if they knew of My Lai village. They said yes. 'We heard about the accidental deaths,' nuns said. 'Americans killed twenty children by mistake. They were looking for Communists . . .' nuns repeated. 'Not twenty kids! Whole village! 300 people or more! Not accident! They brought us to pit, then shoot!' I screamed. But nuns won't listen. 'Stop blaming Americans!' nuns told me. 'Communists are just as bad! Don't forget the Tet '68 massacre in Hue. Communists shot children and put them in pits too!' nuns said. Nuns showed me newspaper photos of Hue. Lots of dead bodies. Nuns showed me television news of Hue. Lots of dead bodies too. Everybody talked about Hue. Everybody blamed Communists. But nobody cared about My Lai. Nobody blamed Americans. I don't hate all Americans. Only hate Charlie Company. That's why I go to America. I go to kill Charlie Company. Why you go to America, Kim?"

"Minh, the nuns at your orphanage were right. Hue also saw unbearable tragedy in 1968. Communists shot innocent people and shoved their bodies in ditches too. I saw that on television but I hardly remember it. 'Bang! Bang! Bang! Lots of deaths. We saw it on television!' My grandmother never bothered with the details. Only Aunty Hung told me the truth. Five minutes into the New Year, rockets landed in our neighbourhood. At first Aunty Hung mistook the noise for firecrackers. Then she saw flames lighting the sky. The sounds of exploding glass and cracking concrete confirmed her worst fears. War had entered her life in the midst of celebrations.

"Minh, my memory of Tet '68 may be hazy but I remember well the end of the war. I saw the whole thing on television. Did you see it too? April 30th, 1975. Do you remember it? What were you doing that day, Minh? Were you out in the streets welcoming our 'liberators' from the north? Or did you stay away, fearing for a future marked with personal revenge? But no, you have nothing to fear. I forgot—American soldiers killed your family. You get Communist credits for that. My father ran off to America in front of the cameras. Communist revenge never came, but I lived in constant fear and shame after that day. I want to find my father in America, Minh. I want to ask him why he left us."

After that talk, Minh and I became closer. I saw through his tough street-urchin mask. Like me, he lived in fear, the fear of loneliness. He witnessed first-hand the destruction of his village. I watched the burning of my city on television. He saw his parents dead. I saw mine receding farther and farther from my reach. Both lost, we needed each other's company. Rubbing his lump became an excuse to share our stories.

The Philippines

Six

Thanks to Minh, I became the owner of fancy objects for which I had no use. I couldn't give them to Aunty Hung. She'd been around our family long enough to know I couldn't possibly own those things. So I decided to give them to the nurse at the dispensary instead. Yes, Joy, the pretty nurse who took care of me during my sickness deserved the best gifts. Perhaps I needed an excuse to return to the clinic. Perhaps I just wanted to see again *my* cot—number four. To relive, if only for a few minutes, a time when my well-being mattered to someone.

I brought a harmonica to the clinic for Dr. Jacques and a jewellery box for Joy. Dr. Jacques not only remembered me, he seemed pleased to see me again.

"Just the person I'm looking for," he said with a big smile. His proposal took me by surprise. "Would you like to help out at the clinic?" Dr. Jacques asked. He needed someone to translate for him since Joy, the Filipino nurse, spoke no Vietnamese. "I am getting tired of doing vet medicine," Dr. Jacques laughed.

"Excuse me?" I asked, not quite grasping the meaning of his words.

"Veterinarian medicine, that's medicine for dogs and cats."

"You mean there are doctors for dogs and cats where you are from?" I said, quite amazed at my ignorance of the West, despite my fluency in its languages. Obviously years of reading French comics and listening to Aunty Hung's American music didn't prepare me for such revelations.

"Plenty," Dr. Jacques replied. "In France, dogs are sometimes more important than children," he said. "People bring them everywhere. Even to restaurants, like pampered babies," he continued.

"In Vietnam people go to restaurants to eat dogs," I told Dr. Jacques. "But no, my mother doesn't serve dogs. Dog meat is a real delicacy. Same with snake meat. You need special training for it. My mother doesn't cook according to training. She cooks according to whims and creativity," I assured the doctor. He smiled as though he liked my reply. The hair on his beauty mark wiggled a bit. And the green in his greenish-blue eyes turned darker as he listened to my description of dog meat. Then he repeated once more the offer.

"Two dollars a week for translation work. I'm on a volunteer basis so I'm not exactly rich," he admitted.

I lost no time accepting Dr. Jacques's offer. The job would make the waiting game more tolerable. I would be spared Aunty Hung's sour grimace. The incomplete California address my mother wrote had become a source of constant mockery. Daily, Aunty Hung cursed my mother, calling her name loud enough for all our neighbours to hear. "What I do with you? What I do with you?" became a mantra she interrupted with the occasional "You want her?" Of course, no one else at the camp wanted me. They all had enough trouble with their own kids to take in another one. Even Titi, who shared my bamboo mat, looked at me in funny ways. So yes, I yearned to work for Dr. Jacques.

The Philippines

Seven

Dr. Jacques intimidated me at first. He spoke impatiently and smiled rarely. But with time I got used to his dry tone and became less afraid of him. Once he even bought me fresh oranges and sweet cakes from outside the camp. But he didn't give them to me free of charges. He deducted their cost cent for cent from my small salary. However, I couldn't complain. I needed the much-deserved treats after a long day translating Vietnamese superstition into a French logic he could understand. If the translation of medical terms seemed difficult, the translation of clashing mentalities sometimes turned my brain to mulch!

To help Dr. Jacques see more patients, I would have to refuse some people. To the people I turned away, I would just give out small self-adhesive bandages. "The bandages help my stomach pain and my headaches," many of them claimed, returning to the clinic for more. Fooling people in their beliefs didn't bother me. Seeing people spread their nonsense to others did bother me. Once, an elderly woman insisted on swallowing a wiggling gecko to treat her breathing problems. Holding the animal by its tail, she came to the clinic asking for a banana. The sliced banana would hold down the gecko. "Easier to swallow this way," she said.

"No, Aunty! Eat caterpillars for breathing problems, not geckoes!" shouted one patient from her cot. I had to scream *"Conneries!"* three times before they stopped their nonsense. As a treatment for illnesses, geckoes

58

seemed popular but not as much as fresh urine from a newborn. The waste after a pregnancy also promised miraculous cures to many people.

"The placenta fed the baby in the womb," Dr. Jacques told me.

"Placentas, full of good stuff, will cure diseases," patients also claimed. So a crowd always gathered outside the clinic the day after a birth. People came from everywhere, asking for a cup of the baby's urine to drink and a piece of the mother's placenta to eat. Of course I didn't translate any of these demands. If Dr. Jacques thought I belonged to these backward people, he would stop bringing me treats.

Dr. Jacques wasn't the only one bringing me treats. Nurse Joy also brought me foodstuffs from outside the camp. Her spicy tomato soup filled the clinic with a pungent smell and produced in us nostalgic cravings for a homemade meal. At first, Joy presented the soup as a gift, but when I asked for it again and again, she didn't refuse payment. In fact, through word of mouth, her soup became so popular at the camp, Joy had to stay an hour later everyday to take orders. And because I translated for her, I also made a cent for every dollar she earned. At the camp only a few months, already I understood the language of money.

My new schedule prevented me from seeing the cross-eyed Minh. He didn't make a big scene—he just avoided me. He stopped sending me firewood, stopped pressuring me into forbidden meetings. He pretended I no longer existed. I had no trouble recognizing his wounded pride. But neither had I time to ponder long over it. My official functions at the dispensary kept me too busy during the day. At night, fatigue prevented me from catering to a boy wanting to be a man. Although I missed Minh's stories, I didn't miss his orphan's whim.

One day our paths crossed in the latrine. He asked nicely to see me again. I couldn't refuse his request. That night I brought an orange to share with him. I peeled the orange and placed pieces of it in his dirty palms. He asked me to put them directly on his tongue. I did and he tried licking my fingers.

"Where did you get the orange?" asked Minh. Then he reached out to caress my hair. I let him continue in this direction. It was the first time my hair mattered more than my right hand.

"Dr. Jacques brought them for me," I replied.

"Is he the white man at the clinic?"

"Yes, he's a French doctor."

"I don't trust white men," Minh said.

"I thought you only have this thing against Americans. Dr. Jacques is not American. He's not Charlie Company," I tried explaining.

"All the same to me . . ."

"It's not the same, Minh! He didn't kill anybody!" I protested.

"You like him or something?"

"No, but . . ."

Minh suddenly grabbed my hair, pushing me to my knees. He pinned me down on the ground, crossed his legs on my thorax, and held me captive under his limbs. Taken by surprise, I couldn't fight back. His muscular thighs pressed hard on my breasts while his arms locked mine in. The back of my head bobbed on the growing lump between his legs. Minute after minute, we held that strange position, not uttering a word. Fear and ambivalence sharpened my senses. I looked up to see a shooting star streaking across the night sky. Then Minh released me.

"Goodbye and sorry, Kim. Didn't mean to hurt you . . ." Minh whispered in my ear as he helped me up.

Minh came back into my life two weeks later. I was on my way to work. I noticed Dr. Jacques a few metres ahead of me. The doctor walked briskly, ignoring all the goodwill around him. Children's waves, mothers' smiles, "Hello Mister!"—he returned none of these greetings. Then a piece of rock came from nowhere to hit the back of his head. To my horror, Dr. Jacques slumped to the ground.

"It's the cross-eyed kid! I saw him throw the rock!" someone shouted. A group of men ran after Minh. Another curious group formed around Dr. Jacques. No one offered to help. Paralyzed by fear, they could only stare. Dr. Jacques eventually woke from his stone-induced nap. He palpated the back of his head and moaned when he felt blood. He got up, staggering to the clinic with his head in his hands. At the clinic's entrance, he turned around, addressing no one in particular: "It's OK—let the kid go. He didn't do it on purpose . . ."

I knew I had to help Dr. Jacques but I couldn't move. Witnessing Minh's violence shocked me. A stone to the head in return for an orange on the tongue. Minh's idea of gratitude spoke more to me than all his stories of sorrows. Yet seeing the extent of his jealousy made me feel wanted.

Nurse Joy rushed out of the clinic calling my name. "Kim! What're you waiting for? Come help me now!" Her words forced me to face a grimacing Dr. Jacques. What could I do for him? How could I cure a bleeding doctor? Self-adhesive bandages, geckoes, baby's urine and mother's placenta were all I knew about healing.

"Kim, take some soap and water and wash my head well. Next take a razor and shave the hair around my wound. Joy will sew the wound but if it bleeds while she's sewing, then you take a clean washcloth and press on it with all your might. Understand? Go! You can do it!"

I followed Dr. Jacques's instructions to the letter. He didn't ask me to, but I also wiped the sweat off his neck. Every time Joy's needle entered his scraggy torn scalp, my sweat joined his to form a rivulet down his back. After thirty stitches, we managed to fix Dr. Jacques's melancholic headache.

Minh disappeared from view after that episode. None of the other street kids knew of his hiding place. His self-exile intrigued them. Then one day he reappeared. I saw him at the fountain filling a bucket of water. The change in him appalled me. A swollen, bruised face and an unsteady gait gave him a look I'd never seen before. The traces of whip on his arms and legs told a story of defeat, of a broken will. Minh wavered as he held the bucket of water.

"Minh!" I called, coming to help him. Minh shook his head when he recognized me.

"Fuck your white doctor!" he growled.

"What? Dr. Jacques didn't do this to you, did he?" I asked, but Minh already turned away from me.

The Philippines
Eight

I wanted to question Dr. Jacques about Minh's bruises but I dared not bring it up. I dreamt about Minh's tattered body at night and woke full of guilt. I wondered who had hit Minh, then convinced myself it couldn't be Dr. Jacques. The complexity of jealousy, revenge and guilt seemed beyond my understanding. While I had yet to earn Dr. Jacques's complete trust, I knew I had lost Minh's friendship forever.

Dr. Jacques avoided small talk. He preferred scientific explanations. He loved showing me the different facets of diseases. In the role of teacher, Dr. Jacques became surprisingly patient. I beamed when he congratulated me for helping to heal his head wound. Medicine seemed to be his passion. Off topic, he returned to his taciturn state.

My job at the dispensary gave me everything I wanted: money, time away from Aunty Hung and patients' respect. I'd even gathered a crowd of admiring children outside the dispensary.

"Big Sister, Big Sister! You have candy for us?" they always asked, intercepting me on my way to work. Of course I didn't have any candy. But these kids placed me on the same pedestal as American GIs during the war. "Mister, Mister! You have gums?" Ah, I felt good!

The first month we worked together, Dr. Jacques called me "*Eh, la Gamine.*" It took him several weeks before he could remember to address me by my real name, Kim. But that didn't bother me. The cakes and oranges he brought me compensated for his lack of memory. I resold those foods at double the price to some of my neighbours. They too yearned for more than rice and peas.

One day Dr. Jacques stopped talking medicine long enough to reveal a bit of himself. He invited me to join him for lunch. At the table, he offered me a piece of his rice cake. Then he told me of his love for the Orient. He described it as an obsession with roots in his grandfather's tales.

"My grandfather taught mathematics in Hanoi, at a time when France still ruled over Vietnam. He devoted the best years of his life to the prestigious Lycée Albert Sarrault. Being a French *lycée*, students learned only French at this Hanoi institution. Local graduates finished their studies unable to read their native Vietnamese language. The students also learned French history, French geography and sang 'La Marseillaise' in class. 'Our ancestors hailed from Gaul,' they recited each week. Yet most of the kids came from pure Vietnamese stock, children of rich families, collaborators of the French. Only through betrayal of their country did the Vietnamese become wealthy," Dr. Jacques concluded.

"My grandmother said the same thing, Dr. Jacques."

"As a young boy I heard many tales of Vietnam. Stories of beautiful women with teeth dyed black intrigued me the most. How can people be beautiful with black teeth, I wondered. My young mind couldn't imagine it. So I wanted to see for myself."

"Did you, Dr. Jacques?"

"No, but I will one day."

"It's an old custom, Dr. Jacques. Most Vietnamese women don't dye their teeth black anymore."

"My grandfather left my grandmother for one of those beautiful black-toothed women," continued Dr. Jacques.

"Oh . . ."

"My mother was only six when her father abandoned his family. He heeded the call of adventure, sailed for Hanoi one day and never returned. The family received a postcard sixteen months later announcing his marriage to a black-toothed Vietnamese woman. My mother remembers her

63

Parisian childhood home as a place of silence and darkness. My grandmother's migraines, which developed after the abandonment, made noise and light unbearable for her. She spent days in bed, ignoring the needs of my young mother playing silently by her bedside. Left alone, my mother invented her own perverse games. She painted her dolls' teeth black and slowly cut off their hair. At other times, she'd chop their hands or severe their heads and bury the whole thing in her toy cemetery in the plant pots. My mother grew up hating all things adventurous, exotic, far away. At twenty, she married her high school sweetheart and settled into a life of domestic calm. As a child, my mother entertained me with her venom. Later, she stopped mentioning Vietnam. She feared my grandfather's restlessness would find its way to me. Of course it did. I became obsessed with the Orient as soon as I could read. So coming here is like realizing a dream."

"I am sorry to hear about your grandfather's disappearance. Must be sad for your grandmother, for your mother, for you. I know how it feels, Dr. Jacques."

"No, my grandfather's adventures didn't pain me. I respect his quest for freedom, his love of the unknown. I only wish my mother hadn't coloured my childhood with her torment."

Working for Dr. Jacques gave me many advantages over my compatriots. Through him, I met important-looking people. These men talked and acted as if our lives depended on them. Our lives didn't depend on them but our dreams did. These immigration men came often to Dr. Jacques for minor ailments. And Fate put me on Mr. Sandys' path one day.

"I'm an immigration officer from America—you know what that means, little girl?" Mr. Sandys asked.

"Not really, sir," I said.

"It means I can get you out of this place one day. So bring me to your doctor now!"

"He will be here soon, sir."

"Why is it that we always have to wait for doctors? And what's a young girl like you doing here? Not a nurse, I hope!"

"I help translate, sir."

"Good for you, but I don't need you."

"Dr. Jacques speaks little English, but he understands well, sir."

"What kind of doctor speaks no English?" asked Mr. Sandys, more as a joke than an insult. Before I could answer, Dr. Jacques entered the room, addressing me in French.

"What does this shithead want?" the doctor asked with a frown. When it became clear to all that Dr. Jacques wouldn't dismiss me, the immigration officer sighed. "Tell him it hurts when I pee. Want to go all the time but nothing comes out."

"*Il dit qu'il a mal quand il ' pee,' Dr. Jacques,*" I said, doing my best to translate, although I had a feeling Dr. Jacques could do very well without me in this case.

"Ask him if there are secretions from his penis. Any pain in his testicles?"

"I am sorry, Dr. Jacques, I don't know the English words for penis and testicles," I protested, embarrassed.

"Same as in French, just pronounced differently," Dr. Jacques replied.

"Yes, he says there is a yellow liquid coming out of his penis," I continued translating in spite of my burning red cheeks.

"Tell him to take this twice a day for seven days and stay away from the girls in the meantime," Dr. Jacques commanded as he handed me some medicine and a couple of plastic packages that he took out of his personal bag.

"Thanks Doc, but I won't need the safes. Got lots of them in my suitcase," replied Mr. Sandys, taking the medicine but not the other things.

"Then use them!" ordered the doctor impatiently. He didn't even wait for the American to get out of earshot before exclaiming, "*Quel imbécile! Quel emmerdeur!*"

A week later, when Mr. Sandys returned with a bottle of wine for the doctor, they acted as if their friendship stretched far back into a nostalgic past. They ignored my services, preferring to converse in a mixture of English and French. How a bottle of red liquid can seal a shaky relationship remained incomprehensible to me.

After that day, the American came back often to discuss wines with the French doctor. The first time Mr. Sandys returned, I wickedly announced, "The imbecile shithead from America is here!" I had hoped to elicit a smile of recognition, but Dr. Jacques only stared blankly. The immigration officer also came for lots of minor ailments. Perhaps the ailments served as excuses to see Nurse Joy? Joy didn't exude joy. I never saw her smile at Vietnamese patients. She never smiled at Dr. Jacques either. With me, she acted like a strict older sister. But in Mr. Sandys' presence, she became a grinning and silly girl. The change in Joy's behaviour got on Dr. Jacques's nerves more than once. But the doctor didn't discourage Mr. Sandys' visits. He liked talking wine too much.

When Aunty Hung heard about Mr. Sandys' visits to the dispensary, she muttered less. She replaced her usual "What I do with you?" with long sighs. One day, as we squatted down for our usual dinner of rice and peas, she pretended not to see me. She filled everyone's bowl with undercooked rice while mine remained empty. When I asked for my bowl to be filled, she ignored me. At the second request, Aunty Hung gave a loud snort.

"Hmmm! I hear there's an American immigration officer coming to the clinic!"

"Yes, Aunty Hung. His name is Mr. Sandys."

"Why didn't you tell me about him sooner?"

"I don't know . . ."

"What's he like?"

"He likes wine and he likes Joy, the nurse. But Dr. Jacques thinks he's stupid."

"He likes the nurse, eh? What's she like?"

"She is pretty."

"Well, well, well! What time does he come to the clinic?"

"I don't know, Aunty Hung. Sometimes he comes around four in the afternoon. Sometimes he doesn't come at all."

"OK, here's your rice. Hurry up, eat fast. And don't forget to wash the dishes before they turn off the water at the fountain!"

The next day, Aunty Hung came looking for me at the clinic. Crusty blood coloured her lips red. Dried mud lined her eyes. She left the top part of her blouse unbuttoned enough to see a trickle of sweat rolling down her chest. A tight smile traced an ungenerous outline on her face.

"Where's the immigration officer?" Aunty Hung asked me.

"He didn't come today," I said.

"Are you sure? I'll wait outside in case he comes!"

"Is the woman OK? She seems to be bleeding from the lips," remarked Joy.

"I think she is OK. She probably bit them on purpose. Self-inflicted wounds to make her more colourful. Or maybe more pitiful . . . I don't know."

Aunty Hung loitered at the clinic's entrance for hours. She walked back and forth, left and right. After a while, she sat on the dirt floor, her head slumped on her bended knees and dozed. People took her for a mad woman when she woke, startled by the sounds of a cooing pigeon, her mud eyes smudged, her cracked lips bleeding and her unbuttoned blouse revealing a pair of naked breasts. She hurled obscenities at the men leering at her. Then Aunty Hung straightened up, fixed her blouse and entered the clinic. "Tell your doctor I want to meet his American friend, the immigration man," she told me. When I translated her request to Dr. Jacques, he only replied, "*Conneries!*"

At Dr. Jacques's request, I had to drag her back to our hut and hand her to her wide-eyed husband. Day after day, Aunty Hung returned to the clinic, but luck didn't walk with her. She never ran into Mr. Sandys. After three unsuccessful weeks, Aunty Hung gave up her mission. She reverted to her "What I do with you now?" complaint.

Mr. Sandys still hung around our clinic. He came mostly for Joy's smiles. He also came to collect French wine stories. But one day he actually came for *me*. That day, a typically hot cloudless day, I almost fainted when he read the names of sponsored people due to leave for Connecticut. He repeated my name three times before I understood my new fate. Someone from a strange-sounding place sponsored me . . . New York, yes, Washington, yes, California, yes. But Connecticut? The unfamiliar name puzzled me. Without an atlas, I could only imagine it as a place in the centre of the world. I kept telling myself there must be some kind of error that would be corrected soon enough. But my heart still leapt like grasshoppers inside my chest.

The Philippines

Nine

"Are you sure you're looking for me—Nguyen Thi Kim? My name is very common. There must be dozens of us with that name here," I asked Mr. Sandys, trying to sound calm.

"Yes, the name's the same. She was born in 1965 which makes her fifteen now. That's about your age isn't it? Dr. Jacques tells me you are from Hue—so is this Kim I have on my list. Come by my office this afternoon and bring me all your official papers. Birth certificate if you have it. I'll see what I can do."

Back in our hut, I rechecked my burlap bag a dozen times. Besides my school diploma and Vietnamese identification card, I found no other official papers. In planning for my future, my mother forgot to pack my birth certificate. Or did she do it on purpose to erase all traces of my past? Once again, I had to face an ambiguous question I could not answer.

When Mr. Sandys saw my two pieces of "official papers," he shook his head and sighed. But not wanting to discourage me, he added that some people with less than that lived new lives in the West. Identities are not hard to create.

"Good thing you're a young girl," he said. "It means you probably have no criminal or undesirable political past. So your case won't be scrutinized for minute irregularities," he continued. "I am glad I found you, Kim. We've

69

been looking for this Nguyen Thi Kim for the last seven months, but nothing came up at any of the other camps. I feared she might have died at sea. But obviously she hasn't! All this time she's lived here! I mean *you've* lived here, Kim. At last, a happy story! I'm so tired of hearing all these tragedies. I didn't go into the foreign service to mope!" At this comment, he laughed so hard, he almost choked. My racing heart slowed down a bit. I too wanted to laugh. But the interview had barely begun.

"When were you born?" he asked. "The Kim I am looking for was born on the 10th of November, 1965."

I was born on the 11th of October but since my identification card only bore the numbers 1965-10-11, I didn't hesitate to lie. "I was born on the 10th of November, 1965. You can check my card, sir. Vietnamese from Hue sometimes invert the day and month when writing the date. It is an Imperial tradition."

"Oh?"

"Yes, sir. Most of our emperors hailed from Hue. The Imperial Court did things differently to distinguish themselves from ordinary people."

"If you say so . . . Let's see. OK . . . it says here your address is 29 Cong Ly Street, Hue. Is that right?"

"Yes, sir."

Fortunately, Mr. Sandys didn't know the home address of "his" Kim. He only had the name of a church in Hue. This Catholic church maintained strong ties with a sister church in Connecticut. The American church, St. Joseph, wished to sponsor the orphaned Kim, since she excelled in school. They wanted to give her a chance at a better education.

Everything sounded fine until Mr. Sandys mentioned "orphan." "His" Kim was an orphan—I was only an abandoned kid. How would my tale live up to his? But he didn't give me much time to think.

"Are you familiar with this church?" Mr. Sandys asked.

"Yes, of course—St. Redempteur Church. It is next door to my school. The sisters from the church also run my school. But they do it discreetly, you know. They walk around in plain clothes since they don't want to attract the state's attention. Communists don't believe in religion. They call Jesus 'that man on the cross'! Can you believe it?" Oh, how I lied, with stories so false they seemed true. "Of course, the church no longer bears a French name. Re-baptized Dong Cuu The, its beautiful spire still pierces the sky," I said. It was the last thing I saw of Hue as I left the city furtively one night, I almost blurted out. No, that wouldn't do. Didn't secretly leave Hue at night —I left with other orphans. In bright daylight. The old nun drove a big bus. We went to the beach for a picnic. Nobody asked any questions. In the evening when all the others returned home for supper, we boarded our boat. The nun waved goodbye from the bus window.

"Kim, what happened to your parents?"

"My parents are dead, sir . . ."

"I know, but what happened?"

Charlie Company slit their throats and signed his name on their chest, I thought of saying. Then I changed my mind. No, no one would believe Minh's story. After all, Americans don't kill innocent civilians. Mr. Sandys of all people would not believe a word of that horror tale. Better spare him the nightmare of the truth. Besides, Charlie Company accomplished his deed in My Lai, not in my hometown of Hue. Too much exaggeration will only get me into trouble.

"It was Tet '68, sir. You saw that on television? Really? I didn't know Americans watched that kind of thing . . . I was celebrating New Year's Eve with my family. At midnight we heard fireworks and saw the sky light up. My parents forced me to go to bed when they saw me yawning. They went outside to watch the fireworks. But they never returned. I found them dead the next day. A horrible sight greeted me on the street. Ruined houses, corpses everywhere . . . Oh, you saw that on television too, sir? Then you must know how bad I felt . . . An exploding car door killed both my parents. Blood still leaked from their wounds when I found them, sir. Their open eyes still looked at the sky, still hoping to catch a glimpse of the fireworks."

"I am sorry to hear that, Kim. Are you OK now?"

"I am alright, sir . . ."

To turn the interview away from the subject of my parents, I showed Mr. Sandys my school diploma, adorned with three gold stars for excellence. He seemed only half convinced. He wanted to know with whom I lived.

"Where is this place—29 Cong Ly Street?" he asked.

"My mother's cousin lived there," I answered vaguely. "I stayed with her for a while after the death of my parents. But Aunty Lan's health deteriorated. She couldn't take care of me. So she sent me to the orphanage a few years ago," I concluded. When I saw Mr. Sandys biting the bait, I stopped exaggerating. Overdoing things is never good. Now that my tale had taken shape in his head, I left it there to germinate on its own.

I also wanted to fill the holes of my future story. I wished to know all about this new life offered me by mistake. What would I do in America? Where would I stay in Connecticut? With whom? And for how long? Mr. Sandys didn't mind answering my questions. He took delight in giving me minute details of American charity. His explanations sounded convincing. Unlike the false promises my mother offered, the immigration officer's story for me seemed as clear as stream water.

"An American church in Derby, Connecticut, sponsored you," Mr. Sandys explained. "This was a goodwill project agreed to by the most important members of the community. Many nice ladies worked hard for years to raise money and support for your cause. Your hosts will be the Thompson family. The church will pay for your airfare and other large expenses, while the Thompsons will provide your food and shelter. You will be under their care until the age of eighteen. Your sole obligation will be to study hard so you can one day become a good citizen of Derby, Connecticut," concluded Mr. Sandys. The mention of studies unleashed my regrets. I thought of my dear old school and the newspaper articles lauding my good work. I wondered if my mother had kept those articles.

"Where is your birth certificate?" Mr. Sandys' sudden question brought me back to reality.

"I don't have it, sir. The nuns at the orphanage forgot to give it to me."

"Um . . ."

"We don't always think of fetching our birth certificates before leaving."

"I see. Now just a few standard questions. I know you should do OK, but I still have to ask them. Formalities, you know."

"Yes, I understand, sir."

"Have you ever been a member of the Communist Party?"

"No, sir!" I said without hesitation, even if I did belong to the Uncle Ho Youth Group. Since I joined the group only for its library privileges, I didn't feel the need to bother Mr. Sandys with such unimportant details.

"Have you ever been in trouble with the law?"

"Of course not, sir!" With these words, I spoke the truth for the first time. I blushed at my sincerity and wondered if he could tell the difference between this honest answer and the previous one.

"Good! OK, interrogation time is over! I'm glad I found you, Kim. I'll cable home tomorrow and we'll make arrangements for your flight as soon as possible."

I could hardly believe my good luck! I had succeeded in my lies. With my crooked story, I had tricked a tired immigration officer not wanting to hear sad tales. Soon I would become some other Kim, a Kim not fortunate enough to make it here on time. I lied like a professional thief caught in the act but still denying the truth. Yes, the camp had changed me.

That night I couldn't sleep. I wondered all night about the whereabouts of this other girl. Common sense told me she had probably drowned at sea. But what if she was still alive and hadn't shown up yet? While guilt kept me awake that night, I smiled at my good luck during the day. My mother, who had always been more practical than moral, would have approved of my actions. My father, who stepped on an old woman to get on the last helicopter out of Saigon, would have done the same.

But what about Dr. Jacques? I hated the idea of deceiving him. After all, he gave me my big opportunity at the camp. I wanted to please him, not tarnish his reputation with the immigration officials. I decided to ask his opinion the next day. If he approved, then good. If he didn't, well, I'd think about what to do next.

Dr. Jacques gave me a big smile when he saw me the following day. "I heard you got sponsored by some American church. Congratulations!" he exclaimed.

"Yes, thank you."

"You will soon leave us—I will miss you."

"I'll miss working for you too," I managed to say. "Dr. Jacques, I don't know if I should tell you this, but there might be some problems later. What if I am not the girl they are looking for?"

"Oh, don't worry about it. If you are not yet the girl they want, you will be! There's no such thing as 'the right girl,' you know!" Dr. Jacques answered with a grin.

Imagine Aunty Hung's puffy face when I told her my story! She felt relieved of her charge. But I saw her unrepressed jealousy. It coloured her face purple. She still hadn't heard from her brother in California. She spent the interminable days playing the waiting game. As if that wasn't insult enough, now she'd have to wash her own menstrual pads! My going to America didn't improve my standing in Aunty Hung's book. She eyed me with suspicion. Her sideways glances in my direction smelled of rotten fish, a fish she'd be only too happy to throw in my face. She smacked her lips in disgust whenever she saw me. Her conversations with our neighbour always came to a screeching halt when I entered our hut. Their private talk disturbed, the women would return to the task of picking lice off their kids' hair. Whenever our glances crossed, their faces would glow with the redness of disbelief. Then as if on cue, the women shook their head and one after the other, let escape a "tsk! tsk!" sound. They all avoided talking to me. Acting as if my fingers carried leprosy, the women all moved out of reach every time I walked by.

Once, Aunty Hung inquired about my period. "Is it late?" she asked.

"No, why?"

"Because a late period means you're pregnant! Didn't your mother teach you that much?"

"I'm not pregnant, Aunty Hung!"

"How do you know? You spend too much time with those men. Stay away from them!"

"You mean the cross-eyed orphan?"

"I mean your French doctor and your American officer!"

"But I work at the clinic. I have to see them . . ."

"Just don't get into trouble, OK? Do you think I'm stupid? I'm not blind. How'd you get sponsored to America if you didn't do dirty things with those men? And I see the fancy gifts you bring home too!"

"No, the gifts are from the cross-eyed . . ."

"Enough! Be quiet now. Don't bring shame to your family, OK? Your mother has enough problems. She didn't raise you to be that kind of girl. So stay away from those men! Stop the dirty things! I know you're doing those things. Don't deny it!"

Since I didn't know which dirty things she meant, I said, "Yes, Aunty Hung" to purchase some peace. Arguing with Aunty Hung about Minh's lump of coal would only get me into more trouble.

On my last day at the camp, I went looking for Minh. I wanted to exchange one last story, a last goodbye and a promise to see each other in America. I roamed the camp and hung around our usual meeting place behind the dispensary. I asked the other street kids for Minh's whereabouts, but no one had seen him. Minh was hiding from me. On a whim, I decided to write him a note. Back in my hut, I rummaged through my burlap bag for a pen and a piece of paper. Finding no spare paper, I wrote my note on the back of my report card. It was no love letter—just a letter of friendship, of reassurance. I wished I had found a similar note in my bag, but my mother mistrusted words. I went back to our usual meeting place behind the dispensary. I found the large rock on which I often sat. With great effort, I moved it a few centimetres. Then I dug into the earth with my bare hands. I placed my note inside the little hiding place, covered it up with dirt and managed to push the rock back to its original position. I had very dirty hands but I had accomplished my mission.

Then I returned to the dispensary to bid goodbye to Dr. Jacques and Joy. When the doctor gave me his hand, I didn't know what to do. This adult business of shaking hands, I'd seen it lots of times. But an adult shaking hands with a dirty kid? Hands were for holding when you were young and later for hitting with a ruler when you were bad. They weren't for shaking in our house.

Dr. Jacques's big white-man hands fascinated me. I shyly pressed my right palm against his. The wetness of his sweat sent a shiver through my body. I remembered his palpating hands on my unclothed abdomen a few months earlier. I blushed at the thought of those hands. But the memory also comforted me. This white man's hands had healed my broken body then. Now they calmed my ruptured spirit.

"We will have to manage without your translation now! The patients will miss you," Joy said, trying to put me at ease.

"Here's my address in Paris. Write to me when you get to Connecticut."

"I will, Dr. Jacques. Oh, one more thing, Dr. Jacques . . ."

"What is it?"

"Can I wash my hands and hair here? I want to be clean for America."

"All right. But make it fast."

I spent my last night in Palawan clinging to Titi. She cried inconsolably. She wanted to go with me to America. I tried talking sense to her, but her tears, which left my breasts wet, flowed nonstop.

"Sshh, you will wake everybody up," I said.

"I can't help it," she sobbed.

"Now listen to me, Titi. I need your help. Next time you see Minh, the cross-eyed orphan, tell him I left a message for him under the rock at our usual meeting place," I whispered in her ear. I stopped my whispering in mid-air when I heard Aunty Hung's unmistakable "Humph!" I expected to hear more unpleasant words, but none came. Instead, I felt her foot groping for me in the dark. A sharp object stuck out from the foot.

"Take it," Aunty Hung said. I reached down and felt a hairpin between her two toes. "Not much of a gift but it's for good luck," she said. I put the hairpin in my hair and gave thanks. "You won the waiting game," Aunty Hung finally admitted defeat. Titi cried louder, hearing those words, but eventually she too fell silent.

Yes, I won the waiting game. I was going to America just like my father.

Connecticut

One

My first plane trip became a memory even before it ended. I recorded everything in my diary. I wanted to remember all the details of this fifteen-hour flight. After the grayness of the camp, everything I saw seemed magical. The colourful food on hot tin trays enticed my eyes. Its exotic smell filled me with cravings. The clean bathrooms, the warm blankets, the music in my ears—I loved it all. So instead of napping like everyone else, I happily read all the newspapers given me. I wanted to learn all about this new country.

John F. Kennedy Airport—the name sounded familiar but the place looked completely foreign. I had never seen such a big and clean space before. With people going in all directions, bags in hand and food in mouth, it looked more like a central market than a place for saying goodbyes. Only this was a market without the spitting, the hawking, the throwing of coins on the ground for lepers. In my state of amazement, I walked right past the group of people waiting for me. I failed to see my name on a cardboard sign. Confused, I headed for the rows of chairs, not knowing what to do next.

Being the only shabbily dressed Oriental kid getting off that plane, I caught the attention of some people. My welcome group soon figured out my identity, so they came toward me. A cheerfully talkative woman stood out from the crowd. She gesticulated excitedly as she approached me. She wore dark orange glasses, pink, dangling earrings and a red hat. A purple scarf complemented her bright blue coat. This colourful woman introduced herself as Mary Thompson. She would be my host mother in America. Her friendliness eased somewhat my nervous anticipation. But her outlandish dress scared me a bit. What if she was a witch?

Mary took one look at my torn sandals and shivering blue toes and screamed, "Oh, my God!" Immediately she unzipped her boots to reveal a pair of red-and-white checkered socks. She handed me the socks, while managing to wave for her friends' cameras. Then she bundled me in her purple shawl. It felt good to be wrapped in these clothes that still emanated heat.

After saying goodbye to all the well-meaning ladies, we set out for our ride to Connecticut. Our ride *home*. But first we got lost. Once in the car park, trying to find Mary's car, twice on the road, trying to find the right direction home. Mary laughed through it all.

"Too nervous to pay attention," she said.

After initial traffic jams getting out of the airport, the road home soon became a long stretch of snowy fields. I couldn't take my eyes off this vast, empty space before me. The America of my dreams was as snow-covered as I had imagined it. Once I even rolled down the car window to catch a snowflake. Mary laughed at my futile attempt.

Derby, Connecticut—its cleanliness and stillness surprised me. No litter on the streets. No honking of mopeds. No shoeshine boys peddling their services. No homeless people claiming a bit of the sidewalk. Where did everybody go? Then again, how could there be homelessness when even cars had a roof over their heads? Mary had pointed the garages out to me on our ride home.

"That's a doghouse. Over there's a tree house, here's a birdhouse. And this is a greenhouse," she taught me. So many shelters for the living—no wonder only ghosts wandered the streets.

"Wait till you meet the family! They're very excited to see you. You'll have a new life now!" Mary exclaimed with much enthusiasm, as we approached a pretty-looking house amongst other identically pretty-looking houses. Only one thing set it apart from the others—a big heart-shaped plate nailed to the door with the words "Home Sweet Home" written in gold letters. 49 Blue Sage Drive, Derby, Connecticut—this would be my new home, and I liked the sound of it already.

Mary's prediction came true. My new life bloomed as soon as I entered her house. I saw colourful balloons on the ceiling. I noticed numerous vases of red roses. I smelled the sweet odour of baked goods. I heard the voices of children screaming, "Welcome home, Kim!" Yes, I had come home to America.

After much filling out of forms, which Mary's husband, Jim, took care of, I became an American! Or perhaps a resident alien? Political refugee? My official status confused me. But I knew I wasn't a Vietnamese boat person who came here on someone else's identity anymore. I became a new person, a *sponsored* person, a legitimate person. To prove it, I had amassed a whole collection of little plastic cards: social security card, medical insurance card, school identification card, library card . . . Strangely, my name changed during this process of becoming legal. I went from Nguyen Thi Kim to Kim T. Nguyen. The usual order got switched around and my middle name transformed to a simple T. Sometimes it disappeared altogether. But I didn't miss this part of my past.

Connecticut

Two

A month after my arrival, I still marvelled at my new life. Daily I touched the soft lining of my new coat to remind me of my good luck. The red woollen coat had white fur trim and silver buttons. It looked gorgeous belted at the waist. My closet overflowed with other pretty things: lacy blouses, flowered skirts, and sweaters made with gold thread. I'd never seen clothes this fancy before.

"Always wanted a daughter to dress in pretty dresses!" Mary said as we giggled like schoolgirls with our purchases. Mary had bought the clothes at a store called Woolworth's. We went there as soon as I'd unpacked and shown her my meager belongings.

If the clothing store looked heavenly, the food store pleased me even more. I had never seen so many foodstuffs under one roof—never seen Coca-Cola bottles or tomatoes so huge. The abundance made my head dizzy. "Don't be fooled by size," my grandmother always said during our usual walks to the market. "Go for the smaller fruit, it's usually tastier. Search for the rare fruit—don't buy what is displayed everywhere," Grandmother repeatedly reminded me. But her words of wisdom fell flat in this country of Big and Plenty. No longer abiding by Grandmother's teaching, I devoured with my eyes all the huge and wonderful food displays. Of course, I also wanted to eat everything. And I did. People gave me free samples of food everywhere I went. This type of American charity overwhelmed me. I loved it. Of all the free food, I enjoyed the most a sweet thing called Pop-Tart. I could eat this all day, but Mary said, "No, you will get fat, honey!" I didn't mind being a bit fatter. Getting skinnier worried me, not getting fatter. Having worked with Dr. Jacques at the refugee camp, I knew losing weight meant trouble. Coughing grandmothers in their final stages of tuberculosis lost weight. Babies dying of cholera lost weight. Most people in their right minds wanted to gain weight, not lose it. But Mary thought differently.

In the grocery store, I also learned about expiration dates. "Food isn't good forever. Even if they still look good, out-of-date items aren't good for you. So you throw them out," Mary explained.

"In Vietnam, food becomes out-of-date when it turns green with moss," I said. "Even then, it is still sold, bought, served in restaurants and happily consumed by unsuspecting clients," I continued.

Mary screamed, "Oh, heavens!" at this tidbit of Vietnamese information.

I wandered from Mary to look for duck embryo eggs. I checked everywhere but found none. Not discouraged, I wandered some more. Then I got lost. Unfazed, I traced my way back to the man with the free Pop-Tarts and stood next to him. I knew American Charity would not let me down. Sure enough, Mary spotted me and screamed, "Kim!"

"Where were you? Don't wander away like that again!"

"I am sorry. I was looking for duck embryo eggs. I wonder if they sell them here?"

"Sell what, honey?"

"Duck embryo eggs."

"What? Chocolate duck eggs? Not now. That would be for Easter!"

"No, not chocolate eggs. Duck embryo eggs. My mother loved eating them."

"Duck embryo eggs? I've never heard of those . . ."

"It's a duck egg with the embryo inside. My mother said the embryonic bones were so tender they bent in her mouth. Timing is everything in the eating of these eggs. Too early and there would be no succulent bones; too late and there would be bothersome feathers sticking to her teeth. So we have expiration dates in Vietnam too. Only it is a matter of hours, not days . . ."

"Oh, heavens!" Mary cried for the second time that afternoon.

The grocery store gave me my first glimpse of American friendliness. Mary greeted everyone with "Hi there!" and received "Hey, Mary!" in return. I collected enough handshakes in an hour to compensate for a childhood devoid of physical touch. "So this must be Kim!" people inquired, as Mary prodded me to respond. Seeing me tongue-tied, the ladies patted my shoulders with understanding. "Welcome to Derby!" they all said with big smiles. The bag boy at the cash looked less welcoming. He stared at me from a distance. Waiting in line for our turn at the cash, I felt his eyes fixed on mine. The cashier scolded him for breaking a customer's eggs. He paid little attention to his job. My foreignness seemed to bother him. He wanted to stare me down. The ghost of a legless leper boy reached out from the past to touch my present. I could throw that dirty kid a coin but he wouldn't have budged. This bag boy wouldn't move either. When our turn at the cash came, the boy stopped working. He looked straight at me and sneered, "Chink!" He pulled at his eyes, stretching them horizontally to turn them into slits. Then he laughed at me. At first, Mary and the cashier stood frozen. Then, as Mary shouted, "Bradley Newton, how dare you!" the cashier smacked the boy on the back of the head. When I asked Mary the meaning of "Chink," she hugged me and said, "Never mind, honey. Believe me, that boy is never going to say that word again after I speak to his mother."

Connecticut

Three

I wrote my mother at least once a week after arriving in Derby. "To my Dear Venerable Mother," the letters always started. But if the greeting seemed convoluted, the rest stayed simple. We never exchanged stories at home. Conversations meant answering my mother's questions—mostly one-line sentences that ended in silence. Or sometimes it ended with a slap on the face. That was a cue for me to get out of her way. There was no fear of a slap in Derby. No raised left eyebrow to silence me. Yet having no clue, not knowing when to retreat, seemed just as hard. So my letters to my mother contained mostly safe, repetitive stuff. I wrote of the snow and cold. I described my nice American home. Never once did I mention the incomplete California address for Aunty Lan. I talked of Mary's weird outfits, but avoided that bit about her warmth and good heart. I also spared my mother the penis-rubbing stories of Palawan.

If my letters to my mother contained only banalities, my letters to Dr. Jacques overflowed with exaggerations. I went out of my way to make fun of the dunces in my class. This *imbécile*, that *imbécile*—I described them all to him. Even added a few "*Conneries!*" and "*Quel emmerdeur!*" here and there to spice things up. Yes, those mean boys making fun of my accent in school received the full treatment. I reserved my best swear words for Bradley Newton, the bag boy from the grocery store. After receiving a smack in the head for calling me "Chink," Bradley retaliated by recruiting a bunch of friends to torment me in the schoolyard. "Chink! Chink!" they would scream every time they saw me. "I'm no Chinese! I'm Vietnamese and I bet you don't know where that is!" I felt like screaming back, but their big arms and towering height kept me silent.

Whereas Dr. Jacques answered my letters, my mother didn't. I wrote more than fifty letters home but received no acknowledgement in return. My family must've left too, I told myself. There's no reply because no one's home. As simple as that. Finding them would be almost impossible now. Only a miracle could realign our paths. But these weren't days of miracles. So I stopped writing home.

Connecticut

Four

I enjoyed American excesses. My sponsor, St. Joseph Church, showered me with more benevolence than my mother ever did. The same thing could be said for the family hosting me. Everyone spoiled me materially. I ate all I wanted without being told to leave some for my siblings. I even had my own room, painted pink with a red carpet. My mother could never afford this type of luxury back home. I no longer had to wash a complaining grandmother. No longer had to scrub floors and sweep streets. No longer had to hunt for branches to cook our food. Mary insisted on doing all the physical chores herself, so my free time remained truly mine. Yet my heart didn't beat with ease. Anxiety about my family dampened my spirits. Not being able to share this worry with anyone made matters worse.

With little to do on the weekends, I spent my spare time filling the blank pages of my diary. I also wrote an incredible number of letters. This seemed to baffle my host family, not used to keeping up correspondence.

"Kim, who are you writing to? Who is this Mr. Jacques from France?"

"He is a doctor. I met him at the refugee camp in the Philippines and worked for him as a translator."

"I don't mean to pry, honey, but did he ever try touching you in the wrong places? Do you know what I mean?"

"No! Of course not! He is a very good man—wouldn't do anything wrong."

"Good! I hear so many awful stories about young girls like you staying in the camps alone. The priest told us about all the rapes that happened on the boats and it just broke my heart! 'I hope it won't happen to our little Kim,' I used to pray every day before you came."

"Thank you, Mrs. Thompson."

"How many times have I told you to call me Mom? Don't forget! We're adopting you now, remember? No more host family. Soon we'll be real family! The paperwork is underway. It will only take a few more months."

"Yes, thank you, Mom. I am very happy, Mom. But what is rape?"

"That's when men do bad things to you. Forcing themselves into your body. Do you understand?"

"Yes—I don't think I was raped on the boat though."

"You don't think?! You either were or you weren't."

"Well, sometimes things are not that clear. I wish they were."

"What do you mean, honey? Do you have doubts about being raped?"

"No, it's just that I don't remember what happened on the boat. I just forgot the whole thing. I remember getting on the boat at night worrying about its safety. The next thing I knew, big, blonde sailors threw us Coca-Colas and took us to the refugee camp at Palawan."

"Isn't that odd? You were probably too stressed."

"Maybe. I also have strange dreams sometimes. It's always the same scene. A man is biting a woman's neck till she bleeds. I don't understand it."

"Did you watch *Dracula* on the flight here?"

"No. I read newspapers on the plane. What's *Dracula*?"

"It's a crazy movie. Never mind, honey. Listen, if ever you want to talk about your departed parents, don't be shy. You can talk to me. Or the priest if you prefer. He is a very kind man. Don't keep your sorrows inside you all the time. It is not good for you. That's what gives you all those nightmares."

In those days, I lived a double life. I deceived both my host family and my mother. Mary interpreted my distress as a sign of belated mourning for my "dead" parents. I had no choice but to play along with the game. I could not bring myself to tell them the truth. When they asked for Vietnam stories,

86

I found myself inventing anecdotes about life in an imaginary orphanage. The more I exaggerated, the more tears Mary would shed, only to conclude that she did the right thing sending for me. She thought she rescued me from some terrible Vietnamese orphanage. And I dared not shatter her belief in her own goodness. In the end, what did it matter if I was not the Kim she had sent for? The important thing was to be safe and to make Mary happy. And I did make her happy. Yet the fear of this faceless stranger sharing my name still loomed. This other Kim from Hue still kept me sleepless at night. What if she showed up one day to unmask me at my game? Would Mary cry? Would I be deported—sent back to Palawan to rub more penises and testicles? No, I'd have to think more positively. This other Kim drowned at sea.

Connecticut

Five

Mary, my adoptive mother, enjoyed company. She hosted tea parties every Monday and Thursday. I usually stayed in my room during those afternoon meetings with the ladies. But my thin walls gave me muffled access to their conversation. Were they discussing my case? Did they know my true identity? Those tea parties, so enjoyable to Mary, made me sweat. The constant fear of detection turned my afternoons into torture sessions. Occasionally I would catch a word here and there, but they made little sense to me. The words "Child Protection Agency" resurfaced often and their seriousness scared me.

"Child Protection Agency? Has to do with putting bad parents away when they hit their kids, honey," Mary explained one day. Phew! Well, if such a thing existed in Vietnam, all parents would be in jail, I thought. Why, my mother would be the first to go. My mother didn't just hit us randomly. She had a whole set of rules and regulations which she followed to the letter. Minor irritations deserved a sharp pull on the earlobes. Low school grades and laziness earned a swift knock on the skull. Bad situations like the time I broke two soup bowls by accident called for a hard slap on the face followed by a "Shut up!"

Mary on the other hand belonged to the fairytale category of mothers. These mothers never raised their voices, never hit, never forced work on their children. They only kissed, hugged and caressed their kids all day.

Naively, they also believed all the lies coming from those kids' mouths.

Mary's husband, Jim, also deserved praise. I never heard him complain. When Mary burned his supper and set fire to the kitchen, Jim stayed calm. He went outside, came back with the garden hose and sprayed water everywhere. Afterward, while Mary cried uncontrollably, he apologized for ruining her hairdo and uprooting her violets. Jim's calmness made him unreadable. His feelings and thoughts eluded me. He looked lonely, even while surrounded by a loving family. I had yet to hear him laugh and whenever our gazes met, he would shift his eyes away. Despite his prestigious job as the school's vice principal, Jim seemed awkward. I often found him sitting alone during Mary's parties. He pretended to be occupied with a book. To avoid talking to others, Jim also kept busy with a ball that he bounced up and down. Only the neighbouring kids gave his ball-throwing act any attention. The other adults looked right past him. If it weren't for my father's surprising feat on the helicopter ledge, I would say these two men belonged to the same mould—they both exuded sadness.

Mary and Jim had a ten-year-old son named Michael. With curly blonde hair framing a baby face, Michael shone in his parents' eyes. If he wanted to, Michael could get away with anything. This boy had neither intelligence nor physical prowess to impress me. Yet his every exploit, which would not have deserved even a nod from my mother, earned generous praises from Mary. She promptly recorded his daily acts in her baby book.

Michael's room piqued my curiosity. I loved exploring its American-ness. He glued posters of actors and comic-strip characters all over the walls.

"You don't have a *Love Story* poster?" I asked him one day.

"Of course not! No love, that's sucky. Only superheroes! Ever heard of Superman, Kim? Or Batman? Or Wonderwoman? You see *Spiderman* in Vietnam?" Michael asked.

"No, Michael. But we have Tintin. Ever heard of Tintin? He's like a superhero too, but he doesn't fly . . ." I explained.

"That's no fun then!" Michael laughed. I pointed to a poster of a bare-chested, tough-looking man.

"Who is this man?" I asked Michael.

"He's Rambo! He's an action hero! You never heard of him? *Rambo* is the best American movie!" answered Michael excitedly.

My adoptive family lived in a very nice two-storey house in a clean, safe neighbourhood adorned with parks and trees. Mary's house by a field had more rooms than I could keep track of. The living room, den and family room confused me. They looked similar but functioned differently. I never knew where to go to watch television. A large, dark room downstairs from the main floor intrigued me the most. Mary called it the "finished basement." Who'd ever heard of underground living with so much luxury?! There, Mary kept not only machines for sewing, washing and drying clothes, she also kept an extra fridge for the storage of extra meat. A whole cow in there, could you believe it? Well, not really a whole cow.

"It's been cut into pieces, honey," Mary said. "Cheaper that way. I bought it at the butcher's three years ago. But I always forget to defrost the meat. Whenever we feel like a roast, I have to go to the store for a fresh one! So besides a missing left shoulder, the cow is almost intact. And after all these years down there, we don't dare eat it anymore," Mary continued. "Expiration dates? Yes, that too, honey. But it's not just expiration dates. The animal is part of the family now. A frozen pet. Who'd dare eat it? Not Michael. He screams every time I try defrosting some T-bone steaks. And by the way, it's a freezer, not a fridge, honey," Mary corrected me.

Back in Vietnam, the only underground living I heard of was the Cu Chi Tunnel bringing Communist soldiers from north to south. I remembered having Communist soldiers coming to school to talk of their Cu Chi experience. No—it wasn't an experience, it was a life. A place where you lived for years in perpetual darkness and silence, smelling only dust, dust, dust. Yet they had tanks hidden down there, even hospitals! But to get to these sites, you'd have to crawl on your hands and feet for hours, in spaces reserved for those fed a lifetime diet of crickets. "Were you afraid?" we asked the soldiers. "No, our comrades were our strength," they replied. "Were you lonely?" we inquired. "No, the comrades were our family," they said. "Did you miss home?" we wanted to know. "No, home is where the Motherland needs defending," they insisted. "It's just Communist propaganda," my grandmother replied after I told her of the underground soldiers. No, I haven't seen the Cu Chi Tunnel but just hearing about it sufficed. I knew it to be a place of self-sacrifice, no matter what my grandmother said about propaganda. The soldiers' emaciated limbs and pale, greenish cheeks told stories of self-denial that I couldn't quite grasp. But here in Mary's house the underground room remained a place of self-indulgence.

Seeing the cheerfulness of the house, I could tell my adoptive family had lived uneventful lives when I entered the scene. After the initial adjustment period, they came to accept me as one of their own. Then Mary itched to show me off to the neighbours. Apparently everyone wanted to hear tales of refugee camps.

"Oh my gosh! A real Vietnamese refugee amongst us!" some of Mary's lady friends would exclaim at those interminable tea parties where I became the guest of honour.

"Is Vietnam still a third-world country? Or should I say developing country instead?" asked Liz, one of the neighbours.

"Yes, it is still one of the poorest countries in Asia," I replied meekly. "Still the poorest despite the end of the war," I added.

"Oh, I see," the ladies said. "Isn't that too bad?" they whispered to themselves, yet in their hearts, I knew they couldn't really comprehend. And if they didn't understand poverty, how could they understand war?

"Do you have televisions there?" Liz continued. She wanted to know what people watched in Vietnam. I told her the nuns at my orphanage liked watching an American show where a nun flew in the air. "They always laughed when the actress floated around," I said.

"*The Flying Nun,* with Sally Field! I can't believe they had that in Vietnam too!" Liz exclaimed.

"Yes, the nuns also enjoyed watching one about a horse that could talk. But they didn't like the one with a witch twitching her nose."

"Oh, my gosh, *Mr. Ed!* And *Bewitched!* I remember those too!" Liz screamed, very excited by now.

"How about Bugs Bunny?" Michael chimed in.

"No. No children's shows. Kids don't matter in Vietnam . . ."

"So, old shows get shipped to places like Vietnam where people don't mind re-runs," remarked Mary.

"But I thought the Communists banned American shows?" Liz quickly asked, beating Mary to it.

Yes, the Communists did forbid American shows. They called our favourite American programs "imperialist propaganda." So they exchanged them for Soviet propaganda instead. These were tiresome peasant movies, made worse by the lack of subtitles. Nobody understood anything. Sometimes they stopped the movie every thirty minutes to explain the story. Sometimes they didn't bother.

"Imagine that! Russian movies with no subtitles, no dubbing!" the ladies remarked. "And they stopped the film every once in a while to explain things!" The ladies giggled in amazement.

Not being used to the limelight, I felt uncomfortable in my new role of storyteller. But with time, I started enjoying the attention of the ladies, an attention I never had as a kid and still did not have at school with my indifferent peers. My tales soon became more and more elaborate. But since I had a fantastic memory, I didn't worry about my chameleon tongue. The storytelling sessions entertained everyone. My crooked words kept a dozen ladies on their toes while Mary beamed with pride.

Connecticut

Six

At home, I did everything right to please Mary and Jim. I cleaned my room, cooked Vietnamese dishes and helped Michael with his homework. I even looked after the kid whenever Mary and Jim went out for a social function.

"You sure you're OK with a young child, honey?" Mary had asked the first time I took care of Michael.

"Of course, we did it all the time at the orphanage. Older kids taking care of younger ones," I reassured her.

"Good. He's hard to put to bed though. Try telling him a story. Bye now! Michael, you behave and listen to Kim, OK? Mommy loves you both!"

As soon as Mary and Jim left, Michael ran down to the basement. He opened the freezer to check on the cut-up cow. Then he screamed "Mooo!" He returned to his room all excited. He wanted to play ball, eat ice cream, and take a bubble bath. My patience almost ran out when he finally yawned and said, "Tell me a story!"

"What do you want to hear? Snow White? Jack and the Bean Stalk? Peter Pan?" I asked, looking through his pile of old books by the night table.

"That's baby stuff!" he whined.

"*Conneries*! You can read, why don't you read one yourself?"

"What did you just say?"

"Never mind. Read your own book, OK?"

"No, Mom always tells me a story at night!"

"Would you tell yourself a story if your mother never did?"

"No! Mom always tells me a story!"

"OK! What do you want to hear then? Have any better books?"

"No. *You* tell me a story," he insisted.

"The same story I tell your mother and her friends or another one?"

"You choose." Surprisingly, Michael gave me the choice.

"OK. It'll be the same story your mother heard. Simpler that way."

"But is it funny?" he wanted to know first.

"Not really. It's mostly sad. OK with that?"

"OK, I guess," Michael replied.

"OK. Listen well. Once upon a time there was a little girl living in a faraway country called Vietnam. Now the little girl looked just like me, perhaps a little prettier, but we have the same straight, long hair worn in a ponytail and the same thick red lips. Being an only child, she was spoiled, just like you. Her mother gave her everything she wanted—all her attention, all her love and whatever she could afford to buy, which was not much as they weren't rich. One day, just as they were celebrating Tet—that's the Vietnamese New Year—war came to her city. It was 1968, the year of the monkey, way before you were born. The whole city, in fact the whole region, came under attack. Since soldiers stayed home celebrating with their families, nobody minded the battlefield. The enemy could only find innocent people to kill, so they did. They went looking for people praying in churches. They took the people out, shot them in the back, then buried them in mass graves. The enemy also shot rockets into the city. The rockets created huge holes in the streets, brought houses down and smashed cars into a hundred flying pieces. What, you'd like to smash a car into a hundred flying pieces too? Stop talking nonsense! You wouldn't like it so much if those flying pieces fell on your head! Oh, you were talking about your toy cars? It's still nonsense to smash your toys! Let me go on with my story.

"Now, the little girl, her name was Kim just like me–it's a popular name, like Michael in this country. Kim was visiting a friend in the countryside throughout this whole awful time. So she was spared the killing. But her beloved parents, who had stayed in the city to work, well, they weren't so lucky. An exploding car door fell on their head and killed them instantly. A neighbour found them two days after their deaths. Blood still oozed out of their brain, their eyes still staring up at the sky . . . You like that part about the staring eyes? No? They scare you? Sorry! I'll make them close their eyes next time . . . When her parents didn't come to get her after many weeks, the little girl understood her new fate in life. So what do you think happened next? Of course! Orphanage! You're right on. But enough for now, we'll continue next time. No. Michael, I said no more and I mean it. Good night!"

So Michael too became hooked on my story. How many times did he beg his parents to go out so I could babysit him! "No party this week? Go see a movie then," he'd plead with them. And since he broadcast my stories to his friends, I soon became a popular babysitter in our neighbourhood. They all wanted to hear my orphan tales! *Bugs Bunny* must've done this to them. It made them tired watching the coyote alive and running, after he'd been blown up a dozen times. I saw that show only twice but got fed up with the Beep! Beep! after ten seconds. Could you imagine years of watching this stuff? After a while you'd want to hear real life dramas, true stories in which people actually suffered and died and never came back. But poor Michael didn't know my stories strayed from reality. And the more I repeated those tales, the more they became truer than the truth.

I soon got tired of repeating the same story about a falling car door. So I changed my narrative to see if Michael was paying attention.

"You know, the enemy didn't send rockets anonymously. They wanted to be recognized. So they signed their names on the victims' chests after slitting their throats. They used the victims' blood as ink. Sometimes, they'd just write their initials. What are initials? It's when your name becomes only two letters. You know, things like VC or CC. What does it stand for? I don't know. Maybe Viet Cong or Charlie C. Or Charlie Company or something like that. Let me go on with the story. Yes, Charlie Company killed my parents by slitting their throats with a knife. How'd I know his name? Because I heard the others calling him, 'Charlie! Charlie Company, come here!' You don't believe my story? I knew you wouldn't believe it. But you believed that story about a flying car door killing my parents . . . Why did I change my story? Because real stories can be so horrible at times. So bad that no one would believe them. Getting killed accidentally by a falling object can happen to anyone, anywhere. Having your throat slit by an enemy who will take his time to sign his name on your chest is something else. That happens only in horror movies, you say? But it did happen in real life to real people. Now you know why I changed my story. It's to protect you from knowing too much of the world's bad ways ."

"The nuns were mean to you?" Michael always asked me this.

"Not really, just strict. Very severe and strict," I replied.

"Like how?"

"Like they never smiled or laughed, not even on Christmas Day. One nun specialized in raising only her left eyebrow while the other stayed still as a dead worm on her face. She loved knocking our skulls and telling us to shut up."

"That's nothing!" he'd say, hoping to hear scarier things.

"Well, sometimes they checked in our underwear to make sure no one stole food or erasers."

"Gross! You loved the nuns?"

"Not really, but I didn't mind them. They were the only people taking care of me. So I was grateful to them."

"You did fun things at the orphanage?"

"Well, sometimes the nuns took us to the beach. They drove us in a big bus. I liked that."

"You were sad to leave them?"

"Kind of."

"Why?"

"Because life there was a routine I knew well." But not life here, I wanted to add but didn't. And before Michael could ask me more, I used the occasion to pose some of my own questions. These were questions I'd been too ashamed to ask Mary for fear of sounding stupid or insulting. "Now you tell me something. Do you know what 'home sweet home' means?" I said, as if quizzing him. And when Michael screamed, "It's like you're happy to be home 'cause your home is the best!" I smiled, satisfied with my discovery. This was my way of learning about my new world, a safe gathering of information. Michael and his friends were a great source of knowledge I couldn't get elsewhere. Oh, how many times did they help me save face?

"Mom said you're a boat people," Michael insisted on telling me during our study period.

"Yes."

"What's that?"

"That's for people who left Vietnam in the middle of the night on a boat."

"Why at night? The captain can't see!"

"At night so we wouldn't get caught. We weren't supposed to leave, remember?"

"You mean it's against the law?"

"Yes, you can say that."

"Wow! And why on a boat?"

"Because there is less control that way. Harder to get caught than on an airplane."

"What happened on your boat?"

"Lots of marvellous things which I won't tell you today."

"When then?"

"Another time."

"Oh, come on, Kim. Please? Pretty please?"

"What if I told you I can't remember what happened?"

"That's impossible. You're lying!"

"Maybe."

"What happened on your boat? What happened on your boat? Tell me! Tell me! Tell me!"

"What if I told you Dracula bit a woman's neck on the boat?"

"I don't believe it! *Dracula* is a movie! I hate that weird stuff! Tell me the truth!"

"OK. Here's the true story. My boat held many people, some of whom I knew, others I didn't. The captain I didn't. My old neighbour I did. Her name is Aunty Hung. No, she isn't my aunt—I just call her that, more friendly that way. I'm an orphan, remember? No family. Aunty Hung used to sell American music in her shop. Then one day she turned Communist. What's a Communist? It's someone who hates Americans like you. OK? Don't ask any questions and let me go on. So Aunty Hung became a Communist after the war. Then all of a sudden she wanted to escape communism. Changed her mind so many times, you never knew where she stood. Anyway, we recognized each other on the boat.

"She took pity on me having no family. She took care of me, shared her clothing with me. Even lent me her underwear since I didn't have any. I became friends with her daughters; we slept together. We considered each other sisters. Those girls carried plain features on slouched shoulders so nobody minded them. I didn't radiate beauty either, but being older, I attracted the captain's attention. He liked me. He'd tell me stories—amazing stories about people I've heard of but never knew existed for real. You know, people like pirates and thieves and all that. Imagine—the captain befriended all these bad people! His stories fascinated me. We met at night while everyone slept. He had a sore back from guiding the boat all day. He asked me to rub his back. In exchange he gave me fancy gifts. But I've given those gifts away to other people. Only kept one thing for myself—a fan that smelled so good, you'd think it soaked in perfume. But unlike perfume which fades, the fan's smell lasts and lasts. Just smelling it brings back all kinds of memories for me.

"Ever heard the expression 'all journeys come to an end'? Means we eventually arrive where we want to go, and that's what happened to me. So one day, poof! We arrived on land, our boat trip ended and we had to say goodbye. The captain didn't want to see me go but I itched to leave him. He had changed by the end of the trip. He started screaming at people, stealing their pieces of wood, ordering them around. Once he threw a rock at a man he didn't like. He planned to kill other men. He wanted to sign his name on their chests. He wanted to use their blood as ink. Revenge obsessed him. He ruminated all day about a man called Charlie Company. His obsession made him crazy. What? What about Charlie Company? Is this the same Charlie that killed my parents? I don't know! Maybe. Wow, your memory is good, you remember my stories! Anyway, let's get back to the captain. I felt ashamed to be seen with him by then. I yearned to reach my destination. You see, my journey didn't end there on land—my journey ended here in America. In Derby, Connecticut, USA. You like this expression, 'all journeys come to an end'? Good! Makes a lot more sense than 'home sweet home,' no? Who's going to eat a home to see if it's sweet?! Ha! Ha! What? Did I love this captain? No, of course not! I didn't know a thing about love."

"Now you tell me a story, Michael," I asked my adopted brother one day.

"Which one? *Rambo*?"

"No. Your family's story. I bet it's more interesting than Bang! Bang! Bang! You know anything about your parents' life?"

"Of course! Mom tells me everything! Sometimes Mom tells me too many things! Sometimes I wish I didn't know them!"

"What? Family secrets?" I asked.

"Yeah, kind of . . ."

"You're lucky. I don't know any family secrets."

"But they are not secrets anymore 'cause Mom tells them to everybody. She believes in honesty, you know."

"So what's your mom like?" I asked.

"Mom tells me she was a crazy girl. Did you know she got married at sixteen? Yeah, she quit school and ran away from home to marry her musician boyfriend! They lived in a dirty room in Boston! Her first husband had hair to his bum! Mom had long hair in those days too. They spent a lot of time braiding each other's hair. They also sang and played guitar in the malls. She could play all the Beatles songs! Cool, isn't it? Mom had a baby girl with her first husband. She'd give the baby Pepsi 'cause it's cheaper than milk. When neighbours saw Pepsi in the baby's bottle, they called the police! That's mean, isn't it? The police put the baby in a foster home. Mom felt really bad after that. You want to hear more? You'll have to ask Mom! You want to hear another secret? Liz says Mom's always looking to replace her baby girl. That's why she adopted you, Kim!"

Connecticut

Seven

"Mom, Michael tells me you had a baby girl years ago . . ." I mentioned one day.

"He did? I thought he forgot all about that. Yep, I used to tell him those stories at night. Instead of reading a fairy tale, I told him my story. Easier to remember!"

"What happened to the baby girl?" I inquired timidly.

"Well, Michael must've told you she died very young," Mary said.

"No, he didn't . . ."

"She died before her first birthday. She had a defective heart—I didn't know it at the time. I never paid attention. I thought her dark lips came from the Pepsi I gave her. They were actually blue lips. She didn't get enough oxygen because her heart functioned badly. I never took her to a doctor—I gave birth at home, you know. At seventeen, what did I know about babies and giving birth? Nothing! I didn't even know I was pregnant, stupid old me! I had a chunky body in those days, so the bulging stomach seemed normal. Just thought I'd gained weight! My periods never came as expected so I never kept track of them.

"One day I had this huge tummy pain. It felt like the worst constipation of my life. So I sat on the toilet bowl and pushed with all my might! The pain made me holler obscenities. After an hour of pushing, I saw strands of wet dark hair coming out of me. Then I felt what seemed like wiggling toes inside me! I freaked out and called Pedro—that's my first husband. He seemed as clueless as me! Well, maybe not. No one could've been as clueless as me! When Pedro saw the baby's wrinkled front coming out of me, he started panting. 'Jesus Christ! Jesus Christ!' he repeated. It took him a long time to calm down. He finally stopped swearing and helped me up from the toilet. Then he pointed to the mattress on the floor. I could hardly walk. I screamed but Pedro kept yanking me toward the mattress. The baby's head peeked out before I reached the dirty mattress full of bread crumbs. A half-dead spider lay on the pillow, its legs twitching. I gave a shriek as I groped my way toward the sheets. Before I knew it, the rest of my baby popped out. Pedro saw the baby falling head first to the floor. He let go of my hand and quickly grabbed one of her feet. Thank God for Pedro's fast reflexes. Otherwise her head would've been smashed! We didn't know a thing about umbilical cords and placentas. We were just stunned at the whole scene. Remember, I didn't even know I was carrying a child! Exhausted, I fell asleep with the baby in my arms.

"While I slept, Pedro went to a neighbour for help. They called the local hospital and got instructions on how to cut the umbilical cord and all that stuff. The hospital nurse wanted me to come in but we had no money for a cab. So we stayed home while Pedro took care of everything. He clamped the cord using my elastic hair bands. Then he cut it with his razor. Blood spurted all over his hands. But he didn't squirm. Only muttered, "*Dios mio!*" over and over. When the placenta finally made its way out, Pedro gave a deep sigh of relief. He had saved the baby. But I let her die a few months later—it's a horrible feeling, honey! I hope you'll never have to experience that guilt. The doctors told me it wasn't my fault. She was born with a bad heart. But guilt still wakes me at night. She didn't even die in my arms—she died in some stranger's house, taken away from me in her last month of life! All because I gave her Pepsi instead of milk. Stupidly, I thought all kids liked Pepsi!

"After her death, I moped all day. Pedro got fed up with my constant sniffling. He disappeared one afternoon and never returned. The message he left with the neighbour only said, 'I'm off to California.' I grew up fast after Pedro left. Survival suddenly became important. I sought help at the local community health clinic. I met Jim there. He worked as a social worker at the time. I fell in love with his calmness. His blue eyes and square jaw also drove me crazy! Jim saw the sadness behind my clueless talk. Somehow my 'blah, blah, blah' made sense to him! So he quickly embarked on a rescue mission by reintroducing me to religion. I resisted at first. I didn't run away from a preacher father to end up with a religious man. But Jim's faith differed from my parents'. No lectures hampered my way. No television pastor bugged me for money. So I ended up marrying Jim. Life has been fine since then."

"Mom, what was your daughter's name? What did she look like?"

"She had a tiny body with dark eyes, straight black hair and olive skin. Mexican blood ran in her, you know. Why, she almost looked Oriental! I named her Kimberley."

"Is that why you adopted me, an Oriental girl called Kim?"

"Oh, honey, what's that all about? Is Liz giving you those crazy ideas?"

"No . . ."

Knowing Mary's past brought me closer to her. But I still couldn't figure her out. The image of Mary staggering down the hall with a baby's head between her legs frightened me. It was a piece of jigsaw puzzle that did not belong to her "home-sweet-home" image. I wondered if she wore strange clothes in those days too?

Connecticut

Eight

As long as she didn't pry too much into my past, I enjoyed Mary's company. She taught me American folk songs and took me hiking to overcome my fear of landmines. In return, I inundated her with enough bittersweet stories to fill her collection of scrapbooks. Alone in bed, I rehearsed my orphan role diligently. I also practiced my lines word for word. Only Dr. Jacques heard my true voice. Dr. Jacques didn't always answer my letters. Occasionally he'd send me a postcard telling me of his activities in a Parisian clinic. "Treating colds, acne, and people's imaginary problems . . ." And although I couldn't hear them, I could imagine the "*Conneries!*" and "*Quel imbécile!*" he must be throwing left and right. One day a letter came announcing his wedding to Arianne, a French lady brought up in Indochina. "We share the same obsession for Vietnam! In fact we met in a Vietnamese restaurant on Avenue des Gobelins," Dr. Jacques wrote. And because of that nostalgia, she understood his need to return to the refugee camp.

Imagine Dr. Jacques getting married! Dr. Jacques who once obsessed about beautiful black-toothed Vietnamese women! Actually the paradox obsessed him more than the beauty. Seduction played little role in his world of sickness and sorrows. I never saw him looking at Nurse Joy in lustful ways. He only eyed her with annoyance whenever she missed a patient's vein.

Dr. Jacques's fiancée, Arianne, stirred my curiosity. Knowing that she had lived her childhood in Vietnam made this curiosity more intense. As a French citizen in colonial Vietnam, she must have led a charmed life. I imagined her surrounded by Vietnamese maids. I imagined blonde pigtails framing a pair of slapped-red cheeks. I imagined a class full of Vietnamese students reciting by heart, "Our ancestors hailed from Gaul!" and daily singing "La Marseillaise." I imagined classmates wanting to hug her, hoping her whiteness would rub off on them. I imagined Dr. Jacques's sweaty palms palpating her naked torso and his ear pressed to her grumbling heart. I imagined my fingers pinching those slapped-red cheeks of hers.

Connecticut

Nine

Strange and recurrent dreams haunted my nights. I dreamt of rushing to school and in a moment of carelessness, boarded an unfamiliar bus. I ended up lost in a strange city, not knowing how to find my way home, not being able to call Mary. I panicked. Then all of a sudden my father appeared on the street, dressed as if going to a party. I called his name but he didn't recognize me at first.

"Father! It's me, Kim!"

"Oh yes, I see now."

"Where have you been all these years, Father?"

"Just travelling around . . ."

"Can you help me get home? I'm lost!"

"Sorry, I don't know where your home is . . ."

"Derby, Connecticut, USA. Can you find this place?"

"Maybe . . ."

The father in my dreams seemed so real—I wished the nights would never pale. Years had passed since I last saw my father in the flesh. I had forgotten the obtuse angle of his shoulders, the blue of his newly shaved chin, the nasal tone of his voice. Details shelved long ago returned to electroshock me out of forgetfulness. I refused to wake up, longing for that state of half-consciousness when I could dream, yet be in control of my dreams. Mary overheard my mumbled talk with my father. She thought I suffered from hallucinations and wanted to call the doctor. Fortunately Jim talked her out of it. "Kim's just sleep-talking. She's tired. Let her sleep," Jim simply said.

When I finally woke up from my prolonged state of semi-sleep, I became aware of my pulsating heart. I gasped for air as if an enormous lump in my throat prevented me from breathing. Sweat rolled down my temples, accumulating in the small of my back. I shivered and coughed nonstop.

Mary convinced Jim to call an ambulance. They promptly whisked me off to Griffin Hospital where I underwent a battery of tests. Because of my background and stay in the refugee camp, Dr. Delucas decided on the spot to hospitalize me. I tried telling him about my malaria-induced trances but he hardly listened. He ordered numerous chest X-rays and skin tests to rule out tuberculosis. To check for strange parasites, I had to spit and defecate into test tubes every day. I had so much blood drawn from me that I became whitewashed by the third day. When all the tests came back normal except for the physical findings of a heart murmur, along with some wheezing in the lungs, I was promptly discharged. What my heart murmured to the doctors, I couldn't tell. But to me, it didn't murmur. It cursed. It cursed my father who left us years ago. It cursed Dr. Jacques who would soon abandon me. It cursed my mother who lied to me about an aunt in California. A dog gave birth to you all! A dog gave birth to you all! it screamed.

"Kim has asthma. Make sure you keep all animals, plants or stuffed toys away from her. Cigarette smoke is very dangerous. It would help if you vacuumed every day to keep the dust down. Give her this pump the next time she's out of breath," Dr. Delucas told Mary.

"Thank you, Doctor, but our house is very clean!" Mary protested.

Connecticut

Ten

I forgot about November 10, my supposed birthday. Mary didn't let me forget. She organized a surprise birthday party for me. Such traditions stayed foreign to me. I froze on the doorstep coming home. My mouth opened wide to let fly silent words. In Vietnam, nobody I knew celebrated birthdays. They only celebrated the death anniversaries of ancestors.

For my "birthday," Mary bought a cake and many bottles of Coca-Cola. She also decorated the house with pink paper garlands. For guests, Mary recruited children from the neighbourhood. Most of them knew me as their babysitter. The kids all sang songs in my honour, then forced me to blow on tiny candles flickering on a chocolate cake.

"No wait, I'll get the camera," Mary said. By the time she came back with the camera, a puddle of candle wax had already formed on the cake. To the kids' laughter, Mary shaved off the ruined icing with her bare fingers. She sprinkled brown sugar to hide the mess made by the melted candles. She lit new candles and told me to blow them out for the camera. In Vietnam, I only posed stiffly in front of cameras—I never acted out a scene. With no prior experience with this kind of thing, my blowing of the candles and Mary's clicking of the camera refused to stay in sync—we couldn't coordinate our actions. After three failed attempts and many groans of "Not again!" from the kids, we decided to take the photo without the flickering candles. I just had to hold a wilted smile in front of a ruined cake.

Being half my age, the kids soon left me to go play in Michael's room. I stayed to wash the dishes with Mary. Then she asked me to open my present.

"I thought I was supposed to open it only when I'm alone," I said.

"Maybe that's how you do it in Vietnam, but here we open it in front of everyone. So, even if you don't like the present, you have to act like you're happy and kiss the giver! Ha! Ha!"

I opened the present, finding a pair of red woollen mitts with a matching scarf, hat and sweater. With that came a handwritten card from Michael: "For the cold winter, with love from your new family." Seeing those words, I could no longer contain the tears I'd suppressed for so long. I cried for the loss of innocence, for the horrible ordeal I must have endured on the boat, which I no longer remembered. I cried for my present state of loneliness, so far away from my real family and country. But I also cried tears of gratitude for hearing the word "love" for the first time.

"You're supposed to kiss me, silly girl, not cry!" exclaimed Mary. "What's the matter, honey? Are you OK?" she continued.

"Yes—no—I don't know! I've never had a birthday present before. I'm very lucky to be here with you but I also feel so sad. It just hit me all of a sudden."

"I understand, honey. You must miss your parents and your old home. But don't you worry, things will get better with time."

Yes, misery ruled my days. I didn't talk much but Mary felt my desolation. The anxiety about my family made me shed tears in front of her. Nobody witnessed my tears before. Not even when a rusty nail ripped through my shoe and into my right foot many years ago. I pulled the nail out myself that day. I also cleaned the wound and walked around with crumbled toilet paper in my shoe for a while. My mother never knew of this accident. I never told her the truth. I feared she would scold me for being clumsy.

Connecticut

Eleven

I felt on familiar ground again with the heat of summer. Snow had fascinated me at first but eventually it lost its charms. When the novelty of ice-skating wore off, I developed cravings for the hot, sunny weather of my childhood. With school over, I spent the summer babysitting for neighbouring kids, thus putting more money into my bank account. I also read everything I could lay my hands on. In no time I had finished the two-dozen books on Mary's tiny bookshelves featuring mostly nature books.

"Oh, Kim, I almost forgot! There's something on the boat people in this old *Life* magazine. Kept it all this time but forgot to give it to you! Here, take a look at it."

"Thank you, Mom. It'll be interesting reading it."

"Not much to read. Mostly photos, but what unbelievable photos!"

"Seems more colourful than what I remember of it."

"What, honey?"

"The refugee camp."

"Does it?"

"Yes," I replied.

Yes, the photos definitely glowed in colours. Dark green palm leaves, light blue sky, shiny tin roofs. The ground revealed itself in half a dozen shades of brown. Why did I remember only an oppressive state of colourlessness? The camps looked overcrowded with people. Yet why did I meet only a cross-eyed orphan? There must have been thousands of worthy stories, but I listened only to Minh's tales of prostitutes and murderers.

Mary noticed me putting the *Life* article away. She came back the next day with more articles. She clipped all the boat people stories she could lay her hands on. *Time, Life, National Geographic, Reader's Digest* went from her doctor's waiting room straight into my lap. "To help you remember your boat trip, honey," she said. "Although I don't know why you would want to remember it," she added. Dutifully I read those articles, but didn't recognize myself in them. The emotions seemed either exaggerated or not fully captured. The articles all followed the same pattern—a traumatic beginning, then a happy or tragic ending. The inevitable line about seeing desperation in people's eyes bothered me. What nonsense, I thought. The Oriental eye—this must be the most passive of organs. The lids often droop lazily. The iris's darkness and lack of light block all inquisitive regard. You couldn't tell anything from them, much less see desperation in them. So despite my initial curiosity, I soon lost interest in these articles. Real-life stories retold to fit a mould—this wasn't good reading. I'd rather have made-up stories anytime.

"Mom, does your doctor keep old magazines?" I asked Mary one day.

"What do you mean, honey? Which magazines? How old?"

"Same magazines you brought me the other day. You know—stuff like *Time, Life, National Geographic*. But I want older copies. Something from 1968 or '69 . . ."

"1968! That's old! I don't think the doctor would keep magazines that old. Why?"

"I want to read about the Vietnam War."

"Oh . . . but why only '68 and not other years?"

"I heard horrible stories from that year. The first tragedy happened in Hue where I'm from. The second one took place in My Lai, my friend's village. I only have vague memories and rumours to rely on. I want to know the truth, Mom."

"Are you sure it's a good idea? If you insist, we can go to the library tomorrow ."

At the library, I found dozens of magazines and books on the Vietnam War. Many articles dealt with Tet '68 and the massacre at Hue. I had less luck with My Lai. So I began to doubt Minh's version of the event. A whole village dead? Almost everyone killed by our American allies? This could not be, I told myself. Then I stumbled on a little book hidden at the back of the shelf. The book contained hundreds of photos of death and suffering. I saw naked corpses strewn on the road. I saw bodies piled on top of each other in a shallow pit. I saw the burnt-out frames of what used to be houses. Then I saw it. My heart quickened. On a corpse, I saw the words "Charlie Company" written in blood. So the cross-eyed Minh didn't lie to me. Charlie Company did exist. And he killed Minh's parents. I trembled uncontrollably in my bed that night.

The more I researched the massacre at My Lai, the more horrified I became. Charlie Company was not a person. It was a whole battalion. One American soldier didn't shoot children by mistake. The whole company went on a rampage to kill as many innocent villagers as possible. Naturally the army hushed up the event for many months. Soldiers blamed stress for their momentary loss of control. In the end, only one American went to jail for this massacre. When his imprisonment caused a national uproar, he was released after a few months. Indignation overwhelmed me. Yet I couldn't share this feeling with Mary. I feared she would take it badly. Mary wanted me to become a patriotic American like her. She wanted me to be proud of the flag, to experience goosebumps when reciting the pledge of allegiance. Deep down, perhaps I wanted the same thing too.

Connecticut

Twelve

Mary's presence brightened my days. I enjoyed her easygoing nature, her generosity of spirit. At home, we regularly treated ourselves to hair-braiding sessions. She loved working on my fine straight hair. I envied her her natural red curls. She liked my flat earlobes. I admired her upturned nose. While we succeeded in Scotch-taping her protruding earlobes into place, we couldn't lift my downturned nose. The Scotch tape blocked my nostrils so we had to cut holes around them. After the third trial, we gave up our silly game of trying to turn me into a white person. We laughed as we hugged each other. During these beauty sessions, I learned of Mary's childhood, growing up restricted by the rules of religion, an only daughter in a preacher's house. She learned of my mother's left-eye-twitch superstition. When not exchanging stories, we would watch television. Mary loved reruns of *The Mod Squad*. Despite her age, she developed a huge crush on one of the young characters, the one with the enormous head of frizzy hair. An "Afro," Mary taught me this word. And so began my apprenticeship as an American teenager.

With time, memories of Vietnam became no more than hazy images and muffled voices. I had so much difficulty visualizing the face of my dear youngest sister, Thu, that I had to dig out the old photograph of my family to see again her chubby face. On the back of that photo, my father had written, "Tet 1972 with Kim, Mai, Thu" (I knew it to be my father's writing for it

112

differed significantly from my mother's scrawl on the back of Aunt Lan's picture). Every time I looked at the address on the back—"16 Spring Street, California"—I laughed so hard, tears rolled down my cheeks.

As I began to forget, an unexpected letter forced me to remember. Dr. Jacques's message from Palawan jolted me back to the past. He had unbelievable news for me. He'd run into my sister Mai at the clinic. She consulted for a broken wrist, the result of a fistfight with her roommates. At first the name intrigued him. Then when her story of private French lessons in the back of the kitchen matched mine, he knew he was on the right track. "My wife Arianne is so excited at this discovery, she wants to do a story on your family," Dr. Jacques wrote. "Your sister Mai is an angry young woman. But what a beautiful angry woman! The rest of your family is still in Vietnam, never got your letters. Confiscated mail. This is nothing new in a place that strips you of your hope for a better future."

Imagine my sister running into Dr. Jacques at Palawan! What an incredible coincidence! And my mother still alive at home! To think that I had already shelved her drowning and death a long time ago! A death I just presumed but never mourned.

"Father, we've found Mai!" I would scream in joy. "Really?" he would say. "Yes, can you believe the good luck! Now we need to find Mother and Thu for us to be a family again. Then we'll pose for photos. All of us on your lap again. Do you remember, Father? 'Tet 1972 with Kim, Mai, Thu.' That old photo has been bent, folded and unfolded so many times. But your smile still comes through clearly. I wonder who took that photo?" "I can't remember," he would say. "It doesn't matter, Father. I promise I won't squirm this time. I'll smile for the camera too!"

Rereading Dr. Jacques's letter, I couldn't help but laugh at Mai's fistfight with her roommates. How typical of her to engage in fights! The years had hardly mellowed her. Although I wore a grin of happiness, I feared reaching out to my own sister. I had lost the way to my family's heart after all these years of silence. The memory of Mai's temper tantrums also cooled my enthusiasm. I procrastinated for many weeks before writing to her.

One day, I finally got the will to write. "Dearest Younger Sister Mai," the letter started. I told her of my happiness at having found her. I wrote of my worry all these months with no news from home. I asked about everyone's health. "Is Grandmother still bad-mouthing the communists from her garden chair? Is she still reciting lines from *The Story of Kieu* or is she already silent? Is Mother still skinning frogs for dinner? Is Thu still innocent like in the days of old? Did anything happen on your boat trip out of Vietnam? Did Mother give you an incomplete address for an Aunt Lan? 16 Spring Street, California? Funny, there is a 16 Spring Street here in Derby, Connecticut. It's a rundown house in front of Griffin Hospital, owned by a grumpy old couple. I checked it out on the way to school the other day. No Vietnamese woman named Lan there, now or ever. Derby, Connecticut, where clean streets lead to nice houses overflowing with the sounds of television. This is nothing like the fanciful America of our imagination. No flying nuns, no talking horses. No witch with a twitching nose. Not even a blonde genie living in a bottle. Only car chases and shootings on TV. Or forbidden tales of husbands beating wives, doctors kissing patients, men eyeing sisters-in-law. And the story goes on and on, forever without end, day in, day out. Very strange shows indeed. The war is also present everywhere on television. Rambo, Rambo, Rambo. He's forever pointing machine guns at you. As if the war wasn't over. As if the war wasn't already lost . . ."

Before I had time to send my letter, another came from Dr. Jacques. This one contained two photos. The snapshots showed a pretty young girl, tall with big eyes shaded by bushy brows. Her fine nose turned upward at the tip. Her smile showed teeth crooked at the right place–on the extreme upper-right side. Because of their position, the crooked teeth became noticeable only when she grinned happily. So looking at them was like peeking at her good fortune. Strategically placed crooked teeth ranked high in my grandmother's scheme of things.

Yes, I recognized the crooked teeth. The upturned nose also seemed familiar. "But where are Mai's dimples? Where is the deep long scar at the base of her neck? Since when did she have such tiny hands? And the knock knees, where did they come from? Did puberty transform Mai that much?" I wondered aloud. I searched but found few traces of my sister in those photos. After hours agonizing over Dr. Jacques's photos, I resigned myself to the truth. This girl he had found had nothing to do with my family. She never tasted my mother's tangy soup, never witnessed her famous slaps in the face. She was just another girl playing the waiting game in Palawan.

How could Dr. Jacques commit such an error? Mary, yes. Mr. Sandys, the immigration officer, yes. But Dr. Jacques too? Were we so alike in our misfortune that no one could tell us apart? We shared a situation, but didn't we all have our own separate stories? Obviously, Dr. Jacques didn't distinguish one girl's sadness from another's. Although genuine, I didn't mention my disappointment in my letters to the good doctor. I only mentioned casually the changes in Mai's face, how adolescence can twist and turn one's features to the point of non-recognition. Like his nonsense obsession for black-toothed women, this nonsensical belief that he had found my sister had to be nurtured. I just had to be on his good side.

Since my letter to my "sister" Mai already lay in an envelope, I decided to mail it anyway. No harm in giving a poor refugee girl some hope about a "sister" in America. As a sign of good faith, I even promised to send her ten dollars if she answered my letter. But she never did write. I only received some of her pencil drawings of the camp. Actually the girl never sent her sketches. Dr. Jacques did. He eventually stopped referring to her as my sister Mai. He only called her Mai. To encourage her finger exercises, Dr. Jacques had bought her paper and pencils. These drawing exercises helped return agility to her stiff fingers. So all day, Mai drew and sketched.

"She has talent," Dr. Jacques assured me. In fact he had already sent many of her drawings to friends in Paris. The sketches would accompany Arianne's refugee camp articles. Arianne's Parisian friends had expressed admiration. Everyone wanted to meet this young refugee with the wise man's vision. "Lots of people draw well. Fruit baskets, street scenes, young nudes, geometric designs, interlocking streaks of colour, all had been done before. But topless grandmothers giving sagging breasts to kids because their own mothers had died on the way to freedom? Yes, withered breasts that hang down to the navel. Not for the milk—there isn't any—but for the comfort of a memory. This hasn't been seen in a while . . ." This refugee girl, a genius? More white-man nonsense, I told myself.

I never wrote to Mai again. Yet I continued to receive, through Dr. Jacques, more and more sketches of the refugee camp. I kept those drawings to remind myself of my dirty beginnings in the world. The drawings also helped me earn A's in class research—one "Life in a Refugee Camp" project versus twelve "Life in Colonial Jamestown" reports. Guess which one wins?

History class, geography class, social studies class, art class, I presented the same drawings over and over. Yet the teachers didn't say, "Stop—stop copying yourself!" They told me to go on.

Connecticut

Thirteen

I spent my fourth summer in America doing the usual stuff. I babysat, read and played hairdresser with Mary. I also indulged in daydreams. I thought about all the penises I could rub. I'd imagine the sex organs of my teachers, my classmates, the bully Bradley Newton and Dr. Jacques. I'd reserve the Iron Fist Squeeze for Bradley Newton. It'd make him scream so hard, he would lose his voice forever. With Dr. Jacques, I'd do it just right. Dr. Jacques's penis made me twist and turn in bed the most. I imagined it smelled like Mary's French perfume. Perhaps I'd bend down to get a whiff of its fragrance.

Nightly I'd go to sleep seeing Dr. Jacques's penis in my hand. Soft, then hard, then soft again. And to still the itching in my groin, I'd rub myself against my pillow. Sleeping on the side with knees bent and a pillow between my thighs kept me satisfied. Mary found me in this position every morning coming to wake me up. Liz, our neighbour, called it "the fetal position." She whispered to Mary some nonsense about me wanting to return to my mother's womb. "Poor child's still missing her parents," Mary sighed. But no, I had no desire to dig through my mother's private tunnel. I just missed Dr. Jacques's masculinity.

Connecticut

Fourteen

When I least expected it, a letter came from Dr. Jacques announcing his intention to sponsor the refugee girl, Mai. "Arianne is too old to have kids. And God knows how much we want kids. This would be the worthwhile cause Arianne has been waiting for all her life. Not just writing about boat people but also raising one. Of course, Mai is free to leave whenever she wants. Paris would be good for her art education. So what do you think of that, Kim?"

What did I think of it? I smiled for this girl's good luck. But I resented her getting a free ticket to Paris on my sister's back. "What are you talking about," my father retorted when I told him this. "Be grateful for what you have. You could've been a Kim Nguyen still stuck at the camp. Cut this free-ticket-to-Paris crap. You should be glad for her," my father said. Then he dissolved into my malaria-induced nonsense.

118

Connecticut

Fifteen

The school year passed by without my noticing it. As usual my marks stood amongst the best. I won many scholarships and became our school's sole student accepted into a pre-med program. I never dreamt of medicine as a young girl. Like my nemesis, Arianne, I wanted to collect stories, then retell them to the world. I imagined reinventing people's fates as in a fairy tale. Yet, I suppressed my instinct to please those around me. Medicine—Dr. Jacques had wished it on me, while pride and money were in it for Mary. While medicine stirred no passion in me, I did feel respect for this field vast enough to challenge my endless memory pit. Bacteria genus and virus subtype—I didn't mind brainwashing myself with them. *Escherichia coli*, *Salmonella*, *Proteus*, *Morganella*—I wished to know them all, to earn Dr. Jacques's respect and love. If I couldn't be his daughter or lover, I could at least be his fellow doctor.

Québec

One

Saying goodbye to Mary at JFK airport proved more difficult than leaving my mother behind in Vietnam years ago. Whereas my mother had stayed dry-eyed, Mary couldn't stop the flow of tears down her pink vest. In the tumult, I managed to shed a few genuine tears of my own. True sadness twisted my intestines as I prepared to leave this woman who had loved me as her own all those years. But unlike my first departure from home, I felt prepared to face the world this time.

Busing into Montreal from Dorval airport, I couldn't help noticing everyone's licence plate. "*Québec Je me souviens*" flashed at me from everywhere, telling me to remember. Remember what? Who knows? But I liked it already. "*Je me souviens* . . . I remember . . ." This was subtle advertisement talking to people's nostalgic longings. "I remember . . ."—a million different things to a million different people, but invariably, we all remember. The poetic propaganda reminded me of my hymns to Uncle Ho. For a moment my mind wandered back to Hue by the Perfume River. But before I could get too carried away in my daydreaming, I returned to reality as the bus hit a pothole the size of a rocket crater. So Montréal tasted sweet but also sour.

Montréal disoriented me. I often got lost going from my YMCA room to the McGill University campus. Telling north from south seemed easy. North meant Mount Royal, whose cross you could see from all over downtown. Differentiating east from west proved more difficult. In Hue, as in Derby, a street got a name, period. No east or west was added to throw you off guard. The McGill campus also confused me. Biology in the Stewart Building, anatomy in the McIntyre Building, biochemistry in the Otto Building. The constant race against the clock brought me to class breathless. Yet I smiled, for in this big, anonymous school, I finally blended in.

With a considerable Oriental presence in town, nobody bothered to stare at me on the street. No one called me "Chink" in school. While my accent bothered no one, my Vietnameseness attracted some people in class. So I made friends quickly. My Vietnamese classmates all shared my ridiculous obsession with study. We soon gravitated toward each other to form a study group. We became a gang of four unrelated girls sharing the last name Nguyen. While I have kept my Vietnamese name Kim, my friends preferred trading theirs in for more Canadian- sounding ones. Cindy, Veronica and Stephanie, they called themselves, but there was nothing Cindy, Veronica or Stephanie about them. Vietnam still flowed in their blood. Thermoses of fish sauce and pho soup still occupied their lunch boxes.

Only Stephanie, a shy and withdrawn student, shared my experience of being a boat person. The other girls came to Canada before the fall of Saigon so never knew the stinky smells of a refugee camp. But since Stephanie refused to talk about her past life, I too kept quiet about my former self. Exaggerating our plights to the North Americans earned us sympathy. Revealing our dirtiness to our compatriots never worked. Both Stephanie and I felt ashamed of this lice-infested period of our lives. We'd rather forget those days living like cockroaches in sardine cans. We hated seeing pouts on the other girls' faces. "Things were different before *you* came to Canada," they always said. Sometimes they acted more Canadian than the real Canadians. You can't slurp your soup here, you can't wear flip-flops to school here, you can't do this, you can't do that, they were forever reminding me. To this I'd reply half jokingly, "Shit, you're worse than the Communists."

I visited my friends at their homes many times. I met their families on numerous occasions. Of course we talked about pre-med school during these visits. The subject of Vietnam also surfaced often. My friends' parents showed me old photos of Saigon in its heyday. They served me Vietnamese food that came close to my mother's. In short, during these visits, I tasted what life might have been, had my real family been here with me. I realized then that for many others, it is possible to be a Vietnamese émigré and still lead a normal life. We were not all equal in our maladaptation.

"Do you have pictures of Hue?" I frequently asked my friends. Some of them had real photos, others only magazine cut-outs.

"You can keep them," they all said. "You need them more than we do. We have our family—we have no use for old pictures. Our parents always remind us of our past, but you, you have no one to remind you. So keep the pictures, they will prevent you from forgetting." At their insistence, I kept the pictures of Hue. I stored them in a shoebox along with my collection of boat people photos cut from *Time* and *Life* magazines. This box of memories also held the old burlap bag with which I left Vietnam.

One day at Stephanie's house, I worked up enough courage to ask her for her boat people story. She looked at me in silence for the longest time, as if saying, why do you want to hurt me? Finally she said, "I don't want to talk about it." I only learned later that she was grieving the death anniversary of her twin sister. I got that story from Stephanie's little brother. Their boat ran out of food on the fourth day at sea. Wanting to help, a young Stephanie suggested they try catching fish with their conical hats. The two sisters went to the front of the boat for this task. The twin leaned over for a better look at her catch. The sea became violent at that same moment. Before she knew it, the sister had fallen into the water. A strong current carried her away. Nobody could save her because nobody could swim, not even the captain. Since arriving in Canada, Stephanie had stopped talking about her twin sister. She kept busy in school in order to forget the past. She wanted to forget. I wanted to remember. I asked for more of Stephanie's story, but her brother only said, "There's nothing more to tell."

I looked at all the Vietnamese students in my class and imagined a dozen worthy tales. Tragic, heroic, funny or even erotic stories—I would like to hear them all. And when I'd heard enough, perhaps I would remember my own story of getting out of Vietnam. But if Stephanie, my own friend, refused to tell her story, who said the others would?

Québec

Two

After much searching, I found a rental room in a grey stone townhouse on Hutchinson Street. Of course I'd have preferred my own apartment in a real building. But this arrangement, found through McGill Student Housing, suited my purse. I had an attic hideaway on top of a houseful of students. "You'll be alone but not lonely," the girl at Student Housing told me.

At the house I made friends easily—philosophy students, communication students, psychology students. These girls came from all over the country, all over the world—Costa Rica, Maryland, British Columbia, Switzerland. With no man around to pit us against each other, we coexisted peacefully. No mind games, no jealousy, no betrayal marred our relationship. We entertained each other with stories of our childhoods, our homelands. Naturally, the girls clamoured for Vietnam stories. Like little Michael in Derby, they wanted to know all about the war, the refugee camps. Once again my storytelling fed others' imagination. But this time my audience heard the truth. No more fake-orphan tales. My refugee camp story troubled my housemates. While the sordid penis-rubbing tales intrigued them, my ambivalence toward Minh offended them.

"He abused you. You shouldn't exchange your body for a gift," they lectured me.

"But what if Minh's gifts and orphan stories somehow helped me get out of the camp? Is he still a villain in your eyes?" I asked.

123

"Yes!" they all answered in unison.

"But Minh was a victim himself. He saw his family killed!" I argued back.

"One bad act doesn't excuse another bad act. Stop defending him. He's a bully," the Swiss girl told me. Bradley Newton is a bully, not Minh, I protested. But no matter how hard I tried, I couldn't convince the girls of Minh's special place in my memory. I couldn't rehabilitate his reputation with my friends. So I left him there, a dubious shadow in my past.

Naturally, none of my housemates believed the part about seeing my father flee on television. "Too much imagination," they said. Yet when I told them I couldn't remember the boat trip, they blamed that on a lack of imagination. "What happened on the boat?" they asked over and over.

"I don't know," I replied.

"Well, can't you at least imagine it?" the Swiss girl said.

"I have recurrent dreams about a man biting a woman's neck. She winced but she never complained."

"And?"

"Sometimes I also hear cries. A young girl calling my name. The voice is familiar but I can't quite identify the person. It's all very strange."

When my storytelling sessions ended, my housemates craved more. They often went to bed perplexed, with questions in their hearts. Without wanting to, I created with my tales a strange midnight thirst in the house. Somehow we all woke up to drink at around one in the morning. These girls were more than my housemates. They were my Hutchinson Street big sisters.

My housemates loved going to the movies. They didn't watch movies to escape. They watched movies to be able to cry again. They wanted to experience fear and indignation again. "Like the time I was six and saw my cat being run over by the neighbour's car," said the Swiss girl from Geneva. "I have forgotten how to suffer now," she admitted in her strange singing Swiss accent.

"We have everything, yet we have nothing. There's a hole in our souls," added the girl from Vancouver. So to satisfy their longing for sad stories, my Hutchinson Street sisters would seek out Holocaust films, slavery films and of course, Vietnam War films. All the while, my Vietnamese friends would overdose themselves on *The Price is Right* and *Jeopardy* in their quest to be more North American. I went to see *Dracula* and thought it rather ridiculous.

Québec

Three

My heavy schoolwork left me little time for serious reading. But I still checked newspaper stores for Arianne's refugee-camp articles. *Libération*, *Actuel, Le Monde*—I perused them so many times the clerk at the Multimag store eyed me with annoyance. Dr. Jacques had mentioned his wife's articles long ago. I knew they would be out soon. On my way home one day, I noticed a colourful *GEO* poster in the store window. The tropical scene stirred something in my memory. I entered the store and asked to see a copy of the magazine. It took half a minute to find what I'd been waiting for for so long. My pulse almost doubled seeing the words "'Histoires de Palawan' par Arianne Jacques." No dramatic photos, no big headlines, nothing about seeing desperation in people's eyes. Instead the article described the games Palawan children played—how they entertained themselves, what they did to pass the time. Ah, the waiting game!

"The children of Palawan, they collect worms, they fight, some even draw. . . ." By the end of the fourth sentence, the story had me totally engaged. This article deserved a special place in my shoebox of memories.

Québec

Four

I spent my first Canadian summer toiling in a lab. Mary insisted I return home for the summer. But I had found a part-time job sterilizing soiled instruments at the Montreal General Hospital. Although monotonous, my work enabled me to bring home a real cheque every two weeks. The hospital job also gave me my first exposure to a French Canadian boy. I welcomed this chance to hear French again. For his part, the boy seemed content to stare at my naturally hairless legs. Working side by side, we couldn't avoid physical contact. Our elbows were on a constant collision course. His were pink, pointy and taking all the space on the table. Mine were round, shy and retreating. Despite the frequency, we never acknowledged these bone-to-bone encounters. Barely a week on the job, I already looked forward to washing soiled test tubes every evening. Sore elbows and a leaping heart sufficed to ground me in Montreal.

Claude, my French Canadian fantasy, spoke four languages. French, English, Chinese and Japanese flew effortlessly from his tongue. Being a linguistics student, he also spoke the language of Liberal Arts. Like Dr. Jacques, Claude nurtured a nonsense obsession with the Orient. He eyed me for hours on my first day at work. Then one day he asked about Vietnam. He wished to learn Vietnamese syntax. So we started talking.

Québec

Five

My occasional meetings with Claude over coffee soon gave way to more flirtatious encounters in restaurants. Of course my mother would've preferred a Vietnamese boy. But the Vietnamese boys in class only obsessed about villous adenomas and hyperplastic polyps. So in my book, French Canadians worked just fine.

One day as we were both cleaning test tubes side by side, Claude took off his gloves, lifted up my skirt and started tickling the insides of my thighs. When his hand moved its way further up, I froze. I told him temptation overwhelmed me but tradition held me back. Losing my virginity can't be a casual affair, I reminded him. My grandmother would not allow the perforation of hymens at the workplace. For her, this act could only be tolerated on the matrimonial bed. Not willing to admit defeat to an old woman, Claude suggested I draw "stop" on areas of my body he mustn't trespass. I agreed. "How about the French 'arrêt'?" I asked. "No, 'stop' is fine, I'm no separatist," Claude replied. The next day I bought magic markers and practiced decorating my body with traffic signs. The first week I had "stops" and "Xs" all over my body. He couldn't touch me anywhere except on my belly button and under my armpits. With time, I started adding a few "yield" signs. Before long, traffic became uncontrollable as Claude's greedy fingers wandered all over my body. I knew I wouldn't be able to resist forever.

After a month of playing the stop game, we finally did make love. It happened one night after a party at Claude's east-end apartment. That day, I impressed all his guests with my imperial rolls. But I also made a mess of Claude's kitchen. So I stayed behind to clean up. By the time I finished, we found ourselves alone in an apartment with only one bed. Somehow, by intent or by accident (I will never know), I had misplaced my house keys. Seeing me searching my purse, Claude smiled. He approached me with a glass of white wine and asked me to stay. He hardly pressured me—in fact he acted like a damn gentleman. "I'll prepare the sofa for you," he said. "The bed looks more comfortable," I insisted. "Are you sure? What about the stop signs?" he asked. "It's the cops' night off tonight. Besides, I'm out of magic markers," I replied.

Yes, I took the lead that night. I seduced him in a way Mary could only dream of. She would have been proud of me. Her romance tips, gleaned from hours of watching *As the World Turns*, worked. Claude succumbed to me, despite the dangerous level of alcohol floating in his veins. No sex before marriage, my grandmother would insist. No sex before marriage, my mother would agree indeed. But I no longer heard those words. Claude's inquisitive fingers had already trespassed on private property. My insides ached with pain, the pain of longing, the pain of pleasure satisfied. All my yearnings in Derby were acknowledged on this night that was turning into dawn.

After our lovemaking, I drifted into a state of dreamless sleep next to Claude. When I woke, Claude had already left to buy us croissants. A pleasant warmth radiated from my belly. Last night's pleasure cried out to be repeated. I penetrated myself greedily and felt a delicious wetness. Then I saw the traces of blood on the bed sheet. It startled me but also reassured me. So I had still been a virgin when I met my lover. Nobody raped me on the boat after all. I had evidence of that now.

Québec

Six

"Tell me about Vietnam, about your city Hue," Claude often asked after our lovemaking.

"In my grandmother's book, Hue is Vietnam's most beautiful city. Historic monuments, a languid river and verdant mountain ranges add charm to this ancient Royal capital. There are frangipani trees everywhere. Bonsai gardens too. I remember playing with the frangipani petals as they fell to the ground. I pretended they were snowflakes falling from above. But people never remember this poetic side of Hue. For the textbooks, Hue is the bloody offensive of Tet 1968.

"What happened in '68? Well, 'New Year's Eve. Boom! Boom! Boom! Lots of deaths,' is what I remember most. The haziness of childhood memories can't be seized. They can't be refocused. Memories are like fog—when you see them, everything else blurs. What I know now, I only picked up from newspapers years after the fact. The Imperial Palace on fire. Women in white weeping over corpses. Bullet holes through which you could insert a fist. A Saigon policeman executing his communist suspect in front of the cameras. The images I remember don't belong to me—they belong to *Time Life*. They belong to us all.

"Any personal recollections? The most vivid image I've carried all these years? It's my mother's sad face. She had to close her restaurant. She took a break from cooking for the first time in many years. School remained

130

closed. I missed my friends. Our neighbourhood seemed eerily quiet. Many people left for the countryside. Others hid in makeshift rocket shelters. We did the same, only it wasn't a real rocket shelter—just a room on the ground floor of a three-floor building belonging to neighbours. They kept their bicycles and junk there. We moved the junk outside and made space for our mats. Somehow having two floors on top of our heads reassured us. All that concrete protecting us from shrapnel and whatnot, we thought stupidly. As if rockets would halt their destruction on the second floor! And the thing about rockets is, you never know when they're coming. Or where they're coming from. No clue at all. We only had split seconds to react. My mother didn't take any chances with those nanoseconds. So we stayed in the shelter for weeks on end, eating old canned food and mouldy leftovers. But the TV functioned perfectly! We watched the battle on the tube just like you did here. I remember being force-fed the news footage every night. Blown-up corpses brought to us in grainy black and white, all to the accompaniment of the *Exodus* sound track. You know, that film with Paul Newman. I don't know why they chose that score but they did. With the dramatic music, it seemed more a war movie than a newscast. Only it didn't end after two hours.

"Do I remember now? Yes. But only bits and pieces. You want to hear more about the war? Everything I know about it, you can find in the library. The little girl running down the street naked. The monk on fire while maintaining the lotus position (he came from Hue, by the way). We saw it all on TV. So much engraved on our collective memory. For years my grandmother painted the enemy as a faceless threat. He was a shadow, a gust of wind. Yet I soon saw through Grandmother's bias. In reality, the enemy had my facial features, spoke my language and shared my history. Civil wars are nasty, hard-to-digest pills that leave a bitter aftertaste. Wounds will heal but guilt invariably lingers on. People tell me I walked on the wrong side of the war—the side that napalmed kids, that dropped Agent Orange on my own land. I erred by going to school as others lay dying. Mine was a sin of ignorance. But I too was a victim of this war, wasn't I?"

"Nobody said you weren't a victim of the war. Stop blaming yourself Kim. Now tell me how you got out of Vietnam," Claude said.

"It was a humid night. I walked with my mother to the beach. A gust of wind almost blew her conical hat away. She didn't say much, only smiled. Sweat rolled down her face. I never thought of them as tears. But they could've been tears. From a short distance I could see our small boat. Already it looked rickety. I turned around and felt the old leper's breath on me. Disgust came over me as he took my right hand. He pushed me toward my mother and together they dragged me to the boat. I ran toward the captain, hoping to free myself of the leper's clutch. Just before boarding, my mother caressed my face and told me to be brave. Then she walked back to the leper's hut before I could say a word. Only the old leper stayed to wave goodbye. On the boat, I sat squeezed between strangers. Somebody's tuneless singing drove me mad. But the familiar lyrics also comforted me. 'Go to sleep, your dreams are still normal. Go to sleep, your dreams are still normal. . . .' What happened next? I am not sure. After all these years, I can still see the leper's bloodshot eyes, still taste the Coca-Cola that Norwegian sailors gave us. But everything in between remains a mystery. Strange dreams of a young girl calling my name used to bother me. I've stopped trying to figure it out."

I felt much relief in retelling my story over and over. Sometimes I would be overcome with sadness, yet even then, the tears would not come. At such moments, Claude would hold me tight. Then he would caress the hair on my neck. It was uncanny how we both knew the exact moment to stop discussing and start renegotiating our way back to each other's bodies.

Yes, I loved this husky French Canadian with curly red hair. Not extremely handsome but gentle and thorough enough in his handling of my body to make me feel like a prized catch. I loved his easy sense of humour, his self-assurance without self-importance. The breadth and depth of his swear words also impressed me. They had nothing to do with bodily functions. No shitting or fucking one's mother here—that seemed too banal for the French Canadians. They swore instead in religious terms. *Tabernacle*! *Calice*! *Calvaire*! Sacred words thrown out in a cavalier way shocked these people. And Claude issued them at a constant rate of five per minute, no matter what his mood. Since my upbringing included no Catholic terminology, these words meant little to me. Thus I didn't mind Claude's "sewer" language that made heads turn on Sherbrooke Street.

Life with Claude went beyond sex and swearing. I loved the things we shared together—the lust for exotic food, the appetite for foreign films, the Sunday-morning laziness lying in bed while others jogged. And so I spent my free time falling in love with this French Canadian, writing bad poetry to remember him by.

"Did you know I used to work in the kitchen of a Vietnamese restaurant years ago?" Claude asked me out of the blue one day.

"Oh? You never told me that," I said.

"Yep, I washed dishes and lugged the groceries in for a whole summer. I was just a teenager working for cigarettes and beer money. One day a CBC journalist came to film all the industrious refugees cutting carrots into flower shapes. This journalist, *not* the owner, asked me to step aside so my red curls wouldn't spoil her filming. *Tabernacle*, can you imagine that! I was very naïve then.

"The restaurant closed for three hours between lunch and dinner. One day, my co-worker, a pretty Vietnamese girl of about twenty, made me an elaborate lunch. She then sat down in silence to watch me eat. She didn't speak any English so I never knew her name even though we worked side by side for months. It was an uncomfortable, silent meal because I knew nothing of Vietnamese culture then. I wasn't sure if, by accepting this great feast, we weren't now formally engaged to wed or some such stuff."

"Claude, Claude, Claude. Did she have painted black teeth?" I asked.

Québec
Seven

While I excelled as a student, I failed miserably as a medical intern. Knowing my textbooks by heart didn't prepare me for the difficult task of caring for the sick every day. All of a sudden, high marks became useless. Professors no longer judged me on what I knew. In the real world of hospital politics, quick wit or social skills mattered more. Making the right diagnosis or being up-to-date in my reading sounded good, but not good enough. Somehow getting the biopsy result before it officially came out the next day counted more. Writing good discharge summaries without being asked to earned brownie points. Dealing with annoyed family members wondering just who was in charge would be the cherry on top of the sundae. In short, we did all the little things that made life easier for the professors. They based our evaluations on these daily mechanical acts. Did we clog the machine or did we help it run smoothly? It all came down to that.

Being sleep-deprived didn't help my mood. The thrice-weekly calls working twenty-four out of twenty-four hours kept me more than edgy. I looked a wreck by the end of my first rotation. Halfway through my internship, I had lost so much weight I became the twin image of my leukemia patients. I looked so sick, my program director had to force a holiday on me.

"Take a month off," Dr. Rosen told me. "Go on a trip. If you have no money, I'll loan you some! You're too good a student to lose to burnout," she insisted.

"So, have you thought about where you want to go for holidays?" Dr. Rosen inquired one day.

"Maybe Paris. I know a French doctor there. I'd like to see him again," I answered vaguely.

"Paris! No, no, that won't do you any good!"

"Why not?"

"Yes, Paris is beautiful but it's grey, cold and rainy now! You'll come back even sicker and more depressed. What you need is a relaxing place. Somewhere sunny with a beach, like the Bahamas or California."

"California would be nice. My mother has a cousin there," I replied absently.

"California it will be then! I'll pick you up at lunchtime tomorrow. We'll go to my travel agent for your ticket," concluded Dr. Rosen swiftly.

"What do you think of California?" I asked Claude that same evening.

"West Coast bullshit."

"I know—primal scream, pet rocks and crystal therapy, to name only a few."

"You got it. Trends for the culturally deprived navel-gazers."

"But all that is finished. Nobody is doing that stuff anymore!"

"Well, they have newer fads. We just haven't heard about them yet. Remember, Canada is a backward country."

"No, I am serious. My program director suggests I take a holiday. I thought California would be nice."

"Why? I thought you always dreamt of Paris?"

"I do. But Dr. Rosen said it rains all the time there. I need someplace sunny and relaxing, with a beach or something."

"Great, how about Puerto Escondido in Mexico? Amazing surf. Cheap too."

"No, not Mexico. California."

"What is so special about California, that you've got to go?"

"My mother has a cousin there—Aunty Lan. I was supposed to look her up after my stay in the refugee camp. But I ended up going to Connecticut instead. I told you about all of this! 16 Spring Street, California, remember?"

"Yes, I know. But she doesn't exist!"

"She does so exist! I have a picture of her somewhere. It's her address that's no good. Or maybe it is good. I'll have to find out."

"How?"

"With you helping me, of course. We'll rent a car and go along the coast, checking out all major towns with a Spring Street. If we have time, we'll go inland as well."

"Oh, boy! Going to Paris sounds less tiring to me! But if you insist, I'll ask my boss for some time off tomorrow."

By this time, we'd ceased washing test tubes at the Montreal General, moving slowly but surely up the respectability ladder. After his MA, Claude found himself a job as a media analyst at Canadian Trend Reporting. This small up-and-coming enterprise run by a former Californian saw the future in newspaper articles. It predicted tomorrow's trends by analyzing today's media. Claude's boss initially hired him as the firm's token French Canadian, but thanks to his no-nonsense approach and peculiar sense of humour, he soon became the boss's favourite.

Being the boss's pet had its disadvantages. Her possessive claws scratched his back but also held him in check. Getting a month off proved harder than expected. But Claude succeeded in negotiating this time away from her.

This trip to California obsessed both my days and nights. The maps and guidebooks I studied returned to disrupt my sleep at night. 16 Spring Street! 16 Spring Street! flashed at me from all corners of my dreams. To my great surprise, there were only four towns with a Spring Street in them: Los Angeles, Santa Barbara, San Jose and San Francisco. By the time we boarded our Air Canada flight to San Francisco, I knew the exact location on a map of each Spring Street in each of the four cities. Now if only I could find a 16 Spring Street with a Vietnamese woman by the name of Lan inside.

California

One

No, I could not locate this Vietnamese woman named Lan. This didn't disappoint me. I had expected it all along. Aunty Lan probably never existed, as Claude insisted repeatedly. My mother had baited me with this Aunty Lan story. And I fell for it. Yet without the proper amount of tears to nurture it, the seed of doubt could never flower into real resentment.

I didn't find this woman Lan, but I found Aunty Hung and her family. After some loitering in phone booths, I tracked them down. Like many other Vietnamese émigrés, they had settled in Orange County, building new lives amidst old bricks. Aunty Hung had opened a pho restaurant catering mostly to American students on the lookout for cheap ethnic meals in an authentic setting. Walking into the Saigon Palace Restaurant, I immediately recognized Aunty Hung's pouting lips. They had dropped even more with the years. Her tight lips refused the slightest smile. Her eyes squinted at all the waiters. Even from a distance, I could hear the loud snort escaping from her nose. Thank God she didn't immediately recognize me.

"There she is—Mrs. Hung. The chubby one ordering the waiters around," I whispered to Claude.

"Who is she again?" Claude asked for the tenth time.

"My old neighbour in Vietnam. I left the country with her family. Shared a bamboo mat with her kids at the camp. I told you all this before."

"Oh yes, left Hue to board a boat in Lang Co, Vietnam. Then arrived in Palawan, the Philippines."

"What's it with you and locations? You remember them all, but can't recall people or important events."

"Well, it's a different type of memory, what can I say? You're the doctor. Tell me which part of my brain is compensating for the part ruined by too much pot?"

"Hush! Here she comes. Don't you mention anything about pot!"

"Chopsticks or forks?" Aunty Hung asked without looking at us.

"Chopsticks please. Cam on," Claude answered, doing his best to suppress his language-school Mandarin accent. That earned us a slight smile, but still no eye contact. When she returned ten minutes later with chopsticks and two Vietnamese-only menus, I finally gathered enough courage to address her in Vietnamese.

"Are you Aunty Hung, formerly of Hue?" I asked shyly.

"Yes, why?" Aunty Hung asked in return, looking at me now with much curiosity.

"Do you remember me? Kim—we were at the camp together . . ."

A long silence ensued before she screamed out the obligatory "Oh my God!" Suddenly Aunty Hung jumped on me, hugging and kissing me all over.

"Tell me about you! Where you live now? How's your mother? Your sisters? What they up to?" She went on excitedly, firing a million questions, to which I had few answers.

"I live in Canada and am training to be a doctor. This is my boyfriend, Claude," I answered meekly.

"Canada! Doctor! Boyfriend! Oh my God! Look how you've grown! Only yesterday you were still little kid. Nice kid but so shy! Nothing to say! So how's your mother?"

"I don't know. I think she's still in Vietnam but I haven't heard from her in years."

"Oh my God! That's terrible! You come visit us tomorrow at home. OK? My oldest daughter also in medical school! Remember her? You two shared mat at camp! You'll have lots to talk about. So what you want to eat? Bill on house of course."

"Do you have any Hue specialty, Aunty Hung?"

"Oh, missing mother's cooking, eh? No, I can't compete with her! Only spring rolls and noodle soup here. Americans like it that way."

"Safe, exotic food," added Claude who, having been left out of the conversation for a while, itched to join in.

"Oh my God! He understands Vietnamese! Wait till I tell Titi about you!"

When I saw her the next night, Titi forbade me to address her as such. Tired of the ridiculous sound of her name, she had long ago given herself an American alias. Titi became Cheryl and she greeted me with a set of braces so shiny they competed with her mother's diamond collection. To me she was still Titi, the five-year-old so bad in school, her mother had to bribe me to do her ABCs. First-year medical school now, can you imagine!

At her house, Aunty Hung welcomed me with an exaggerated hug and an overly sweet smile. Even the pout in her lips did a U-turn. She wore a fine silk suit that smelled of newly sprayed perfume. A heavy jade pendant dangled from her neck, making a worrisome clunk against the marble table every time she bent to slurp her soup. A piece of green onion protruded from the gap in her teeth, but nobody bothered pointing it out.

Aunty Hung ate and talked merrily. All evening she entertained us with tales of American awkwardness. "Imagine hoisin sauce in pho soup! And soy sauce on spring rolls! Actually they like the fish sauce but if you tell them 'fish sauce,' they ask for soy. Same with Jewish people asking if there is pork in my rolls. Of course there is! But I tell them ground veal. They like it better that way! Maybe they can tell difference, but they aren't complaining!" Aunty Hung said with a mocking laugh.

Like her mother, Titi couldn't stop talking throughout the evening. She bragged about her excellent school performance. She named all the boys running after her. She listed all the sports trophies she had accumulated. Her Americanness bothered me. The self-confidence with which she carried on rang false. She acted as if she had never shared this Vietnamese past with me in Hue, never slept on my slimy mat in Palawan.

139

I wanted to talk about our boat trip out of Vietnam. I wondered if she remembered. "Nothing dramatic, just real bad stomach pain," Titi said.

"Must have been your menstruation starting," I suggested.

"No, I was too young for that. It was the constipation. Hard to shit over the boat railing. The shit couldn't come out so I kept it in for ten days."

"What about urinating?" I wondered.

"Oh that. We just peed in the boat. Then threw seawater on it to clean up. We scooped the whole mess and threw it overboard using our hats. It stunk. Why do you ask all this? Can't you remember? You were there!" Titi exclaimed.

"No, I forgot," I said hesitantly.

"Then good for you. Sometimes it's better to forget," she replied.

"Do you remember a French doctor called Dr. Jacques? No, he doesn't have crossed eyes. That's the orphan Minh. Dr. Jacques took care of me during my sickness at the camp. Later I worked for him. He once told me about his obsession for black-toothed Vietnamese women. I used to dismiss this as nonsense. You know, typical white male fantasy for beautiful savages. Now I understand him better. He didn't obsess about the women. He obsessed about our country, so beautiful yet so rotten. Dr. Jacques is married and back in Paris now. He adopted a Vietnamese girl called Mai from Hue. He thought the girl was my sister Mai, but she wasn't. Years ago somebody at the camp mistook me for an orphan called Kim. All these convoluted pasts and mixed identities, there must be many more. My two sisters and mother probably met the same fate. They are probably somebody else's daughters or wives by now. Or worse, they could be dead at sea. I still write them the occasional letter but they never answer. I know I won't ever find them again. And wherever they are, I wish them restful dreams, for there is nothing worse than twisting in your bed wondering about what might have been."

"Do you remember Vietnam?" I asked Titi.

"Kind of."

"Do you feel Vietnamese?" I inquired.

"Not really."

"Do you feel you belong somewhere?"

"Of course—here in L.A."

Ah, yes, Titi had found her niche in Los Angeles. I guess I could call Montreal home too. We had adapted. But how many others hadn't? A boat person here, a refugee there. A soup shop here, a convenience store there. People trying to patch up former lives as best they could, smiling and nodding their way through odd jobs in faraway lands. Putting up facades of normalcy when nothing remained normal . . .

All these thoughts buzzed through my mind but I couldn't share any of them with Titi. Our conversation went nowhere. Talking served no purpose except to further deepen the melancholy between us. What Titi did, what she bought, what she accomplished—our dialogue centred only on her new life. I had hoped to reminisce about our old Cong Ly Street, about my mother's famous restaurant and her mother's American music shop. I wanted to laugh with them, looking back on those hot Palawan days playing the waiting game by counting flies on garbage. I wished to exchange memories with these people who knew me from way back then. But that conversation never materialized. No one wanted to remember.

Titi talked me into another get-together for the following Saturday. "The biggest Vietnamese wedding in town this year. The bride is my best friend, you have to come," Titi insisted. "The groom's father, Dr. Vu, is a well-known plastic surgeon. Both Vietnamese and American women run to him for an exotic experience. Imagine nose jobs under acupuncture! You and Claude have to come!" Titi insisted again. And so we did.

Claude seemed less than happy in his tight rental tux but the prospect of witnessing a real Vietnamese wedding made up for the inconveniences. At the Blue Lotus Restaurant, the fanciest Chinese eatery in town, guests showed up in sequined gowns and black ties. Dozens of Vietnamese girls in strapless dresses gathered around Claude. They giggled as he pulled out his I-speak-Vietnamese act. He grinned as if in heaven, so I left him there. Titi, as maid of honour, also stayed busy all night looking after the bride's ten-foot-long veil. Left alone, I sought the company of Titi's younger sisters and brothers.

"Do you remember Pham Duy's song 'Go to Sleep, Your Dreams Are Still Normal'?" I asked John, one of Titi's younger brothers.

"Mom listens to it all the time. It's very popular with her friends. Sounds corny to me."

"The old Vietnamese crowd loves that song. Your mother sang that to you as we were getting on the boat in Vietnam years ago."

"Oh?"

"Do you remember?"

"No. What about it?" he asked.

"For many years I couldn't get that song out of my mind. I used to sing it to myself at night before going to sleep. It's like a daily prayer."

"OK . . ."

"Don't you think it's strange to tell someone to go to sleep, go back to your ordinary dreams? In the West we'd say have sweet dreams, wishing you nice dreams. Nobody wishes for ordinary dreams."

"It's just a song—don't kill yourself trying to figure it out," John replied.

"But in our unfortunate country, we can only hope for ordinary dreams. Ordinary dreams to forget the suffering."

"If you say so, Kim."

"You know, fate spared your family the worst of the war. But for many others, death remained a constant companion. Generations of orphans never tasted the lightness of being." I was about to tell him Minh's orphan story but he cut me short.

"Know what? Your tendency for drama is getting on my nerves," John waved to dismiss me.

Having little success with the younger kids, I approached their father, Uncle Hung. He sat alone, nodding to the music as his wife waltzed herself around the room.

"Uncle Hung, what happened on the boat?" I asked, waking him up from his daydream.

"What boat?" He looked perplexed.

"The boat that brought us out of Vietnam years ago."

"Oh. Nothing dramatic. We ran out of food and water after a few days at sea. But nobody suffered major illness. Soon after, we got picked up by a freighter and brought to Palawan."

"That's it?"

"Yes, why?"

"I don't remember anything about the boat. So I thought maybe something really bad happened . . . ?"

"No, you were just too young to remember. That's all."

"But I remember the camp, and I was young there too."

"Well, you spent a lot more time at the camp than on the boat. So you have more memories of it. It's normal," Uncle Hung said.

Could that be it? Not remembering the boat trip simply because it didn't last long enough to imprint itself on me? Like an instant Polaroid picture with no negative for you to file? I found this explanation unconvincing. So I continued my conversation. "Uncle Hung, I have had recurrent dreams since the boat trip. It is very strange—I don't understand it. I see blood trickling down a woman's neck. I hear a young child calling my name over and over. Sometimes I even see a woman's head inside a barrel of water. Can you understand it? Did any of that really occur?"

"Kim, let the past stay in the past . . ."

"But I just want to know. Did anyone get killed on our boat? Did anyone drown?"

"No, nobody died. Listen to me, Kim. Stop worrying about the past. There is no point in doing it."

"But if nobody died—why is there a head inside a barrel of water?"

"I told you nobody died! Stop asking questions," Uncle Hung said, then got up to join his wife on the dance floor.

At about one o'clock in the morning, the kids went wild. The sickly sweet music of Pham Duy gave way to punk noises. I felt tired and decided to drag Claude away from his hordes of admirers. On the way out, the bride asked us to sign a guest book. Leafing through the pages, I noticed a distinctive scrawl. I instantly recognized both the name and the handwriting. How could I not? How many hours had I spent staring at the photo and rereading a hundred times the few words written on its back? "Tet 1972 with

Kim, Mai, Thu." The handwriting matched the one in the guest book.

"Are you OK?" Claude asked.

"Asthma attack! Give me the Ventolin pump, please!" I pleaded.

"Alright, here it is. Calm down. Breathe the stuff in. That's better. Now what's the matter?"

"I don't know. I think my father was here tonight."

"Your father! You haven't seen him in more than ten years! How could you recognize him?" Claude said.

"I didn't see him. But I saw his name in the guest book."

"Lots of people have that same name! Didn't you tell me half the Vietnamese in America are called Nguyen?"

"Yes, but his handwriting. I . . . I recognize it . . ."

"So? Many people have similar handwriting. Doesn't mean anything."

"But . . ."

"How can you recognize your dad's handwriting anyway? He never wrote you!"

"No, but I have an old photo with his writing on the back."

"Where's this photo?"

"Who knows? Somewhere at home. Must be in my box of Vietnamese photos and Time Life refugee stories."

"When was the last time you looked at that photo?"

"Don't know. Years ago. But still . . ."

"Oh, come on, Kim. Let's go back to the hotel. I'm tired."

"OK. I need some sleep too," I agreed.

California

Two

Claude still doubted my story the next morning. "There must be lots of men with the name Thiet Nguyen," he said. "How could you possibly recognize your father's handwriting after all these years? He disappeared ages ago in Vietnam. He couldn't just show up at a California wedding now!" The whole story smacked of absurdity to Claude. But I couldn't dismiss it. I knew I had seen my father's signature last night. Getting no sympathy from Claude, I turned to Aunty Hung for help.

"You saw your father last night?" Aunty Hung exclaimed with much disbelief when I told her my story. "Can't be! I would recognize him! Even with lots of people there. Even with the low lights. I tell you he wasn't at the wedding!"

"No, I didn't see him. Only saw his name in the guest book. It was his handwriting. I recognized it, Aunty Hung."

"Still can't be. I know all the Vietnamese around here. If he lives here, I already tell you!"

"Maybe he doesn't live in L.A. or Orange County. Maybe he lives somewhere else?"

"No! Thiet Nguyen is a common name!"

"Could you at least ask Titi for me? Maybe her friend, the bride, would know something."

"Titi's very busy with school. Don't want to bother her with this." Aunty Hung dismissed the idea, reverting to her usual difficult and pouting self.

"Please help me, Aunty Hung," I pleaded. "My father left our family so long ago. I never knew why. My mother never talked about it. I remember the shame I felt in school, having no father while all my friends had one. With time, the war claimed their fathers too. But theirs was a heroic end to a life of self-sacrifice. The whole neighbourhood went to their funerals. But me, I lost my father to unknown circumstances. No, he couldn't be in the army. He had a hunchback, remember?"

"Maybe he left for younger woman," Aunty Hung speculated aloud. "But your mother's nice-looking too," she said, more to herself than to me. "Lots of men looking at your mother too."

"You knew my mother in her youth?" I inquired.

"Of course. We went back a long time! Knew your father as a kid too."

"Really?"

"He lived few streets away. Same neighbourhood."

"You never told me this in Palawan."

"Too much worries in Palawan. No time for idle talk then."

"Aunty Hung, what was my mother like?"

"Very beautiful. Men falling for her left and right. She loved the attention."

"Oh? I always remember her as serious and hard-working. Not one to care about men's attentions."

"Hard-working, yes. But who doesn't want attention?"

"Funny, I could never picture my mother as a flirt."

"Not flirt! But there are lots of things you don't know about your parents. Better that way."

"Yes, but . . ."

"Look, mothers weren't always mothers. Once foolish like you young people now." I wondered what Aunty Hung meant by that. If Aunty Hung knew my family's secret, she didn't feel like divulging it. At least not now.

146

"Sometimes I wish I knew my mother more. And my father, he's a mystery to me. Yet I dreamt about him all the time in Palawan. We had imaginary dialogues with each other at the camp and in Connecticut. I had no one else to confide in, in those days," I said with as much regret as I could muster, to touch something in Aunty Hung's cardboard heart.

"Wonder what your mom saw in your father—a hunchback!" Aunty Hung said, then quickly added, "But he was a nice man." She wanted to console me.

But I didn't need any more consoling. I smiled, for I knew I had hit her soft spot—speculation and gossip. Aunty Hung, too, yearned to know my father's story. With all her Vietnamese contacts, she would prove helpful in my search for this elusive man my mother once married.

The disappointing truth came soon enough. Indeed, my father never attended the wedding. The Thiet Nguyen signature I saw belonged to a 20-year-old UCLA student from San Francisco. His father, Bao Nguyen, carried no hump on his back. Aunty Hung and Claude were right. "Thiet Nguyen," like "Robert Smith," exuded commonness.

"Don't be sad," Aunty Hung said when she saw the grimace on my face. "Guess what? One of Titi's friends saw a short hunchback in San Francisco's Chinatown last month! She noticed him because he swore to American ticket cop in Vietnamese. He was double-parking with a Mercedes. Imagine, a shorty in a fancy car! Hey, maybe that's your father!" Aunty Hung said jokingly, wanting to cheer me up. When I failed to smile, Aunty Hung adopted a more serious tone. "Your father must be here somewhere. You saw him getting on American helicopter, right? You're sure? OK! So he must be around! You come back visit me next year and we find him. OK? I know all Vietnamese around here. I have friends in New York, Dallas and D.C. too. They'll help find him. Don't worry. Now come, I tell you some secrets."

California

Three

What if I had run into my father at a California wedding? I repeatedly asked myself. The thought, not improbable, lingered on. After all, most Vietnamese immigrants did settle in California's Orange County. And being a close-knit community, everyone would show up at such an important wedding. I imagined a short hunchback in a tuxedo too long for him. I imagined as well a new wife by his side, also short but not hunched over. As I introduced myself, his crossed eyes would flicker incessantly. Would my father be happy to see me? Would he show signs of remorse for disappearing from my life? Or would he simply be nervous? With polygamy a crime in this country, perhaps he would dread my mother showing up to put him away. Finish off his American dream. If we did meet, what stories would we tell each other?

"Why did you leave us?" I would ask.

"Not sure if I can answer that," he would respond. "But I will tell you the story of your mother and me. Did she ever tell you that story?"

"No. She never told me stories."

"Well then, I will. Where do I start?" he would say.

"I remember your mother as one of the most beautiful girls in our neighbourhood. Clear skin, fine straight nose, large eyes, slim waist—she carried all those features with grace. Unlike most girls her age, she walked with steady steps, as if knowing exactly where to go in the Central Market. At fifteen, she became the most sought-after girl. Matchmakers lined up in front of her house for a peep at her famous white-girl nose. Every mother on the block wanted this good-looking yet strong and hard-working person for a daughter-in-law. Since my family owned more buffaloes than we needed, I had a better chance than most suitors. Thus, despite the fierce competition, despite my hunchback, I won your mother's hand.

"I remember the wedding as an elaborate affair. One hundred invitations in all. So many people, guests had to bring their own chairs! My father hired two cooks to prepare rose-shaped dumplings. My aunts took care of the suckling piglets roasting in the garden. My cousins helped with the fireworks. Even my grandmother busied herself distributing tea. The feast pleased everyone. My dear departed mother would have been proud. I met your mother only a few times before the wedding. We'd seen each other at the market. She knew me as one of her best suitors. She knew she'd end up marrying me someday. Yet she never smiled, never acknowledged my presence when our paths crossed on the street. If I dared say "hello," she'd turn around and run away from me. Not like a shy girl would. More like an irritated woman woken up from a daydream. At the wedding we talked for the first time. I told her 'Thank you for accepting my marriage proposal.' She answered 'Thank you for asking.' And that was it for the rest of the ceremony. No more conversation.

"On our wedding night she refused to sleep with me. She preferred spending the night on the floor with the dog instead. 'I'm not ready for us to be intimate,' she said. This went on for months on end. I stepped on her foot by mistake one night getting out of bed, going to the bathroom. Unlike the dog withdrawing his paw, she only moaned 'awww' in her sleep. She didn't move her foot one bit. So I tripped over it, almost breaking my own. The next morning we saw our feet covered in bruises. My father gave me a big smile. He thought we'd spent the night engaging in forbidden acts. In fact, we only exchanged silences. After a while I traded places with your mother. Felt too guilty seeing her on the floor like that. She didn't make a fuss, didn't insist on my having the bed as most wives would. She only said, 'Thank you, that would be nice.' And instead of raging in anger, I counted myself lucky to be her doormat. Yes, I loved her very much in those days. Stupidly, I thought our union would work. But it remained a one-sided affair from beginning to end.

"I slept ten months on the floor before your mother granted me her presence. Love and communication lacked during our lovemaking sessions. She never smiled at me spontaneously, never touched me out of free will. Every night I had to take her reluctant hands to guide them along my face, my chest, my groin. Once she touched my hunchback by accident—she immediately withdrew her hand and screamed, 'No!' Yes, our whole marriage smelled of lovelessness. Her coldness terrified me. I had nightmares about sharing a bed with a corpse. But I couldn't bribe her into tenderness. I couldn't sweet-talk her into loving a hunchback. During the day your mother acted the perfect wife. She managed the house beautifully and cooked the most wonderful meals. The warmth denied me at night radiated freely from her each morning. My family loved her. My father called her 'My Daughter,' a term used with genuine care and not with hypocrisy, as is often the case in father–daughter-in-law relationships. My grandmother, who had lost her appetite years ago, suddenly craved your mother's bird nest soups. Everything your mother undertook became a success. Clients flocked to her beauty, to her talents, to the flirtatious smiles she granted them. Her restaurant in Hue, her clothing stores, embroidery shops, flower arranging schools, they all made more money than we could keep track of. No, she didn't work for money—she worked for the sheer joy of working. Or perhaps she worked to avoid seeing me . . . As for me, I never worked. People thought I taught schoolchildren. But I only taught the dog tricks. Despair feeds on uselessness. Rejection helped breed the super-rats that gnawed at my soul every night.

"When you were small, I took care of you. As you grew, so did my need to escape. I wanted to flee this false marriage. I resented this woman, so much better than me at being a man. I feared playing shadow puppet to her. So I left without saying goodbye, without leaving a trace. I didn't want her to find me again. I didn't want to explain anything to anyone. I wished to start anew. Was there another woman? No. No other woman haunted our desolate bedroom.

"Don't get me wrong. Your mother never pushed me out of the house. My sense of failure and worthlessness did. Despite her frigid fingers handing me my bowl of rice, she stayed a faithful woman. Her sense of responsibility was unmatched. You could always rely on her in time of trouble. Did your mother ever tell you the story of her younger sister Lan? No? Then I will.

"No, Lan never lived in California. Was there a cousin also called Lan living in California? 16 Spring Street? Perhaps, but I don't remember— why? But let me go on with my story first. Promise me this will stay a secret between us?

"If your mother's beauty attracted admiration, Lan's shone even more. But being underage, Lan was spared the inquisitive looks of matchmakers on the prowl for a prized catch. Unlike your mother, Lan tended toward laziness and clumsiness. Her attitude earned her many slaps in the face. But those slaps only fed her stubbornness. Soon after your mother's wedding to me, Lan wasted no time in rebelling against her family's values. She decided to quit school at thirteen. Neither beating nor pleading could bring her back on the right path. A girl stopping school at thirteen was not unusual in Vietnam in those days. Girls stopped to go work in the fields. They stopped to get ready for marriage. But for your mother's family, this seemed unacceptable. Don't forget, your maternal grandfather had taught school. Education, even for a girl, ranked high in his mind.

"Unfortunately, family traditions meant nothing to Lan. She quit school to keep company with a bad bunch. Nobody knew what she did during the day. In the evening, she came home laughing and sweaty. At sixteen, she announced that she carried a child but didn't know the father's identity. 'He's American!' was all she said. Imagine one sister in a traditionally arranged marriage, the other with a bastard kid! The family became devastated at the news. So your mother stepped in to help. Through her many contacts at the shops, she arranged a disappearing act for her younger sister. Lan would spend the rest of her pregnancy in Lang Co, away from the curious eyes and mean tongues of our native city. At term, she would be assisted by the village's midwife. Her child would then be given up for adoption, so she could return home with her head held high. What's that? Lang Co, that's the leper village south of Hue, ever heard of it? Yes? You've been there? You're afraid of lepers? Lepers = death? Never heard of that before. But you're the doctor, you know better than me!

"Anyway, let me continue. A wonderful seamstress in Lang Co worked for your mother. She provided her store with pajamas so beautifully embroidered no one suspected they came from a leper's hands. Funny how fingers become more nimble knowing they could fall off anytime. As if they worked harder trying to prove their worth to you. But let me finish my story . . .

"Your mother arranged the trip to Lang Co for her sister. She thought she could manage people's destinies like she managed her shops. But fate doesn't follow plans. The delivery went well. The midwife did a good job bringing to life a beautiful half-breed baby girl. But Lan didn't stop bleeding after the birth. The midwife tried all her tricks yet Lan still bled. Unfortunately no doctor worked in the village. They didn't think lepers worthy of a doctor. So Lan died, drowned in her blood and amniotic fluid. Your maternal grandmother mourned the death for many months. She blamed your mother for Lan's demise. She cursed the whole village for their lack of medical care. She resented the village's chief, and by extension, hated all lepers. Then one day your grandmother snapped out of her sorrows. She convinced herself life would be worse had Lan come home, unmarried, with a half-breed in her arms. As for your mother, she became stricken with remorse. The guilt changed her completely. Overnight she went from a self-assured young woman to a sullen, controlling lady. The guilt may have stiffened her smile and slowed her gait, but it added agility to her hands. She began to hit you during that time. What? Black and blue? Don't exaggerate. You were only a few years old then. She wouldn't have hit a toddler black and blue.

"What happened to the half-breed? What do you think? Your mother decided to atone for her mistake by keeping the child. She adopted it as her own to make peace with the gods. Yes, you are right—the child is Mai, your second sister. The one always fighting with you. After all these years, I haven't forgotten! Yes, Mai is actually your cousin. An unwanted child from conception to birth. The one that killed her mother and ruined her family's reputation. The object of nobody's love. Her maternal grandmother hated her while your mother merely tolerated her. I tried to be as fair as possible with Mai. But her difficult character turned all thoughts of tenderness into quarrels. I sometimes wonder if she knew her true origins. I promised your mother to keep my lips sealed about this story. I have kept the promise so far. Now it is your turn to keep this secret.

"Who did your mother love the most? You. Yes, you. Of course, we all spoiled Thu, the baby. But despite the hitting, your mother loved you the most. Her first-born—such a quiet, easy child, yet such brains! You never felt it? Well, what can I say? Did I leave Vietnam on a helicopter on the last day of the war? I don't know what you're talking about. Now, tell me about yourself and the rest of the family."

"When you left us, I was still in school. I took the long road coming home that afternoon. I wanted to check if the lotuses had bloomed in the mossy water of the Citadel's moat. Some had, so I stayed awhile, looking at their pale pink petals. When I finally got home, Grandmother met me at the door. Furious at my late return, she punished me with a few hard knocks on the head. In the kitchen, Mother was cooking as usual, but when she saw me, she looked up from her skillet to inquire about the time. I still didn't know what had happened. 'Your father is late but we won't wait . . .' said Mother. We left your bowl, chopsticks and a dish of lemongrass beef on the table. The next morning, the food remained untouched, so I put it away. I sensed anxiety in the air. Yet Mother acted as if nothing had changed from the days of old. She continued cooking as usual. We left you a different meal every night—spicy, sweet and warm. Every morning we woke up to the scent of pungent vegetables and old, uneaten rice. This went on for four days. On the fifth day, Mother told me, 'No need,' as I prepared to set the table for you. That was it—no more setting the table, no more waiting for you. While Mai and Thu eventually stopped mentioning your name, I never ceased talking to you in my daydreams. You never answered my questions but that didn't discourage my constant pestering of you. Of course I asked why but I also asked how. How did you manage to hang on to the helicopter ledge without falling? Yes, I saw you on television on the last day of the war. Don't deny it. I saw the whole thing on Aunty Hung's television. As you fled hysterically, we calmly watched television. Can you imagine it? With time, things became better for my sisters. Our baby Thu soon got the honour of sharing Mother's bed. Mai was glad because this freed up some room for us on the mattress.

"Our mattress on the floor stayed as you knew it to be, lumpy and stained. One night as I lay on that mattress I felt Mother's hand shaking me. She said nothing, only gestured with her fingers. I didn't understand, yet I understood instinctively. I walked with her all the way to Lang Co that

153

night. I felt tired but overjoyed. I thought we were going to join you in America. At the last minute, Mother handed me to Aunty Hung, our old neighbour in Hue. 'We'll meet again in America with your sisters,' Mother promised me. But the address for her American contact proved no good. I never found this person Mother intended for me to find. So I lied and cheated and reinvented myself to survive. I became an adopted daughter to a strange but wonderful woman. And there is an equally nice French doctor in Paris nurturing my spirits and answering all my questions. But where were you when I needed you so?"

***

Seeing the effects of her words on me, Aunty Hung continued her tale. Her revelation of my family secrets strained me but I yearned to hear more. With an open mouth and wide eyes, I listened. "Yes, your mother worked hard. Unlike her dead sister, Lan, that wild one. While Lan ran around with Americans, your mother slept with a hunchback! Poor woman! Pre-arranged marriage—she couldn't get out of it! Yes, your father had twenty buffaloes —so what? Young girls care about muscles and looks, not buffaloes. And your father had big ugly potato-nose on top of the cross-eyes!" Aunty Hung exclaimed. At this, we both laughed.

Québec

One

Flying back to Montreal, I couldn't help rehashing Aunty Hung's words over and over. Her portrait of my family kept me wide awake on the midnight flight. Claude thought it worthy of Reader's Digest. Imagine running into Aunty Hung after all these years to discover my true connection to Mai. Mary would hoot at such a convoluted story. Ah, the stories we tell and the stories told to us . . .

Québec

Two

I finished my internship with average marks. The infinitesimal world of microbiology seduced me. I spent days caring for HIV patients and nights reading about malaria-induced hallucination. While old and new microscopic fiends kept me challenged, obstetrics brought a smile to my face. The maternity ward echoed with both screams and laughter. Pain and happiness don't often hold hands but they do in obstetrics. During those moments of elation, I often thought of my aunt Lan whom I had never met. Lan, who died in childbirth because her uterus didn't contract to stop the bleeding. Life would have been different had a doctor with the proper medication been on hand. A shot of oxytocin and some IV fluid would have saved her. Then my sister Mai would've known a mother's love instead of an aunt's guilt.

I also started thinking about my sisters and mother again. No, I actually never stopped thinking about them all these years. With medical school, Claude and Mary to occupy me, they just became less prominent thoughts. But they never got demoted to shadows in my puppet theatre of the absurd. Whenever I passed a Vietnamese restaurant, I never failed to stick my head inside for a breath of sesame oil, fish sauce and coriander. The pungent smell knew no borders. A whiff of this odor always brought me back to my mother's restaurant in Hue. At such times, I had no trouble seeing again my grandmother with her favourite book in hand, my youngest sister's sweet smile and my mother bent over her skillet. But where did Mai go? She must be on the street picking fights with Aunty Hung's kids. No, wait a minute—Aunty Hung's kids live in California . . . And as my memory kicked back into gear, the daydream would unravel until it became nothing more than a big question mark. Where was my family?

None of the refugee stories I collected proved useful in my search for my family. Even Arianne's articles, while beautifully written, deceived. Her story of sisters separated by fate, then reunited by chance, strayed from the truth. The Mai she thought she had found for me belonged to another family, another past. The refugee camp articles brought back some details of camp life, but they could not retrace old ties. I had only doubts to keep me company.

"Do you think there were two Lans?" Claude asked, out of the blue one night.

"What?"

"Lan, your mother's dead sister, and your mother's cousin in California. Were there one or two Lans?"

"You mean was there a real Lan in California or did my mother invent her? I have been asking myself that for many years. I don't know."

"Isn't it a coincidence they both have the same name?"

"It's a common name for girls in Vietnam. Like Mary or Jennifer here. Lan means orchid. Every girl wants to be an orchid, a rose or a chrysanthemum. Sounds nice. Peach blossom is a bit tacky."

"I agree. What about boys' names?"

"Courage, Bravery and Might are popular."

"What do you want for a boyfriend, a 'Courage' or a 'Bravery'?"

"How about a 'Hottie'?"

"Seriously! What was your father's name again?"

"Thiet, it means honesty."

"Ah, yes . . ."

"Know what? I think there is a real Lan in California. We haven't found her, that's all. My mother wouldn't lie to me."

"I guess not. After all, she did marry a guy called Honesty."

Québec

Three

Soon after California, I was already pondering my next trip. That trip, of course, would be back to the refugee camp that saw me rub penises for Seiko watches. An urge to outdo Dr. Jacques kept me obsessed with Palawan. Night and day I studied the few articles written about it.

Dr. Jacques never ceased writing to me over the years. We kept a regular correspondence despite our busy schedules. Yet he hardly noticed my entry into womanhood. The occasional daring photos I sent him earned no response. As always, he answered my letters in a maddeningly passionless voice—a voice that spoke of medicine and Vietnam, of the refugee camp and the Philippines, of food and magazine articles. Never once did he acknowledge my long-distance longings for him. Never did he reveal anything of his physical self. Claude satisfied me, yet my mind couldn't help but wonder, what if?

In his last two letters, Dr. Jacques had urged me to do international volunteer work. "Beware of time that kills all youthful idealism. Do it now before it's too late," he wrote.

"Things have changed. It is quite safe to return to Vietnam now. No more communist re-education camps," the doctor reassured me. He must be right. Like everything else, things must've evolved in Vietnam also. Like me who had changed skin, the youth of Vietnam must've moulted too. Fifty years of struggle digested, metabolized and eliminated in less than one generation. I wondered if I should rejoice or scream.

Médecins Sans Frontières, Doctors Without Borders, Doctors Without Borders, Doctors Without Borders—Dr. Jacques repeated it a dozen times in his letters. Southeast Asia remained ravaged by viral hepatitis these days. I knew I could put my expertise to practice there. And what better place to start than in a refugee camp? "Admit it, it's not the volunteer work that interests you, it's Michel Jacques who's tempting you," Claude said. Claude took my interest in Palawan as a personal affront to his manhood. His jealousy, which at first I interpreted as a compliment to our love, became harder to handle with time. His protectiveness of me, reassuring at the beginning, I now found difficult to distinguish from possessiveness. He feared my unanchored feet. He thought I'd move away again like I had done so many times before—from Vietnam to Palawan to Derby to Montreal. A perpetual traveller, forever searching for a place called home. Claude wanted to plant my roots in Montreal, in its fertile soil where his family had lived for six generations. He wanted our future kids to have fixed identities, stable lives, a house with a basement. But I dreamt differently. I wished to move on, to change locales. Claude wouldn't hear of it. His job didn't allow him the freedom that mine did.

"Come with me," I said.

"What would I do in a refugee camp? Sit around and write refugee articles?" he asked sarcastically.

"Why not?"

"'Cause I'm not Arianne," Claude replied flatly.

"Then you'll wait for me till I come back," I said, trying to sound light.

"Sure. While you run off to tease Michel Jacques."

"No, Dr. Jacques won't even be there! I'm doing it for myself," I protested.

"For a change, why don't you do something for us?"

"Why can't we talk anymore?" I pleaded, more sad than upset.

"Because I'll never be Michel Jacques in your eyes."

It's true, no one else could be Michel Jacques in my eyes. But what did it matter? Dr. Jacques was just an idea I'd carried around since the refugee

160

days. He should be no threat to Claude, who shared my bed in the flesh . . .

After that day, Claude and I drifted apart, becoming less a couple and more like roommates who occasionally bedded. We didn't argue and still talked to each other, but mostly of mundane things. We ceased teasing each other, so laughter became rare in our studio. Sex, without its usual foreplay, became an act of raw necessity—more his than mine. Even the fiery licking of sex organs could not heal the resentment in our souls. To avoid further conflict in our relationship, I gave in to his desires—making phony grunts to cover the sadness engulfing us. I wanted to cry but feared being caught in the act. As if it were forbidden for separating couples to regret each other, to mourn the passing away of their common path.

Yes, I gave Claude up for a Southeast Asian venture. Traded in the love of a man to follow my destiny. Or perhaps to follow the footsteps of another man? Like a criminal returning to the scene of the crime, I itched to go back to the place that made a liar of me. Beneath the doctor image lurked an illegal immigrant girl who could've been deported. I must acknowledge her.

Nostalgia played no role in my longing for Palawan. After all, who gets nostalgic for stinking shithouses overflowing with fat maggots? Who yearns for a horizon filled with barbed wire stretching into the night? Not me. This craving tasted stronger than nostalgia. But I lacked the words to name it. My silence resembled that of a starved child not able to vocalize what she desired most.

"You're just running away from me," Claude sighed. "Just like you ran away from Mary. You are fleeing us."

"Claude, oh Claude, that's not it at all."

The Philippines
One

The camp had changed—no doubt about it. Modern bathrooms had replaced latrines. The familial gardens planted during my time had grown into full-blown trees, giving much-needed shade to children, still naked, playing in the mud. A school had been built to force education on a generation of kids born and bred here. A blonde TESL teacher waved to welcome me back to Palawan.

The straw city that I knew had evolved into a brick one. It seemed less boisterous, less crowded. With many refugees resettling in North America, the place looked almost desolate. Only the difficult cases with no solution stayed behind. Even the United Nations had given up hope on these unwanted pegs not fitting any holes. So they lingered on, fertile wombs reproducing every two years, bringing into the world a litter of children to legitimize their over-extended stay. These children of Palawan who had never seen a horizon free of barbed wire scared me with their lack of reaction. No screaming, no fighting, no crying out for their mothers. They seemed abnormally passive even by Oriental standards. On the other hand, their elders had turned frighteningly rough and tough, having lost their patience long ago. Petty crime kept people indoors even on hot windless days. Prostitution became the only waiting game still played. Moral languor allowed the deflowering of thirteen-year-old mistresses in the family hut.

The camp would've rotted were it not for the generosity of the local

162

Catholic Church. Christian donations modernized the refugee camp and kept it going. The money also helped build a chapel near the schoolhouse. Yet most Vietnamese worshipped Buddha, or even their ancestors. But what the hell—the Vietnamese were practical people, after all. They'd pray to whoever would get them out of the camp first. Believe in Jesus and we'll build you more bathrooms! Yeah, but how about exit visas? Nothing in life came without strings . . .

The Philippines

Two

I wandered the camp searching for a short young man who would look at you, yet beyond you. Minh's eyes had left a definite mark on my memory. Messageless, they deceived with their lack of words. Finding a cross-eyed man in the camp proved harder than I thought. I checked the medical clinic for traces of his passing or illness. I harassed immigration officers for proof of his departure. Every day I returned to the office to study old files. Thousands of black-and-white miniature portraits stared at me from these files, but I recognized no one. Minh was not amongst those lucky enough to officially leave the camp.

To facilitate my task, I sought the help of street kids. If I once avoided these types, I wished now to engage them. Like the hoodlums of a generation before, these kids came with an attitude. Their blasé outlook reflected not an absence of feelings, but rather an absolute control over nagging emotions.

"Take me to your boss," I said to a dark-skinned boy chewing on strands of oily hair.

"What boss? I don't have any," he responded nonchalantly.

"You must. Who takes care of you around here?"

"Hey, Big Sister, mind your own business! I take care of myself!"

"Good! Ever heard of a cross-eyed man called Minh Nguyen? He must

164

be around 27 now . . ."

"No, but for $10, I can ask around. You pay $5 now and $5 later when I find him. Make it American dollars. I don't want anything else."

"OK. Come to me as soon as you have some news. I'm at the medical clinic. I'm the new doctor from Canada."

Of course, I never heard from that kid or any other kid I met. A cross-eyed Minh, the boss of all street kids, no longer patrolled this place. I imagined him in America under another name—a new identity, just like me. Despite my disappointment, I felt happy for Minh.

I vaguely remembered the rock that sheltered my secret message to Minh. It stood behind the clinic, at a place where I first lost my innocence. A place dear to me because there I also gained the street smarts that allowed me to survive. But the clinic had been extended so the rock no longer stood in its original spot. Unable to work alone, I recruited a team of street kids to help unearth my message of long ago. The first two days of digging brought no result. I gave a sigh of relief and contemplated calling off the project. But doubt kept me digging alongside dirty-nailed kids. On the third day, my heart sank when a torn scrap of paper peeked through the earth. I retrieved it and recognized my handwriting. The decades had not disturbed this naive message of hope. In a way, it was also a message of love. But those words never reached Minh.

"Palawan, December, 1980.

Minh, I haven't seen you for a while. Where have you been? Why are you avoiding me? I am writing you this quick letter to say I leave for America tomorrow. How sad that we can't exchange goodbyes . . . When I left Vietnam, my sisters were sleeping. I couldn't say goodbye to them either. But this time, things are different. I will go to America! Minh, if ever you end up in America one day, promise me you won't kill Charlie Company. That's the only way for us to meet again. Do you believe in Fate? Fate brought us together here. It will bring us together again one day. But only if you don't kill. Fate can be mean to those who kill. My grandmother said so . . . Your friend, Kim."

A few days after retrieving my letter, I received a surprise visit from one of the street kids. He ran into the clinic excitedly screaming my name, "Big Sister Doctor! Big Sister Doctor!" When he saw me, he couldn't put a lid on his excitement.

"Big Sister Doctor! There's a crossed-eye Minh Nguyen here. He's short too!"

"Tell me about him. Where is he? What does he do now?" I asked nervously.

"You pay me $5 first!"

"OK. Here's the money. Now tell me . . ."

"He takes care of girls, Big Sister! He gives them jobs. You want to work for him, Big Sister?"

"No, I already have a job at the clinic. Don't need another one!"

"But he pays girls lots of money, Big Sister!"

"How do you know?"

"Girls who work for Minh always dress nice. Fancy clothes. Short skirts, high-heeled shoes, necklaces, makeup. Very beautiful! You want to meet him, Big Sister? I tell him about you?"

"No, don't say anything please!"

"Why not? You not looking for Minh anymore?"

"He's probably not the same Minh Nguyen I'm looking for. Let me see him before you mention me. Where does this Minh hang around?"

"I hear he goes to church every Sunday morning."

"Thank you, Little Brother. Here's an extra $2 for your help."

That Minh earned a living as a pimp disappointed me. Yet it didn't surprise me. But a practicing Catholic? Did the nuns' propaganda at the orphanage convince him? Did he find salvation during mass? Did faith dampen his hate for Charlie Company? Minh's true motivation escaped me. I had to check him out.

Sitting at the back of the small church, I had no problem recognizing Minh. He walked with the same self-confident stride of years ago. The leader of the street gang, the meanest of the bunch—it all came back to me. He wore a slinky white shirt and tight-fitting jeans, proudly showing off the lump of coal between his legs. He looked older, cleaner, better dressed and more endowed, but the crossed eyes stayed unmistakable.

A group of heavily made-up girls followed his every movement. They sat one row behind him and nodded every time he turned around to check on them. He smiled at them and made hush signs for them to stop their talk. Looking at his face, I saw peace of mind. The years may not have erased Minh's memory but the immediacy of revenge no longer claimed his heart. Charlie Company had probably ceased haunting his dreams. When our paths crossed on the church's steps, I smiled timidly at him. Minh walked past me, showing no sign of recognition. It took me much courage to call out, "Minh!" He turned around, gave a victory sign and cried, "Love ya!" in English to the group of girls behind him. He thought the call had come from one of them. The voice that shared midnight stories with him belonged to a past so foggy it had become unredeemable. Minh remembered neither my face nor my voice. And if he did remember me, he showed no desire to resume our tales. These days only silence connected me to this boy who shared my first Palawan stories years ago.

The Philippines

Three

To turn my attention away from Minh, I concentrated on my work. The medical clinic had changed drastically since I last saw it. Bigger and better organized, it functioned more like a hospital than a dispensary. The local staff, polite and efficient, took care of most clinical duties. While they dealt with sick patients, I dealt with paperwork. I had come here to organize a hepatitis screening and vaccination campaign. This kept me busy during the day but freed my evenings. I spent those free hours seeking out stories.

I wanted to hear as many Palawan stories as I could digest. These Palawan stories, I collected by the dozens. Tales quickly noted on bits of paper to be stored in empty jam jars. They were meant as an epilogue to Arianne's refugee articles published ten years before. Telling the stories of those still unsettled, left behind and forgotten.

Of course, the stories that interested me most came from those who once called Hue home. After all, aren't we more drawn to people sharing our peculiar accent, our culinary habits? When all connections with the motherland paled with time, the scent of a mother's soup still lingered to tease our memory. Yes, I returned often to sections K and M of the camp where a majority of former Hue people gathered—a society distinct from the others. Even here, where everybody ate the same rice handouts and defecated in the same bathrooms, Hue people still considered themselves special. In their memories, they remained citizens of an Imperial City. In their fantasies, they all thought themselves related to the former emperor. But this provincial egocentrism didn't contaminate only the minds of Hue's citizens. Those from Saigon and Hanoi suffered similar delusions of grandeur. And so, after ten years living in a Filipino refugee camp, we still stayed a divided nation, snubbing our compatriots to give ourselves a phony sense of importance.

The Philippines
Four

Of all the Palawan anecdotes I heard, one sounded familiar enough to send a shiver down my spine. "Her name is Thu, she's from Hue like me . . ." recalled Cuc, a voluble young woman who had shared Thu's boat getting out of Vietnam. Upon hearing the name Thu, I became so excited, Cuc had trouble starting her story.

"What's her whole name?" I interrupted.

"Nguyen Thi Thu, why?" Cuc wanted to know.

"Sounds like someone I know, that's all. Same name."

"You're from Hue too, Big Sister?" Cuc asked.

"Yes. What did Thu look like?" I continued.

"Pale skin, full lips and pretty, despite crooked teeth and chubby cheeks."

"How old is she?"

"Maybe 17 or 18 when I met her, 19 or 20 now."

"Was she alone on the boat?"

"Yes, like me. Her family left Vietnam years ago."

"Please tell me more," I begged Cuc to go on.

"I had spotted Thu the moment I boarded our boat. She sat alone in one corner, pressing a burlap bag against her chest. Her trembling hands and

170

clacking teeth spoke of fear. I recognized her loneliness and slowly moved next to her. We squatted in silence while our thoughts darted in all directions. I imitated her every gesture—eating when she did, sleeping when she closed her eyes. But I didn't dare address her for fear of ruining our silent pact.

"One day our captain ordered us to throw overboard all our personal belongings. With more passengers than expected, the boat had listed dangerously to the side. Some people reacted to this order with sneers. They used a rich-people language to mock the captain's decision. Thu understood this language of exclusion for she nodded here and there to their comments. I finally decided to speak to her.

"What kind of language is this?" I shyly asked.

"A mixture of French and English plus some other words which I don't know. Maybe Chinese. They don't want others to understand their private talk," Thu whispered back.

"What are they saying?" I continued.

"They don't want to throw their belongings away. One woman said she had diamonds in those bags. Her husband snapped, 'Shut up or they'll all go after us!' Another man replied, 'We can't bloody eat your diamonds, can we?' Then the woman sitting next to her said, 'Hide them in your underwear.'

"But getting rid of our personal belongings hardly changed the boat's weight. It still tilted to the left side. The next day the captain ordered us to throw extra bags of food overboard. Once again, some people grunted at his foolish decision but we all obeyed. When I saw people line their shoes with dried fish, I did the same. But freeing ourselves of the extra food didn't save our jinxed boat. In fact, the bobbing bags of clothes and floating salted fish left a traceable trail for pirates on the lookout for vulnerable people. Thus, within hours of dumping our food, a motorboat carrying flat-nosed, brown-skinned men approached us.

"Speaking a language nobody understood but with intentions we knew all too well, the gun-toting men came into our lives. They all carried around their necks the gold pendants of fat Buddha. 'Buddha, number one . . .' one pimply-faced man repeated mockingly, as the others searched our most personal body spaces for hidden jewellery. I can't tell you what happened next. The memory is still too fresh and awful despite the passing of years. Sometimes I wish I could forget the whole damn thing . . . but I can't. The worst thing was watching. Watching and waiting in line for your turn. Watching them force long-barrelled guns in and out of other women. In-between their legs. From behind. Into their mouths. We couldn't resist. We had to watch. Watch and imagine the pain that would soon be ours. The rest is too horrible to describe.

"Let's just say the pirates took everything with them—the rest of our food and personal belongings, our pride, our hope, our innocence. After they left, our boat sank, instantly drowning all children and any women bogged down with the weight of clinging babies. I survived by hanging on to a floating plank. Looking around me, I noticed many others in the same position—hanging on to a piece of wood for dear life, not quite believing what had just happened, not quite knowing what to expect next. I floated like that for two nights and two days. My limbs ached from trying to hold on while between my thighs, a sharp pain tore itself into my belly. The choppy water of the ocean took away my shoes and hidden fish. For food, I stayed alive on the single piece of dried plum Thu had shared with me just minutes before the pirates brought sorrow into our lives. I must have passed out from having so little food in my belly. The next thing I remember was waking up in a huge ship full of foreign officers. I felt some relief seeing Thu amongst those rescued. But I trembled with fear knowing half of us had drowned. You see, in my superstitious mind, I imagined being haunted by their ghosts —spirits that would come back to demand why I had lived and they had not.

"Seeing Thu again was like reuniting with a long-lost sister after a painful time apart. Only I have no sister, no brother. My father died in the battle of Tet '68. I grew up with only a mother for a family. But she too left me five years ago, a victim of wasting disease. I felt desolate, all alone in our house. I kept hearing my mother's coughs although she no longer breathed. Scared, I packed my bags and left home one evening. On the boat I met Thu. She turned my nightmare into a dream. She became the sister I had always wanted. How could we not be soul sisters? After all, her dried plum had saved my life.

"At the camp, we shared a hut with three other girls but we preferred spending time with each other. We didn't mind the other girls' coldness. In our intimate world, only the two of us mattered. We spent days telling each other stories. We dwelt on the distant past rather than the present. With time, we became true sisters in that hut under the scorching sun. From Thu's need to tell me details of her childhood, I knew she too grew up lonely, forever longing for the attention of a busy mother more interested in running a business than running a family. Was Thu an only child? No. She had two older sisters who left for America years ago. What's that? What are the sisters' names? I don't remember. Maybe she never told me, or I never asked. What does it matter? Might be someone you know? Sorry Big Sister, I can't help you with that. What? What kind of shop did Thu's parents run? I don't know. Restaurant? Maybe. No, Thu didn't mention anything about her mother's cooking but it must've been good otherwise she wouldn't have had those chubby cheeks. But aren't all mothers' meals good? Certainly way better than the canned food we have here! Now let me get back to my story. Yes, with Thu, I found happiness despite my misfortune. Yet this soon changed. Four months after our arrival, some men approached us for help at the school. They needed people to keep the children from ruminating bad thoughts all day. We both welcomed this opportunity to do some meaningful work.

"The next day when we showed up at the schoolhouse, we saw a line already forming. Three dozen people waited patiently for an interview. You remember life at the camp, don't you, Big Sister? Line-ups everywhere, even to volunteer your services! My interview went well. I got the teaching job. What about Thu? As soon as they found out she spoke foreign languages, the men assigned her the afternoon adult classes. She became assistant to Mark, the American teacher from California. Unfortunately, the very place that gave me some sense of importance also robbed me of my Thu.

"Yes, Thu went from my arms straight into Mark's grip. Mark obviously noticed Thu's pretty face in class. He soon fell for her charms the way bewitched men do, passionately and without foresight. She also fell for his blonde curls and American passport. They wedded only five months after meeting at the school. The marriage and paperwork delayed Mark's return to America. But he didn't seem to mind. Love fluttered in his heart, so time flew for him while it crept for us.

"Soon enough the time for their departure came. I cried for the loss of a friend, a sister. Thu left an address in California where she could be reached. She promised to write as soon as possible, but so far neither of us has made an effort to contact the other. A part of our past has been deleted from our memory. We are no longer soul sisters kept alive by her dried plum many moons ago . . .

"And that's the story of my friend Thu," Cuc concluded.

Thu, Nguyen Thi Thu—a polyglot young girl from Hue with two sisters already in the West and a hard-working mother. Could this be my youngest sister Thu, whom I missed so much the first few years away from my family? Yet with time, I'd ceased to obsess about her, just as I'd stopped worrying about the rest of the family. I'd pushed all that nagging material away, putting a lid on all futile longings.

I bought Cuc's story even without solid proof. Cuc wanted me to find this girl Thu as much as I did. "If you find her, give her a box of dried plums as a gift from me," Cuc asked me as a favour. This request started me dreaming of a future meeting with my sister. I imagined her surprised reaction at the mention of Cuc's name, her smile at the sight of the dried plums. Their symbolism would not be lost on her. I pictured myself once again in California, but this time searching for a real person with a real address, instead of this 16 Spring Street, California nonsense.

Yet even in my eagerness to swallow it whole, Cuc's tale of a cute girl named Thu still left me with an unpleasant aftertaste. Yes, the prettiness, the chubbiness, the easy-going exterior corresponded with my mental image of my sister. So what bothered me about Cuc's story? Perhaps the vagueness of the details, the incomplete recollection of facts. No, she did remember her boat trip, much more than I did mine. Or did she? Had she invented it all? This girl Thu probably existed, but didn't Cuc exaggerate a bit? After all, what good were words without our imagination blowing life into them? I once concocted a story to fool a whole family, a whole community. Why couldn't Cuc do the same? Ah, caught at my own game! Served me right for lying about life at an age when most kids lied about their homework not being done.

"Did Thu say what kind of shop her mother ran?" I asked Cuc the following day.

"Restaurant," Cuc said without hesitation.

"You sure?"

"Yes, Big Sister. Why?"

"Yesterday you weren't so sure."

"Now it comes back to me. Thu even said her mother's cooking was best in town."

"Oh?" I said surprised.

"Yes."

"Did she mention her sisters' names?"

"I don't remember. Maybe Mai or Lan or Dung. Everybody has a sister with one of those names, no?"

"Yes, they are popular names. Did she tell you how the sisters left Vietnam?"

"On a boat too, like us, I presume."

"Did she tell you how she learned foreign languages?" I continued my inquiry, as if trying to unmask Cuc, when in fact I wanted to believe her.

"In school I suppose."

"But they taught mostly Russian in school after the Revolution," I protested.

"Oh yes. I forgot, Big Sister! Maybe she got private teachers giving private lessons at home."

"That's unlikely since her family wasn't rich. It costs a bundle for private lessons."

"But you know how it is with Vietnamese parents. They sacrifice everything for a better education. Starve to death maybe, but little one will get best teacher!"

"What about her father, what happened to him?"

"Didn't I tell you? He died in the war of '68, like mine," Cuc replied without regret.

No, no—he didn't die in '68. Only disappeared in '73. May be in California now.

"Did she tell you where she lived in Hue?"

"No, I can't remember, Big Sister. Thu only said she could see the spire of the cathedral from her street. But couldn't we see it from almost everywhere in Hue?"

"It's strange that you're also from Hue but you didn't talk about the city with her."

"No, we talked about our childhood and feelings. Our city wasn't hurting us as much," Cuc answered.

"Did Thu mention anything about an aunt in California named Lan?"

"No. But with so many Vietnamese settling in California, don't we all have some relatives there?" Cuc exclaimed without irony.

"Do you?" I asked politely.

"No. Both my parents were only children. So I have no one in the world except Thu."

"I'll be sure to tell her about you as soon as I see her," I promised Cuc, still not revealing my true identity. And before she could go on with her I-am-alone-in-this-world monologue, I swiftly resumed my questioning. Having no family was bad but having no contact in the West was worse. It meant no sponsor, no resettlement, no getting out of the camp. Since I didn't want to dash Cuc's hopes, I thought it better to continue with my agenda.

"What was Thu's mother like, do you know?"

"She worked hard, but aren't all our Vietnamese mothers hard-working when left alone to deal with the house, the kids and the grandmothers?" Cuc replied in her now-typical way, answering a question with another question.

"I guess so," I said, resigned to vague answers formulated to please me. By this time, Cuc understood too well my interest in this girl Thu, *her* soul sister. Was I a cousin, an aunt, a sister? Since I revealed little of myself, she could only guess. Cuc wanted my Thu to match hers—she wished me to locate this girl in California as much as I did. We were two strangers bound by fate—the same fate that separates whole families.

The Philippines

Five

"Big Sister, why you write down story?" Cuc's roommate asked, obviously very curious about my presence there.

"I am collecting stories so they may be published one day," I said.

"Big Sister, you writer? Not doctor?"

"Yes, I'm a doctor. The stories are for my friend. A French journalist called Arianne. She lives in Paris."

"Your stories appear in Western newspaper?" Cuc's roommate wanted to know, more excited than ever.

"Hopefully."

"Then let me tell my story!"

"Well, I don't know if it will be published," I hesitated.

"Please give me this chance. It's only way to find my son . . ." she pleaded earnestly. I couldn't refuse her.

"My name's Tuyet, like pure snow. But my life's not pure. I was born to poor peasant family. At fifteen Father sent me to Saigon to find work. I do what poor peasant girls do in cities. Cleaning up dirt of well-off families. Very hard work, so little pay. But after only two months, they threw me out. I didn't understand what's wrong. 'You're too pretty,' maid next door said. Boss's son looking at me all the time. That's no good. Boss also eyeing me

177

at night. That's even worse. So Boss's wife threw me out. I got another job. But again, thrown out. Get job, lose job. Get job, lose job. Like that all the time. One day while in market, a fat lady approached me. 'Come work for me. It's a bar on fancy Tu Do Street, you'll like it,' she said. So I followed her. To a place called the Pink Night Club. It was fancy alright. All kind of red and pink lights on ceiling. Big mirrors on walls. And everywhere heart tables and shiny pink chairs. Fat Lady was good to me. Taught me English words. 'Hello what your name?' 'Buy me drink?' 'How much?' Fat Lady taught me to dance. Taught me to drink beers and smoke cigarettes. But I always choked and coughed. 'Don't worry. You're so beautiful they'll go crazy for you. Just touch them a lot and sit on their laps like kids,' Fat Lady told me.

"After two days, lessons over. I went to work. She was right, men crazy about me. Young ones were shy, turning away when I smiled. But older men not shy, they approached. Lifted me up in air like a baby. Or put me on their laps like a kid. Fat Lady liked that. She smiled often. 'Older men are richer. And much more important. They're not poor eighteen-year-old GIs. They're colonels to these GIs. They're advisors to people who send GIs here. So be real nice to them,' Fat Lady said. Of course I was nice to them. Danced with them, kissed their neck, sat on their laps. But they wanted more. They wanted to take me to their hotels. Fat Lady said I should go. So I listened. The first one, very nice to me. Very gentle. 'Such young girl, you're still a kid,' he repeated all the time. He spoke Vietnamese, but very hard to understand him. Terrible accent! First time was so painful. First Man so big, too big for me. Lots of blood on sheets. First Man said, 'Oh my God, I didn't know!' After that he's even nicer to me. Came back often for me. First Man taught me more English words. 'I love you,' 'You are beautiful,' 'Touch me here!' Real nice words, I liked. Other men didn't say nice words. More like orders. 'Harder! Harder!' 'Deeper! Deeper!' 'Easy now! Easy now!' Didn't like those other men too much. First Man is my favourite. He also liked me more than other girls. 'I'll bring you to America,' he said. But I didn't want to go. 'No, my family here, my country here,' I answered. So he smiled and shook his head.

"Fat Lady always worried about me. 'Got your period? Got stinky stuff down there?' she always asked. One day, told her I had itch down there. Right away she took me to doctor. 'Can't afford dirty girls,' she said. At doctor's I was checked inside and out. 'You're pregnant,' doctor said. 'How could that be, she had periods,' Fat Lady argued. 'It can still be,' replied doctor. 'How many months?' Fat Lady wanted to know. 'Maybe four,' said doctor. 'Too late to get rid of. But can still work two more months before things show,' Fat Lady sighed. Soon my belly showed. Couldn't go back home. Unmarried and pregnant, Father kill me first. 'Why you so sad today?' First Man asked. 'I'm pregnant,' I told him. 'Oh my God! Child is mine. I bring you both to America,' he promised. From that day, First Man brought me sweets every night. And fruits and canned drinks. Very gentle. Said 'I love you' more often. Kissed me everywhere.

"My belly showed too much. No man wanted pregnant woman. So I stopped working by sixth month. But Fat Lady kept me on. To clean floors and wash other girls' clothes. Many men asked about me. 'Where's beautiful child?' they demanded. 'Back home visiting parents, will return next year,' Fat Lady promised. 'Did First Man come?' I wanted to know. 'No, doesn't come any more,' Fat Lady replied. So I looked for him at his hotel. 'No longer here. He went back to America,' hotel people told me. Can't be, I thought. He'd come for me and baby first. But couldn't argue with hotel people. They kicked me out.

"'Don't worry. You go back to work after baby is born. But baby goes to orphanage, understand? Can't afford crying babies here. Bad for work,' Fat Lady said. So I listened. Only wanted pregnancy to be fast over with. I was tired of heavy belly. Tired of scrubbing floors and cleaning toilets. I wanted to get back to old work. Dancing on floors. Caressed by many men. Treated so well. Didn't mind pain in bed. And money afterward, was so good. Father never made this much.

"Fat Lady kept promises. Took care of everything. Brought baby to orphanage four days after birth. 'You claim him later when you older. No time to think about babies now. Go back to work make money first. You claim him later, never too late.' She insisted. So I listened.

"Saw and held baby for four days. He cried all the time, he exhausted me. My breasts hurt so much, too much milk inside, they wanted to explode! But Bobby won't take my milk. He threw up every time I tried feeding him. So I gave the milk to American men back at Pink Night Club. American men loved sucking my breasts in bathrooms. Very glad Fat Lady took baby to orphanage. I didn't like his crying and vomiting. But he's cute. Curly brown hair. Big purple eyes with brown dots all around, imagine! Never seen such eye colour. 'Mixed-breed kid. Some Vietnamese, some American, all mixed together. That's why you get strange combination,' Fat Lady said. But she too agreed baby is cute.

"Fat Lady called baby 'Bobby'. That's the name of her favorite client. No, I didn't love baby Bobby. Just duty. Like duty sending money to Father. Didn't love Father either. Only loved my job. On bar stools in fancy clothes. Feeling wanted.

"Visited Bobby because of duty. Every year at Tet, brought him toys or sweets. But he cried when he saw me. Wouldn't let me hold him. He clung to nun's dress. He acted like I'm mean monster! So I liked Bobby less. He'd bang head over and over on bed railings when he sees me. Or rock himself to sleep. 'Don't worry. That's normal for orphans,' nuns told me. Bobby was teased at orphanage. 'Mixed breed! Mixed breed! Eat potatoes with skin on!' Older kids always screaming this to him. Imagine the insult! Who eats potato skin? Nobody! Even poor farmers throw it to pigs! Only dumb people eat potato skin. So Bobby teased for being mixed breed. Lots of mixed breeds at orphanage. They stick together. Look out for each other. Half black in one gang, half white other gang. Vietnamese kids not even looking them in eyes.

"One day I come by orphanage but can't find Bobby. It was April 8, 1975. I think. Or maybe April 9, can't remember. 'All mixed breeds gone. Americans came by, took them all to America. All two hundred kids in big plane,' nuns said. 'Not plane that crashed last week?' I ask. 'Yes, we saw that on television too. 'Operation Babylift,' they called it. But plane crashed and killed half those kids. Those that survived took next plane out,' nuns explained. Dead ones brought back to orphanage for burial. Nuns didn't remember seeing Bobby dead. But they can't be certain. 'Can you dig up corpses?' I ask. 'Of course not!' nuns said. 'Any official papers for dead babies?' I ask again. 'No, we don't have time for that kind of thing,' nuns replied. So Bobby may be in America. Or may be dead. I don't know. Not knowing is hard. For first time I missed him.

"End of Saigon was bad time. All bars closed. Americans gone. I had no job. Lived off savings for years. Even then, nothing to buy in markets.

Meat, very rare. Vegetables, old stuff. Fruits, rotten. Survived thanks to zookeeper crazy about me. Fed me food meant for lions. Good red meat three times a week! Could never get that selling flowers in market. Zookeeper's secret got discovered finally. So he was sent to re-education camps in North. Imagine, nothing for people to buy in market but there's meat for zoo animals! That's socialist equality! Years pass. I never hear from my friend again. And my father dies. And I'm getting older. Nothing left for me in Vietnam, cursed country! So I left on boat too.

"Boat trip was OK except for third day. Third day, bad men came. Lots of them. They spoke Thai language. I know it. Heard it before at Saigon bars. Not just Americans at bars. Also French and Japanese and Thai men. They all asked for me at Pink Night Club. All taught me their language. Thai difficult but I learned fast. So I understood bad men's talk. I told them, 'Come to me!' I'm used to this. *'Ma ti ne, qua lai'*? Come here, what you afraid of?' I repeated. Did it all the time at bar. 'Leave other girls alone,' I said. Bad men surprised I speak. Their mouths all open. They're used to silence. Silence or crying but not speaking. Nobody spoke to them before. They laughed at me. Then one came to me. Tore my clothes. Tied me down. Grabbed my hair. Others just looked. Everyone laughed. But I still talked. 'Slow, slow,' I said. 'Deeper, deeper,' I repeated. When he finished, others spit on floor. Then walked away. Bad men left us alone after that. Nobody else hurt. Boat people looked at me in funny way after. Saved their lives. But nobody said thanks. 'Just bargirl,' they said. 'Just a whore,' they laughed. That's what I'm good for. Good for looking down on. Two days after bad men left, we ran out of water. Nothing to drink for days. No rain, no clouds to protect us from sun. A baby next to me cried then stopped crying. He turned blue. I took baby in my arms, offered my breasts but no milk came. He died soon after, but I liked holding his quiet body. Then a stinky smell formed on boat. The captain fought with the parents for dead baby. He snatched it from them and threw it into sea. What terrible thing to watch! Then we saw land.

"Been thinking lots about Bobby. Would be nice seeing him in America. Not to ask favours. Just to say sorry. Sorry I was not better mother. Sorry I gave his milk to American GIs. If your stories get published, maybe I find him. This my true hope . . ."

The Philippines

Six

As I took leave of Tuyet, the prostitute, a dirty-looking young boy approached me. His trembling purple lips and flickering eyes caught my attention. Underneath his torn T-shirt, I noticed limbs no bigger than the branches I used to gather for firewood.

"Aunty, Aunty . . ." he hesitatingly called out to me.

"Yes?"

"My teacher, Aunty Cuc, says I should tell my story too."

"OK, your turn. But make it fast and call me Big Sister, I'm not old enough to be an Aunty," I told him with a smile. I took him far away from Cuc and Tuyet's hut. We sat down on a pile of empty coconut shells, our faces hidden from each other by the swaying leaves of a palm tree. For a long time he didn't utter a word. "What happened?" I asked him gently. He answered with a shrug and a clearing of the throat, then fell silent once more. I asked him his age and he showed me ten fingers. I asked him how long he'd been at the camp and he stuck out four digits. I asked him if he was alone and he nodded yes. Our meeting went on like that for a while until I too fell silent. Finally he decided to speak.

"I miss home, Big Sister. I don't know the name of my hometown. But I remember the number of our house—nine. My mother said that's a lucky number. There's nobody at home now. I can't go back anymore. My father

182

died many years ago. My two brothers left us also a long time ago. They went to America but we never heard from them. I went with my mother on a boat, Big Sister. I don't know what happened. There was a big storm. Then my mother disappeared. 'Your mother went to heaven,' people told me. I was so scared. I didn't want to go to heaven with her. I didn't want to see ghosts. I closed my eyes all the time on the boat. People force me to rub their backs here. Or I go find firewood for them. Sometimes old men touch me inside my pants. They give me money so I won't tell anyone. I was sick on the boat. I vomited on the other people. A nice aunty took water from the sea to wash me. 'Stop vomiting or your mother's ghost will come back,' someone told me. I was so scared I shivered all the time. At home I only shivered when I swam in the lake at night.

"We had a nice house, Big Sister. I used to climb our mango tree in the garden. I helped my mother pick the mangoes for her salad. I had a dog called Loc. One day he just disappeared. Mother thought the neighbour at number 12 ate him. I go to school here, Big Sister. Aunty Cuc is a nice teacher. She tells us lots of stories about her town Hue. Sometimes I have nightmares about my mother. On the boat I always sat next to her. She always held my hands. She didn't want me to get lost. I don't know how she disappeared in the storm. One minute she was there. Next minute she was gone. It happened so fast. I didn't see anything. The boat moved up and down. Up and down. I felt a warm liquid climbing up my throat. I let go of my mother's hand for one minute to cover my mouth. I had to stop the vomit from coming out. When I put my hands back, I couldn't find my mother's anymore. I opened my eyes. She was already gone.

"In Vietnam I had grandparents. But they died during the war. My mother said Grandfather was nice. The old men here are not nice. Sometimes they want me to touch them down there too. I hate licking them with my tongue. It smells bad. But they give me more money when I do it. Sometimes they give me candy.

"Aunty Cuc says I'm a smart student. Is that true, Big Sister? She says I'm an orphan just like her. Do you think she likes me, Big Sister? I miss home so much, Big Sister. Can you give me some money, Big Sister? I need to buy incense for my mother. My mother will be sad if I don't burn incense for her. She'll think I forgot her. Maybe she'll come back to remind me. I don't want to see her ghost, Big Sister. Give me money, Big Sister!"

The boy rambled on and on. As the thread of reality unravelled with each sentence, he became more excited. But my crying prevented me from hearing more.

*

The Philippines

Seven

At the refugee camp only a few months, already I had heard many stories, met many people. My notes, quickly penned on bits of paper, kept everyone intrigued. "Why are you collecting all these stories?" Joanne, a colleague from Toronto, inquired.

"They are for a journalist friend who started telling such stories a decade earlier. It's my way of thanking her for giving voice to my nameless camp mates," I said. "Tales of real people that the world forgot need to be retold," I added.

"Aren't these stories also for you?" Joanne asked.

"Perhaps," I said. While I had forgotten my boat trip, others remembered theirs in minute detail. And the more I listened to their memories, the sharper my past became. Their stories, although unique, seemed all too familiar. How could I be sure their tales were not also mine?

"Have you been back to Vietnam, Kim?" Joanne asked me one day, as we rested for lunch.

"I would like to, but I'm afraid," I admitted meekly.

"Vietnam is safe now, Kim. My Vietnamese husband has been back four times. No problems! Communist re-education camps don't exist anymore. Don't you have any family there to make the trip worthwhile? What? A mother still back home and you're hesitating to go back?! Kim, go

185

find your mother, for heaven's sake!"

Joanne saw through my excuses. A dozen unworthy reasons delayed the ultimate trip back to my mother. A hundred childish indignations kept me from being generous, even in thoughts, to her. I knew I could not run away forever. I must stop this hide-and-seek game.

Vietnam

One

Saigon's Tan Son Nhat Airport—I'd seen it a dozen times in documentaries but nothing prepared me for its oppressive humid heat. Even the walls sweated dusty droplets too lethargic to roll down.

"Vietnamese citizenship or foreigner?" asked an airport official, not bothering to look up.

"Foreigner," I said, handing him my American passport.

"Purpose of trip?" he wanted to know.

"Tourism," I replied.

"Ah, visiting old country for New Year!" He smiled before giving me the thumbs-up and obligatory "America number one" act. We both knew I didn't come back to sightsee. Like many other boat people, I came back to make peace with the past. To reconnect with the country I had given up for adoption years ago. Fleeing a mass hysteria that turned out to be more benign than intestinal polyps. But what did he care about all this? "Any American propaganda?" the airport official went on.

"No," I said.

"What about this?" he asked, pointing to a Filipino videotape he'd just fished out of my bag.

"Filipino film for my Canadian boyfriend wanting to learn Tagalog," I explained. He wouldn't hear any of it.

"Electronic American propaganda," he said, louder this time. "And this?" he inquired, showing me my travel book.

"*Lonely Planet Tourist Guide to South East Asia*, nothing wrong with it," I answered patiently. Nothing wrong except it was Australian backpackers showing me my way home.

"Why *lonely* planet? Talking in codes? More American propaganda?" he screamed out for all to hear.

"What happened to the 'America number one' thing?" I sighed.

"Still number one, but I need money for my children's bikes," he replied softly.

"Oh, I understand. Been away too long, forgot how things work around here," I excused myself. Discretely, I slipped him a $10 bill and we both wished each other a good day.

"Welcome to Ho Chi Minh City," proclaimed the banner, as a mob of taxi drivers screamed for my attention and U.S. dollars outside the airport gate. Ho Chi Minh, everywhere regarded as a hero, except in North America where I had taken up residence. Ho Chi Minh, the only honourable communist legend left after all the others had turned into horror stories. Ho Chi Minh City, one of the last bastions of communism in the global village welcomed me home with half-opened arms. Riding into town on a cyclo, I tried to imagine the old Saigon in its heyday but I couldn't. I tried picturing my father running for the last helicopter out of this hellish city but I had trouble remembering that scene. Too much diversion kept me from focusing on my task. A cacophony of noise and impossible traffic sent exhaust fumes straight into my lungs. Everything reflected a greyish undertone. Even the asbestos-covered trees failed to exhale oxygen. Saigon of the late twentieth century seemed more like a dilapidated, overgrown version of its old self.

The city core smelled like a funeral parlour. The sweet stench of too many too-ripe flowers hung in the air. The flower-sellers with their special Tet goods hogged all the space on the street corners. Orchids, chrysanthemums, cherry blossoms for sale lined the sidewalks. Families bought them to welcome the New Year. The flowers also brought good luck, something to appease the Kitchen God at this time of year. "Lan! Lan!

Orchids! Orchids!" a vendor screamed in my ear as I zigzagged along sidewalks made for squatting. "Lan! Lan! Orchids! Orchids! Best quality for Tet!" shouted another. "OK, I'll take a branch of your spring orchids," I said. I too needed good luck. "Do you remember Tet '68?" I asked as my vendor scrambled to change my one-dollar bill. "Were you selling flowers that year when rockets showered on us?" I continued.

"Hey Sister! I was just a kid then!" she protested. Sorry, so was I.

After two days in Saigon, I had had enough. Too many street hustlers prevented me from walking in peace. They spotted me miles away—an easy target, a returning Vietnamese with a pocketful of American dollars. "Give me a dollar, Big Sister! Do you have candy for me, Aunty? Hey Miss, want to buy silk blouses? Sister, you need taxi to airport? Where do you live in America? I have cousins in California! Aunty, you want to change dollars? I have good rates! What you mean you don't speak Vietnamese? Don't give me that mother-fucking shit! You whore!"

To escape these hawkers keen on hijacking my nostalgia, I took refuge in the Continental Hotel. There I inspected the room Graham Greene used when he wrote *The Quiet American*. I also drank lots of iced tea to cool down. No, I had no obsession for this overcrowded city people still called Saigon. It was Hue that beckoned me.

Vietnam
Two

Going down the Perfume River toward Hue, I didn't fail to notice the innumerable unidentified objects floating on its grey water. The Perfume River hadn't changed. It still smelled of macerated fish bowels. Yet I had waited more than a decade for this moment. I would finally see Hue again by the banks of the Perfume River.

I felt no disappointment. Unlike Saigon, my hometown hadn't changed for the worse. The day I came home, frangipani trees still speckled the sidewalks with their white petals. The incompatible odours of seafood and incense still permeated the Central Market. Despite increased traffic, fresh air still floated from the sky. I didn't use my Ventolin pump once in this city of artists and tai-chi adherents.

With the war long buried in everyone's mind, Hue exuded an aura of peace these days. The city had changed face to welcome the trickle of tourists lured there by the promise of poetic scenery. Yes, poetry still enveloped the old part of town. The Marble Mountains, the Perfume River, the Pagoda of the Celestial Goddess—their mere names made me dream again. Without wanting to, I found myself smiling to strangers on the streets. With a mixture of sadness and joy, I began whistling all the sorrowful tunes written about Hue. And my heart murmur sang along every time I recognized a city landmark.

Looking for my mother's restaurant proved harder than I had imagined.

I got disoriented on the cyclo ride that kept turning right when I thought it should turn left. All of a sudden, the cathedral loomed in front of me when I expected it to be at my back. Coming back to Hue, I lost my way, just as I did the night I left it years ago. My old neighbourhood greeted me with chaotic nonchalance. Clutter defaced streets where once a sense of order had reigned. Quickly built homes erased all symmetry from my neighbourhood. But at least lepers no longer ruled the markets.

We stopped for direction four times before finding 29 Cong Ly Street. To reach my mother's restaurant, I had to enter a new bicycle-repair store, go through its back door, then along a narrow dark corridor before I could finally make out the number 29. I had arrived at last, but no lemongrass scent greeted me at the door. The restaurant now functioned as a karaoke bar, complete with video games for the newly rich of the classless society. Where was my mother? The new owner of the place, a man of about thirty, hadn't a clue. No greasy walls, no mausoleum for cockroaches greeted him when he took over the place four years ago. "There was no restaurant. It used to be a language school here, run by some retired professor from the college," he said.

"Do you know his name?" I asked.

"Professor Son or something like that," replied the man. The name resurrected dead images of an old man expertly blowing cigarette smoke to form letters. I used to marvel at the O's, I's and U's coming through his yellowed teeth.

"Of course—Professor Son, my old French and English teacher!" I cried excitedly. "Where is the teacher now? You don't know? Well, could I at least look around?" I asked.

"Sure why not, if the other tenants don't mind," he replied.

"How many people live here now? Four families? Oh!"

The little courtyard where once we washed dishes now supported a tin roof to house a complete family of four. The living room where my grandmother kept the altar to our ancestors now functioned as a home to another family of four. This used to be our ancestors' room, a place of holiness and silence. While my grandmother could enter this room every morning to offer Buddha and deceased ancestors fresh fruits in exchange for personal favours, we tiptoed in only on special occasions. The death

191

anniversaries of ancestors counted as very special occasions. During these spooky events, my grandmother allowed us to join in an elaborate feast, eating heavenly foods. Meals prepared for ghosts naturally came with rituals attached. First we had to say our prerequisite prayers to the ancestors asking for their blessing and forgiveness for soiling their good names. With incense in hand, we then bowed to a charcoal rendering of their faces. Next, we sat around waiting for the ancestors to "finish their meal" before we mortals could tackle ours. I never wondered how dead people came back to eat real food. I just accepted it as more of my grandmother's nonsense.

After a brief tour of the living room, I headed for the bedroom that I once shared with my sisters. It now housed a family of three. Once sparsely furnished, the room now overflowed with junk. Yet even with carton boxes littered everywhere, I still recognized my old teak desk. This was the only piece of decent furniture in our room full of old beds, lumpy mattresses and chairs used for storing clothes. Yes, the desk belonged to me. But that didn't keep my sister Mai away. Her doodling fingers left distinct traces on the wood. Inspecting the desk, I smiled as I saw some of her old graffiti. At least half a dozen instances of the name "Mai" and as many lotus-shaped drawings interrupted the wood grain. Were it not for my mother's famous knocks on the head, my old desk would have been covered with Mai's nonsense drawings a long time ago. A small inscription near the bottom of the left leg caught my attention. "So much sadness! Thu, 1983," it read. Did my sister Thu write this? Or was it some other Thu who, having inherited my desk, had not hesitated to keep track of her soul on its wooden legs? I had no way of knowing, no way of recognizing Thu's handwriting. Her alphabet still ran wild and undomesticated the year I left her. When I last saw her in my mother's bed, she was laughing in her dreams. Because of this, I did not squeeze her hands goodbye. I did not want to deny Thu her sweet dreams that night. How I regretted not waking her up, not giving her hope that we would meet again. I left her the way our father left us—cowardly with no forwarding address. I wondered if she ever forgave me.

After thanking the tenants for the brief visit, I left our old house, not knowing where to go next. None of the tenants had heard of my mother, her restaurant or Professor Son, my old language teacher. The names Thu and Mai meant nothing to them. Did I leave a lifetime ago or only ten years ago? These strangers who came out of nowhere to claim our house, our furniture

—who were they? How far back did their memory stretch? Casually forgetting the previous owner to avoid my reclaiming a bit of the past. But I had no interest in reclaiming my old house. I only wished to find my sisters again.

Of course I also wanted to find my mother. The same mother who had pushed me out of her life ten years ago, forcing me to fend for myself at fifteen. We were separated not only by time and distance, but also by my fear of her. Only the memory of her cooking brought warmth to my heart. Everything else about my mother represented pain for me. But Aunty Hung saw things differently. "She did the right thing, sending you away," Aunty Hung had said in California. "Your mother gave you a future that no past can compromise. Whatever your recollection, just forgive her. That's what mothers want in old age. To be remembered and to be forgiven."

Yes, my mother had opened the door of hope. I felt thankful for that. But my rancour, reinforced by years of doubt, still poisoned my heart. Yet this feeling wasn't immutable. One tender word, one friendly gesture from my mother and my defensive wall against her would break. Whatever the outcome, I knew I had to see my mother again. Finding her became an obsession that first week back in Hue. Obsession, yes—but where to start looking?

When no one in our old neighbourhood could help with my search, I went to my former secondary school. After all, Professor Son once taught there. Somebody would know of his whereabouts. Once located, he would tell me where to find my mother.

"Professor Nguyen The Son? Never heard of him," the school secretary answered flatly.

"Would someone else know?" I persisted.

"Try the girl in the library."

Thank you—oh yes, thank you. The library, how could I have forgotten? Didn't I spend hours in my youth browsing through its old books? Pretending to be a good communist to gain access to its texts? Ten hours of street cleaning for one of library privilege—it all came back to me. Yet this place, so prestigious in my memory, took no more space than a small bedroom. It also looked shabby with its disorganized piles of books dispersed everywhere on the floor.

"Professor Son? I don't remember anyone by that name. What did he teach?" asked the librarian, slowly looking up from her book.

"Foreign languages. He taught English and French before the revolution."

"That's a long time ago! Try Professor Tung, the new English teacher. He might know . . ." She then dismissed me by returning to her novel.

Almost by luck, Professor Tung entered the room at that moment. He didn't act surprised at the mention of his name. He knew his popularity spread beyond the school's walls. "Everyone wants to learn proper English nowadays," Professor Tung said. "A shoeshine boy's command of English might have worked with GIs during the war but not anymore. The new invaders come from fancy international business schools these days. They are here to check out the emerging Asian markets, not to mention the world's cheapest labour. These people talk slick. They are educated, well-travelled fellows expecting the best since they've always received the best. So no, 'Five thousand, cheap, you buy,' won't work anymore. To do business with these people, you have to speak at their level," Professor Tung explained.

"Sir, do you know Professor Son? I wonder where he is?" I asked, interrupting his speech.

"Professor Son? Must be very old if not dead now. Try his daughter's English bookstore on Le Loi Street. I send my students there since their prices are better," the Professor continued.

"What about French, who's teaching it now, Professor?" I managed to ask before he disappeared down the hall.

"Nobody. Who wants to learn French these days! Better Japanese or Mandarin. Lots of them doing business here too."

I spotted the English bookstore owned by Professor Son's daughter a block away. A crowd of young people in jeans trying to look cool blocked its entrance. As I fought my way in, I heard whispers of "She's an overseas Vietnamese! Who does she think she is, butting in like that?" The bookstore impressed me. Besides dictionaries and language-related textbooks, I saw shelf after shelf dedicated to English-language authors. And on the top shelf, away from the reach of dirty-handed children, was displayed a prized collection of the newest Barbie dolls. No longer in their original cartons and plastic boxes, the dolls now stood protected from the dust of the streets by a simple plastic sheet. These toys sold like hot cakes to adolescent girls. They giggled as they admired Barbie's fashionable outfits. They acted as if they had never known the luxuries of childhood. Perhaps they hadn't.

"You were his old student?" asked a skeptical-looking cashier.

"Yes, but I left a long time ago. I want to pay my respects to the professor now. Without his teaching, I wouldn't be where I am today," I said.

"Come in the back, I'll tell him you are here. Big Sister, what's your name?"

"Kim. He also taught my sister Mai."

I entered the back room with nervousness. Professor Son lifted his eyes from a well-worn copy of Hugo's *Les Misérables* to look at me.

"Kim, Mai . . . Kim, Mai—uhmm, wasn't there another one?" Professor Son asked.

"Yes, Professor, you remember right! You also taught my youngest sister, Thu. We took lessons with you in the back of my mother's kitchen. The Ba Tam Restaurant, best place in town."

"So you've come back after all these years!" Professor Son exclaimed. He looked old but far from senile. As if proud of his intact memory, he suddenly sprang to life, excitedly rolling a cigarette with one steady hand while the other forcefully clasped mine.

"Yes, I came back. I am looking for my mother and sisters. But I can't find them. Perhaps you can help me, Professor."

"I see all those years in the West did you no good. Where's your tact? Didn't even inquire about me and already demanding a favour!" He scolded me like in the old days when he taught me not just foreign languages but also a foreign way of behaving. *Savoir faire* and *savoir vivre* he had called it. It is the art of conducting yourself in a white society. But I could never absorb his civic teachings—only the grammar went down smoothly.

"Please forgive me, Professor, for forgetting my manners. But I didn't forget to bring you a copy of *National Geographic* and a carton of Marlboro cigarettes. I remember you enjoyed them."

"Bribing me will get you nowhere, but I'll take them," Professor Son said with a hint of a smile.

"And how have you been all these years, Professor? I heard you ran a language school at our old restaurant."

"That's right. Must have been around '84, after your mother closed her restaurant. By then, I could teach English freely. I no longer had to hide in the backs of kitchens. But the school only lasted a few years since I lost my patience for teaching. And my eyes aren't so good anymore, so how could I correct homework? (But photos are fine so I'll keep your old copy of *National Geographic*.) My daughter opened this store about two years ago. I help her out. Most of the time I just sit around smoking and watching bad television. Where was I? Ah yes, your mother's restaurant. She closed the restaurant soon after your grandmother's death. When your grandmother died in '83, your mother became restless. Or rather spiritless. She stopped looking people in the eyes. She stopped cooking. I never saw her cry but only words of regret came out of her mouth. She must've shelved her smiles in some forgotten closet. I underestimated her attachment to her mother. Unfortunately their tenderness for each other bloomed only in the darkness of their souls. What did your grandmother die of? Old age, nothing dramatic. Due to joint pain, she stayed bedridden for many years, sitting up only to eat or do her business into a pot. Death tormented her thoughts day and night. "My time has come," she said to me on every occasion I visited. She forced your mother to buy a coffin that she placed beside her bed for many years. "Best wood, best lining," she proudly announced to all willing to look inside, but nobody dared inspect. We all took her words for truth. Why buy a coffin when you're not dead? I guess she wanted to be ready!

"But fate sometimes plays dirty tricks on us. By the time your grandmother actually passed away, termite infestation had claimed half the coffin. Yes, the poor old woman ended up buried in a second-rate replacement, a cheap wooden box. Does choosing your own coffin bring bad luck? I don't know. Maybe. I guess yes, if you are superstitious. Your grandmother lived by superstitions? That's what you remember most about her? Ah, but people change. Don't forget, superstition works best amongst the young or young at heart. Those still hoping for the best, yet fearing the worst from life. But for the older folks who've come to terms with their mortality, who have nothing more to lose, superstition no longer matters," Professor Son explained, relishing once again his role of wise teacher.

"What about my mother and sisters? What happened to them, Professor?"

"Your sisters just disappeared one day like you did, so I figured they too left the country. We weren't fooled when your mother told everyone you went to Saigon to get married! She hid everything from us but we knew better. Your grandmother wasn't so good at keeping quiet. I got bits and pieces of the truth through the old woman. What's that? Did they receive your letters? I don't know. Your grandmother never mentioned your letters. Did they look worried after you left? Of course! What do you think? I've always wondered why your mother didn't leave herself after '83. What kept her here besides the rotten bones of her mother? I have always known your mother to be strong-willed and independent, not one to be held back by sentimentality. Perhaps I read her wrong. Poor woman! She did her best to hold her family together. But a graced life escaped her grasp. She suffered one calamity after another. Can't blame her for becoming tougher with each turn of bad luck.

"Yes, I knew your mother as a child. Her father taught me in grammar school. I came by their house often for private lessons. She treated me like an older brother. Your grandfather would give the lessons with your mother on his lap. I remember them as inseparable. Later, when Lan was born, your mother would be sitting by his feet playing with her baby sister. Did you know your mother had a sister called Lan? Yes? Did you hear that from your father? No? You didn't meet him in America? Too bad. You heard the story from Aunty Hung the neighbour? Ah, she's a special one! I always found her rather irresistible! I hope she is doing well. Yes? Good! Anyway, going back to your father. He was one of your mother's calamities. Theirs was an arranged marriage, a marriage of convenience to someone she didn't know or love. You're aware of that? Your mother's marriage was a respectable way to get her family out of debt. You see, her beloved father had died the year before, so the family had run out of savings. Starvation marched down the street, ready to knock at their door. Marrying off your mother meant one less mouth to feed at home. It also meant the occasional spare cent for your grandmother since the groom belonged to a generous family. Can you appreciate your grandmother's cleverness? She didn't choose the smartest or best-looking man for your mother, for what use would that be if he also had a taste for concubines? No, your grandmother picked the ugliest and weakest man belonging to the most generous family. And that all worked to her advantage. You know the real story of your aunt Lan? Good! Imagine one sister married through matchmakers, the other carrying a fatherless half-breed! Was your mother happy? I don't know. But one thing I do know. She didn't love her husband. She only did her duty. She excelled at doing her duty. Did she love someone else? What a question! Is the human heart made of stone? Your mother had lots of admirers. She looked like a movie star while your father carried a hunch on his back! So of course there must have been someone else. But I don't know who. If she loved, she suppressed it well. She bartered flawlessly with her heart. Without drama, she sacrificed her happiness to fill her family's stomach.

"Did I love your mother? Didn't I tell you she looked beautiful? Her thick red lips and ample chest drove me crazy. So maybe yes, I loved her in my dreams. But she never noticed me. She never noticed your father either. We were like two distant brothers to her. Yet despite her marital indifference, she suffered when your father left. It looked bad, having your husband disappear like that. She lost face to the world. Why didn't she marry another man after your father's disappearance? That's another stupid question! Ever heard of honour and duty? The duty to wait for your husband? The duty to take care of his children without bringing a stranger into the house? Obviously you don't know what I'm talking about! But your mother knew about duty and family honour. She knew it too well. You never saw her laugh or cry? Never saw her tenderness? Well, what can I say? She sprouted bark to protect her damaged soul. What's that? She disciplined you harshly? So what's wrong with that? An occasional slap didn't do you kids any harm!"

"Do you know where my mother is now, Professor?" I asked.

"I haven't seen her in over two years."

"Oh . . ."

"Try the new nursing home near the Citadel."

"I think she's been waiting too long for me. It's time for me to find her, Professor."

"Good luck and give her my regards. Tell her my arthritic feet hurt so I don't go out much these days. You can also ask her who she loved!"

"I will. Thank you so much, Professor, for everything you did for me—past and present. I'll keep in touch," I said, then took quick leave of him to go find my mother.

I could not imagine my mother's world smelling of melancholia instead of ginger. But what did I truly know of my mother besides faulty assumptions based on vague childhood memories. All these years resenting her personal strength, her great power over people, I had so misjudged her. Blowing up my childish impression of her to turn her into some kind of horrible dictator nobody could depose. Yet vulnerability also claimed her. Depression masquerading as perfectionism and exaggerated sense of duty, I could spot it half a mile away in my patients. Yet for my own mother, I allowed myself to think of her as immune to loneliness, guilt, pain. And now it was late—but perhaps not too late to reverse my heart's tendency.

Vietnam

Three

The nursing home may have been new but like most buildings in this city, its interior walls already reeked of ageless humidity.

"Mrs. Nguyen Anh Tam, around fifty-five years old? Yes, she's here. You're her daughter from Canada? Come this way. I'll call her doctor," said a more-than-friendly nurse, upon hearing I lived in Canada. She too had relatives in Montréal.

In the room that she shared with five other patients, my mother looked at me bewildered. The messy hair, drooling mouth and stench of unchanged diapers caught me completely off guard. This was no depression. This was dementia before its time.

"Did you check my mother for other reversible causes of dementia? You know, things like neurosyphilis, temporal epilepsy, Parkinson's? I don't know what else. There must be a cause. There must be a treatment. She's too young to have Alzheimer's disease!" I exclaimed to her doctor.

"Rest assured we did all we could for your mother. Of course, we don't have the latest equipment you get in the West, but we are not bush doctors either!" Dr. Tran said politely, then walked out of the room, leaving me to face my mother. And after all these years, I still feared being in the same room with her. Still expected to be shredded to pieces with her criticism or belittled by her famous raised left eyebrow. But of course my mother voiced no criticism. She raised no left eyebrow. Neither did she attempt to slap me. Only her lack of reaction scared me now.

"Mother, it's your daughter, Kim! Do you remember me?" Silence answered my query. "I've come back! I was in America, then Canada all these years! I worried so much about you. I had no news of home!" I continued, hoping to elicit some kind of reaction from her.

"Canada . . ." my mother repeated, amused by the rhyming sound of the word.

"Yes, Canada. Not California. Aunty Lan, I couldn't find her. Her California address wasn't good, maybe she moved . . ."

"California . . ." my mother tried saying, but this time she seemed less amused by the tongue twister.

"Mother, do you know where Mai and Thu are?"

"Mai, Thu?"

"Yes, your other daughters. My two sisters. Where are they now? Did they go to America?"

"Don't know, don't know."

"Mother, we were all supposed to meet in America, remember? You promised me that."

"Oh?"

"I waited so many years for that reunion. It never came."

"No?"

"Mother, did you put Mai and Thu on boats by themselves too?"

"No! Oh no! Oh no!"

"I bet you did. And it was a good thing you did. You wanted us to be strong like you. You wanted a better future for us. I understand now."

"Mai, Thu?"

"Yes, you remember! Mai, she's a famous artist in France now!" I continued, in a falsely cheerful voice, the false story I was fed.

"Oh?" asked my mother with surprise.

"Yes, Mother. A well-known French journalist adopted her. They live in Paris now. You know what else, Mother? She has a father now! He's a great French doctor called Michel. I've met him!"

"You?" asked my mother, as in "Who are you?" but I chose to interpret it differently.

"Me? I'm a doctor in Canada now! I know you're proud of me, but won't say it. You never do! It's alright, I don't mind."

"You doctor?" my mother asked again, this time with an anxious look.

"I'm not here to give you shots, Mother. I'm not *your* doctor, don't worry!" I tried to reassure her.

"You not doctor . . ." repeated my mother, more confused than ever.

"Yes, I'm a doctor," I said, trying hard to quell the disappointment rising like yeasted dough in my stomach. No, I couldn't even have this bit of accomplishment to show my mother. Once again, like so many times before, my mother refused to acknowledge me. As if for her I had never existed, not now or in the past.

"Mother, what happened to Mai and our little Thu?" I asked, once again trying to trigger her recollection with familiar names.

"Don't know."

"Yes, you know, Mother. You're just not telling. Or remembering. Try harder."

"No, no, no, no!" stammered my mother.

"I think your mother is tired. It's past her rest time now. Come back tomorrow," suggested a nurse, walking in on our ever-so-loud conversation.

"Yes, you are right. Sorry to bother you, but did my mother bring any personal belongings here? If I can find an old photo of us, perhaps she can remember better."

"It's all in her suitcase over there. You can look while she naps."

Going through my mother's almost empty suitcase, I had no trouble locating our family photos. Held together by an overstretched elastic band, the photos found a safe resting place amidst a few other objects. A couple of old embroidered *ao-dai*, a jade bracelet, a sandalwood comb and the lacquer box with our ancestors' names engraved on wooden slats. A lifetime's worth of belongings not even taking up a third of a suitcase. So few mementos to mark the passing years—no object precious enough to become

202

indispensable.

Looking at my mother's suitcase, I wondered where my father's dear old camera went. What had happened to the beloved gadget he didn't bring with him when he abandoned us in 1973? That orphaned camera had tricked us. We thought if Father had left it at home, then he must've left us without premeditation. Perhaps forced to go against his will or disappearing at the whim of the moment, which too seemed forgivable. But he had probably planned his getaway exit years in advance! I remembered too well my father's camera. How many times did he point its unforgiving lens at me? More times than I cared to count. This machine that gobbled up precious money, to give in return tiny, often out-of-focus photos, kept my father entertained. And when this indulgence produced clear photos, you could see everyone's tired smiles waiting impatiently for the camera's at-long-last click. A professional photographer would be so much cheaper and better, my mother had complained. But in this matter of capturing instants for posterity, my father held his ground. So as kids, we had many photos taken, many more so than the average merchant's family. To record what? Fake smiles and a pretence at happiness?

Instead of selling my father's camera, my mother began toying with it. Making a belated effort to understand her husband's lifelong interest, my mother discovered a passion outside the kitchen. Like everything else she did, my mother succeeded in taking good pictures. Her photographic skills outshone my father's amateurish eye. This difference in quality helped me to sort out the photos. The blurry pictures belonged to a happier time, taken before '73 and the detailed ones after '73. I had no trouble identifying my father's trademark out-of-frame fuzzy pictures. His photos focused on the swaying trees in the background. My mother's pictures focused on our unsmiling faces. Looking at those photos now, I had to mock my own naivety. All those years living with her, how could I not have noticed Mai's Americanness? Her Occidental genes showed in her white skin, large round eyes and fine nose. What about Thu, did she look more like me? Yes and no. Yes, as a little girl with straight black hair and chubby cheeks. But she became almost unrecognizable as a haggard-looking adult. The more I studied Thu's later photos, the more unease I felt. Something looked wrong, my doctor's eyes told me. The yellowness of her eyes. Her hollow cheekbones. The spider angiomas on her forearms. The bones sticking out from her skin. The swollen belly. Didn't I see some of this at Palawan recently? Chronic hepatitis in its final stage. How can I deny the evidence in my hands? No, Thu didn't end up in California with an American teacher named Mark. She's probably dying in some Hue hospital or already dead by now. Killed by a common virus endemic to this part of the world. A virus that could've been prevented by vaccination—a box full of those vaccines still lay unused in my suitcase! In this miserable country, health and sickness, unfortunately, were just a matter of timing. Dead at birth, dead in life, dead until death . . .

That night, I couldn't mourn my youngest sister's death. She had died so many times in my imagination, and from my lack of concern for her, that I had little sadness left. Only anger animated my thoughts. I stayed awake all night raging against the bad karma of this place I used to call home.

The next day at the nursing home I tried a gentler approach with my mother. Certainly she must've been aware of Thu's sickness. I would have to extract information from her somehow. Had Thu's death precipitated my mother's dementia? Did she forget to spare herself sorrow? Did she fall sick so she could be taken care of?

"Mother, it's your daughter Kim again. Did you sleep well last night?"

"Yes."

"Good! Do you remember me, Mother?" I said softly.

"You new doctor?"

"No, I am not the new doctor. Just your daughter."

"Oh!"

"Mother, I found some old photos—would you like to look at them?" I asked, in a voice often used by nurses addressing mental patients.

"Photos?" Mother repeated on cue.

"Yes, look at this one of Thu and Mai. Do you remember?"

"Who's this?"

"That's Mai, my sister. Isn't she beautiful? She's an artist in Paris now!" I replied. Then I changed my story.

"Yes, Mother, that's Mai in the photo. Mai, my difficult sister who's in fact my cousin. Don't you worry, Mother, our family's past is no longer a secret to me. Aunty Hung told me all about it. Did you know I met her in California? She's still the same, still talking non-stop. She's living a good life in America these days, running her own restaurant. But her food doesn't come close to yours, Mother. Mai? No, she doesn't live in Paris with any French doctor or journalist. I simply don't know where she is. She has disappeared from our life altogether. So you can stop relying on her.

"I may as well tell you the truth. All these years making up stories for others, for myself—I am tired of this deceit. And Thu? She's probably dead, most likely killed by a lowly virus. You must know more about it than me. And Father? As a kid, I thought I saw him on TV. For many years, I believed he went to America on a U.S. Army helicopter. Now I am not so sure about that televised flight. But the hope of seeing Father again kept me going during my first years in Connecticut. No, our reunion never took place. Like Mai and Thu, Father is not to be found. So there's only me and you left, Mother. Just the two of us to share our tales. Do you realize we have never told each other stories? And now it is too late to hear yours. I only know you through the judgment and recollections of others. I see you only through Aunty Hung's words and Professor Son's praises. I hear your voice only through my own faulty memory and distorted imagination. Now I understand why you kept your stories silent, why you never spoke to us. You wished to spare us the sad details of your life. You didn't want witnesses to your disappointment. I see it now. Tell me about your bus trip back to Hue that night I left you to board a boat. You must have been burdened with worries, seeing me go off by myself. Yet you hid your feelings well. Tell me about all those unbearable months waiting for my letters that never came. You must have been stricken with grief, thinking of the worst scenarios. Yet I wrote you so many letters, Mother. If only you could see them now! Describe for me your loneliness after Grandmother's death. Share with me your despair after Thu's disease took her away from you. What happened in my absence to transform you so?

"What can I tell you about me? After you left me in Lang Co so many years ago, my mind went blank. For weeks, memory escaped me. Then I ended up in a refugee camp, where I met a wonderful doctor who changed my life. Luck held my hand throughout this whole adventure. Do you know, Mary has been more of a mother to me than you have? Don't worry, I'm not blaming you, Mother. That's just how things turned out. Remember how you used to smile at me, then turn around the next minute to hit me? My feelings for you followed the same path—one day loving you, the next day resenting you. Unpredictability and contradiction characterized our relationship. But Mary functioned differently. Her love for me stayed unwavering. She was predictable, oh yes, very predictable. What more can I say? You're still my venerable mother, Mother. Nothing can take that away. Yes, I'm glad you sent me away at fifteen. That night on Lang Co Beach, you gave me a future that was denied poor Thu. It took me many years to see this. Now I know.

"All these years I ruminated on my lost memory. Now I realize it doesn't matter anymore. Remembering the boat trip wouldn't have added anything to my life. You have forgotten a lifetime of memories—what are my two weeks compared to your fifty years?"

"Mai, Mai. Your name?" Mother asked, more confused than ever.

"No, I'm Kim, Mother."

"Mother, what mother?"

"You're my mother."

"Oh?"

"Yes. And *your* mother is dead, remember?"

"No."

"And Thu, look at her here in this photo. Where is she now, do you know?"

"Don't know."

"Mother, do you remember your restaurant, Ba Tam? You were a great cook!"

"I cook?"

"Yes! Remember the shrimp and sweet potato cakes you made for us?"

"No."

"But I do. That's what I missed most at the camp. Your cooking. So many hours spent over the stove to nourish us—this was your way of loving us. You couldn't show it otherwise—you didn't know how. And you know what, Mother? After all these years, I've never tasted anything better than your cooking!"

"Really?"

"Yes, Mother," I said, trying to soothe her perplexed look.

I reached out to touch my mother's dry, wrinkled hands and felt them flaccid for the first time. Those strong hands of hers had scared me so much as a kid, for I never knew when a slap would come my way. Now, they felt lifeless as in a short-circuited home—dark, cold and silent. Timidly touching each other's hands, this was our first physical contact since my departure ten years ago. Yet her bewildered look told me to go no further. Embracing her now would only confuse her more. So I held back. I only gazed into her clear eyes not yet clouded by cataracts. Seeing my mother so different from my memory of her didn't overwhelm me with guilt. No, it was a feeling more generous than guilt, more tender, certainly better. It was a forgiveness of all past misjudgments, both hers and mine.

"And you?" Mother asked, lucidly pointing to me.

"You want to hear my story, Mother? Well what can I say? I left Vietnam on a rickety boat with Aunty Hung's family. You arranged it all for us, do you remember?"

As I looked at my mother's blank face, the fog finally lifted on the ten years of my suppressed memory. I began again.

"Many people asked if sea pirates hijacked our boat. No, no pirate boarded our ship. Only our captain betrayed us. I remember now. I remember hearing Aunty Hung singing 'Go to sleep, your dreams are still normal. . . .' I remember the silence as the children one by one fell into deep sleep. Then the captain came. He pulled Aunty Hung from her seat and pushed her to the front of the boat. There he stripped her of her smelly clothes, laughing as she tried to cover her nakedness. Titi and I watched in disbelief the grotesque maneuvering the captain forced on her mother, while her father pretended to sleep. Wooden rods of all sizes were jammed into her mouth to keep her from screaming. The captain made her kneel on all fours like an animal. He took off his pants and tied them around her throat. Then he pulled Aunty Hung as he would a leashed dog. The more she gagged, the harder he penetrated her. When she choked and vomited, he grasped her by the hair, and pushed her head down a barrel of water to wash off the mess. To keep her from fainting, he bit her neck till it bled. Then he spit out the blood. The scene terrified me. The captain re-enacted the same spectacle for a week. Night after night, we saw the captain strangling Aunty

Hung as he forced himself into her mouth. 'Deeper! Stop breathing and take it in deeper!' he screamed. I stopped breathing too during those moments of shame. One night, no longer able to hold my breath, I cried out, 'No more!' The captain stopped his thrusting movement and came looking for me. He lifted my blouse, saw my underdeveloped body, and laughed. Then he gave me two slaps across the face and kicked me in the chest with his right foot. I fell backward, my head hitting a wooden crate. Then I went into a deep sleep.

"The first face I saw when I woke screamed at me harshly, 'You're a stupid ox, Kim! From now on keep your mouth shut! Understand? You got us into trouble yesterday! Captain threatened to deliver us to Thai pirates next time someone complains!' grunted Aunty Hung. Then she wiped my head wound with the sleeve of her shirt. The sea water she used to wet the shirt stung me. I cried out in pain. But Aunty Hung ignored my moan. She only said, 'Hush! Stop complaining! Sea water is good for keeping wounds clean!' So I stopped complaining. I put a lid on the bile stewing in my heart. We all did. What else could we do? Our lives depended on this captain. Aunty Hung had no choice but to give in to his demands. We had no choice but to turn a blind eye and trust him.

"After a few days, we perfected our business-as-usual act. We let the wind carry Aunty Hung's suppressed sobs into the night. Only Titi and I, holding tight to each other, didn't pretend to sleep. 'Kim! Kim! Stay with me,' she pleaded. We watched this show every night, and in the morning thought it too strange to be real. Must have been something we dreamed up, Titi said. Must have been our imagination playing games under the shadows of a half moon, I told her. Must have been my malaria acting up again, I thought. Or else why didn't anybody do anything about it? Why wasn't Uncle Hung protecting his wife? Why did Aunty Hung treat the captain as if nothing had happened? Still calling him 'Sir Captain' and still smiling at him the next day? How could she still sing, 'Go to sleep, your dreams are still normal . . .' every night, knowing the captain would soon come for her? We couldn't understand such things. This was no normal dream, we told each other. This was a bad dream we wished to forget. And so we did forget. Aunty Hung, how I scorned her all these years . . . It is only now that I realize the extent of her sacrifice. How she suffered for us on that boat! She played the blackmailed pawn in this game of fate. And poor Aunty Hung acted her role so well! Not once did she complain. Not once did she risk our safety. Only my stupid outburst put us at risk. So I deserved very much the crack in my skull. And I truly deserved that loss of memory. I remember now . . . Yes, I remember now."

"You doctor?" Mother asked for the nth time.

"Yes, I told you that yesterday, Mother. You remember!" I said, squeezing her hands for emphasis. "I know you can still remember." I smiled, but exhaustion prevented me from mouthing more hopeless encouragements.

Seeing my mother a dozen times more didn't bring her closer to me. It felt wrong watching her senile moments. I remembered her as a fighter, not one to give up hope. Yet in the end, she did give in to life's bad luck. As I mourned the passing away of her strength, I regretted the vicious thoughts I had nurtured against her all these years.

Each and every time we talked, the same "You doctor?" question surfaced. I could only answer "Yes," then "No." Her memory didn't improve in my presence, and the old photos didn't do the trick. So I decided to leave, taking with me some of those photos to remember the rest of us by. By all standards, I failed as a daughter. Leaving my mother to die alone in a nursing home broke my heart. But my asthmatic lungs craved the crisp Canadian air. I took my mother's repetitive muttering as an order for me to go. To board a plane and leave her once more. So I left to book my return ticket to Montreal.

On my last visit to my mother, she spared me the usual "You doctor?" question. Silence replaced our one-way dialogue. My mother snored peacefully as I sat by her bed waiting out the Valium. But the Valium never quite fizzled out. Its effects stretched longer than I expected. "Your mother can sleep like this for two days in a row. It's normal for her. Don't worry, she'll wake up at some point," reassured her nurse. But I couldn't wait two days. I had to catch a plane home that very afternoon. The prospect of missing my plane stretched my nerves. If I had left my hometown reluctantly a decade ago, I wanted my departure to be brief this time. Somehow missing my plane became more dramatic than leaving my mother without saying goodbye.

As I rushed out of my mother's room, the head nurse came after me.

"Your mother gave this paper to me yesterday. It's been in her blouse pocket for years. We couldn't get it away from her. She'd scream every time we tried to remove it. I don't know what this paper is all about, but I think it is for you." With these words, the nurse handed me a crumpled piece of paper. Being already late, I couldn't afford the luxury of reading a piece of old, yellowed paper. I thanked the nurse, took the paper and rushed out to find a taxi. The thought of missing my plane and being stuck in Hue turned my brain into a piece of Swiss cheese. The adrenalin shot holes in my grey matter and left my reasoning a wreck.

I remembered my mother's piece of paper only three hours into the flight. At 40,000 feet above sea level and a million teardrops away from Hue, I finally inspected the crumpled paper. It was an official piece of paper, typed on paper so thin, it looked almost transparent. A red seal, a calligraphic signature and a 1973 date told me this was no joke. A death certificate lay in my trembling hands.

Years of forgetfulness almost succeeded in erasing the name of the deceased. I had to shine a light on the paper to make out the name Thiet Nguyen. Almost twenty years later, I learned that my father had accidentally died stepping on a landmine. No, he didn't die a heroic soldier. Neither did he push an older woman away to steal her place on the last helicopter out of Saigon. My father was neither hero nor coward. He was just a victim of the times. Another ward of history. Not knowing why, I rubbed my fingers back and forth on my father's name. I caressed the death certificate as if it were my father's own hands. I had found him after all these years. I didn't want to lose him again.

Sitting alone on the Air Canada flight back home, I cried for the father I had hardly known, for the mother I no longer recognized, and for the fate that befell our family. Learning of my father's death twenty years too late pained me. Learning about it at nine years old would have been worse. I understood now my mother's motives in hiding this tragedy from us. She wanted me to believe in a father in America. She wanted me to believe in a dream named America, a dream that she lived through me.

If my mother came out of her forgetfulness to give me this memo from the past, then her dementia was not beyond hope. I made a mental note to contact her nursing-home doctor as soon as I got home. Perhaps a treatment would be found. Pharmaceutical companies were on the verge of patenting anti-HIV medications. I'd read all about it in my medical journals. If we could beat a deadly virus, we must also offer hope for all the consciousness slowly fleeing us. When personal and collective recollection fades, what would be left of civilization? Without people's memories, who will make sense of history?

Connecticut

One

I stopped off in Derby to visit Mary. She loved the dried *longans* I brought back from the Orient. "So much like dried plums yet so much more delicate," she exclaimed with pleasure. Mary hadn't aged a bit, with her youthful enthusiasm, crazy hairdo and rainbow-coloured outfits.

"Tell me about your trip!" Mary asked, eager for details. So I did. I told her of my work in the refugee camp. I described my meeting with the teacher Cuc, and the boat stories heard through her. The tale of a prostitute named Tuyet looking for her half-breed son brought a sad smile to Mary's face. The story of the young boy whose mother had disappeared mid trip also touched Mary. She dabbed her eyes a couple of times listening to that one. Of course, I also told Mary of my trip back to Vietnam, where I met again a member of my family who seemed depressed to the point of dementia. I was not recognized, completely forgotten and erased from this person's memory. But I didn't feel rejected. Somehow, I became part of that person's unconscious. An unconscious where past faces and events, digested, no longer caused any trouble. "Don't we still have an unconscious even if our conscious mind left us long ago?" I asked. At this point in my story, Mary cut me short to ask if this person was my mother. Since I could only answer her with silence, Mary took me in her arms, whispering, "I'm sorry I asked that, honey." So Mary knew, perhaps had always known, my true origins. And she had played my games all these years. After that episode, we never again mentioned my Vietnamese past.

Michael emerged from his room when he heard my voice. He had grown from a spoiled kid to a tall, handsome young man. His horn-rimmed glasses gave him an air of seriousness I had never noticed before. He offered me his muscular shoulders. I nested under his biceps for what seemed like an inappropriately long time. His musky sweat reminded me of Claude's body on mine and I felt ashamed for thinking of Michael in this way.

"I miss your stories, Kim," Michael said.

"But they weren't real. I'm sorry . . ." I answered.

"It doesn't matter. I'll always remember your bedtime stories, Kim. The orphanage story, the boat story, the Palawan story. They fascinated me. I never heard stories like that. So unexpected and out of the ordinary. You intrigued me even more when I learned you invented all that stuff. By the way, you can call me Mika now—I've changed my name. I am fed up with being Michael, being ordinary."

"A new identity? Like the one I brought to Derby?"

"Yes . . ."

Identity—some people hide from it at all costs. Others pay fortunes to find it. Sometimes you stupidly think you recognize it in horoscope charts. Or in your great uncle's twitches. Yet when it looks you in the eyes, you mistake it for something else. Michael loved ambivalence since he had never experienced uncertainty. I, on the other hand, only yearned for normal dreams. "Go to sleep, your dreams are still normal . . ." I wondered how Michael knew my true origin, but I didn't ask. I had probably given him hints of the truth throughout the years. I had probably unmasked myself with each lie, with each story of deceit. Perhaps I wanted my secret to be exposed.

***

"Honey, I've packed you some old stuff to bring to Montreal. It's too bulky to mail by post. Now that you're here, you can take them with you," Mary said the next day, as we ate breakfast while Jim perused his day-old newspaper. Since retiring, Jim spoke even less than before, so although he sat with us, we didn't pay him much attention. We both knew his mind already loitered elsewhere, but we loved him as much as ever.

"Of course. What's in the package?" I asked.

"Oh, just some old stuff so you won't get homesick. Old clothes, old photos, that kind of thing." Mary showed me old lacy shirts, photos of me on my sixteenth birthday and some rolled-up posters of the Mod Squad.

"I didn't know you kept all this stuff!" I said.

"Yes, I did! Show them to your boyfriend, Claude. It's a part of your past he doesn't know. Maybe he'll appreciate seeing it!"

Québec
One

I finally worked up the courage to call Claude three weeks after my return. He seemed pleased to hear from me—happy to know I had made it back home in one piece, both emotionally and physically.

"I've been having flashbacks of my boat trip. Bits and pieces that don't make much sense yet. Titi and I squeezed into a nook, holding onto each other at night, staring at her half-naked mother . . ." I said, eager to tell him all my tales.

"I've been having flashbacks myself. Our California road trip. You and I squeezed into a corner of the car, holding each other . . . I miss you. I want to see you," Claude said, finishing off my thoughts. I could've replied, "*Tabernacle!* Let me finish my story first!" but I knew it was time to forgive the past its faults. Time to dump recycled memories once and for all. I had Claude to look forward to. And Mary and Dr. Jacques. And last but not least, I had my career patiently waiting for me at the Montreal General Hospital. Stripped of my nonsense, I knew that now I could be a good doctor.

EPILOGUE

Soon after her return from Vietnam, Kim ceased keeping track of her life on paper. Her diary, which ended abruptly, stayed untouched and unread for many years. Later when she finally agreed to be dragged into psychoanalysis, the diary became a tool for her therapy. It spoke when she couldn't utter a word; it remembered what she had forgotten. However, the sessions lasted a mere four weeks. Kim, forever thrifty, could not indulge in this strange habit of telling stories to a hired listener. "You want one hundred bucks an hour to listen to my stories?"

Thirty-eight years old and long married to Claude, Kim is now a staff microbiologist at the Vancouver General Hospital. Tired of the long Montréal winters, they moved to Vancouver in 1995. As owner of West Coast Trend Reporting, Claude predicted the rise of environmentalism years before "global warming" became a household phrase. In Vancouver, they renewed ties with Titi, Aunty Hung's daughter. Titi, as a conscientious objector to George Bush's policies, decided in 2003 to relocate to Canada to practice social medicine. Always on the cusp of trends, yuppie-turned-activist Titi literally pulled Claude to his first anti-war protest, just as she pushed Kim to her first psychoanalysis session.

Still in Derby, Mary is now proud grandmother to a healthy, year-old baby boy, offspring of Michael and his Chinese wife. After graduating from Yale, Michael, who became Mika, traded the comfort of home for the challenges of Brooklyn. There he took on the Vietnamese pen name, Minh Nguyen, to write exotic blogs for a whole generation expecting the unexpected.

Dr. Jacques, retired from medicine, spends his time researching and collecting rare wines. He and his wife, Arianne, finally visited Kim in Canada one summer. The meeting was at first awkward, with Claude mistrusting Kim's friendly welcome. But Dr. Jacques's bald head and bulging belly told Kim her French fantasy belonged to a distant past that should be left undisturbed. In his old age, Dr. Jacques became a wine mentor to Claude, who kicked his beer habit without a fuss. No longer distrustful of Arianne, Kim spent hours with the former journalist, sharing tales of Palawan.

Back in Vietnam, Kim's mother died in 2003 at the age of 61, after living 13 years with a dementia that outlasted itself. Twice Kim had returned to Hue to see her mother. She showed the older woman photos of her life in Canada. Again and again, she told her mother stories of her new life. Tales of Vancouver, of Claude, of her job in the hospital were whispered to the older woman. But each time, Kim's mother only looked at her, bewildered—afraid of the mysterious new doctor who claimed to be her daughter.

On the eve of her death, her mother had brief moments of lucidity, uttering, "Doctor, my daughter!" These were semi-intelligible words that had not been heard from her in years. The nurse in charge, thinking the old woman was asking for her daughter, presented herself as the daughter, only to be screamed at. When Dr. Tran was called in, he reassured the mother that he would immediately call Kim in Canada. But nothing would calm the old woman's anguish until he took her by the hands and showed her a photo of Kim standing in front of a Vancouver hospital, and repeated over and over, "Yes, your daughter is a doctor…" With this, she finally smiled, closed her eyes and returned to her short slumber, before death took her away the next day. Her mother's only and final word of approval never reached Kim's ears or heart. At the time of their uttering, Kim was working as usual on the other side of the globe. It was a routine weekday with all the chores that needed tending to. Kim didn't feel any twitch of the eye nor strange intuition connecting her to her mother's last words. Only Dr. Tran and his nurse witnessed that brief outburst of love.

The day Kim's mother died, Claude was protesting the Iraq war in downtown Vancouver. Seeing the "No More Vietnams" signs around him, Claude's thoughts, of course, turned to the old woman left behind in Hue. He'd never met Kim's mother, but always considered her the ultimate war mother. She was a mother like so many before and after her, a mother who lost children to bombs and displacement. He knew the anti-war rally wouldn't change much. Yet he felt a duty to speak out for those mothers nobody heard.

In Los Angeles, Aunty Hung in her old age looks better than ever before. Having sold her pho restaurant, she now spends her days taking care of ten grandchildren, while their parents pursue their American dreams. When asked about her past in Vietnam, especially how she ended up in the States, she only tells the grandchildren, "Live for the moment. No looking back, no looking forward. No regretting the past, no fearing the future. These are the words of Buddha." So Aunty Hung, the real survivor in all of this, the only one with an intact memory, chooses not to make a big deal of it. And that's all for the best.

Unfortunately, the Palawan stories Kim had collected never saw the light of day in print. More than thirty years after the end of the Vietnam War, movie stars still re-enact jungle battles, but few bother speaking out for the people American GIs tried to liberate. No Hollywood movie ever starred flat-headed, fingerless people. Yet these victims of Agent Orange live on, passing their mutant genes to generations of joyless kids.

Palawan is now an international resort frequented by well-heeled foreign tourists. They come by the planeload to admire the white sand beaches and crystal clear water of this Filipino island. The refugee camp no longer exists. In its place is a Vietnamese town where thousands of former boat people not sponsored by the West settled. Cuc, the former teacher from Hue, and Tuyet, the former prostitute, are now co-owners of Saigon Nights, a Vietnamese restaurant and karaoke bar catering to tourists hungry for a bite of history. The two women are also adoptive mothers to the young orphan boy whose mother vanished in mid trip.

And Minh? Well, when tourists need more excitement than Saigon Nights can offer, street kids will steer them across town to the My Lai. There the cross-eyed owner in his silk shirt and designer jeans welcomes American ex-GIs with a broad smile and a catalogue of good-looking girls. While waiting for the girls, he freely entertains clients with tales of refugee camps. Unbeknownst to him, a blue-eyed Minh Nguyen is spreading those same stories across the Internet from a small Brooklyn studio. Ah, the stories we tell and the stories told to us . . .

ACKNOWLEDGEMENTS

My many heartfelt thanks go to the wonderful people who accompanied me on this literary journey.

Mario Laguë for believing in me when I started this story so many years ago.

Arianne and Clara for putting up with my absence during the months of rewriting.

My mother for caring for me and replenishing my memories of Vietnam while I wrote.

My publisher Ian Shaw for his invaluable editorial review and hard work in bringing this work to fruition.

Liz McKeen and Katherine Ovens for their skillful copy-editing and Katie Cunningham for her meticulous proofreading.

And Quan Pham, Bich Ngoc Diep and Charles Kiddell for the many anecdotes that inspired this novel.

Caroline Vu

CAROLINE VU

Caroline Vu is an exciting new voice on Canada's literary scene. Born in Vietnam, Caroline spent her childhood in Saigon during the height of the Vietnam War. She left Saigon in 1970, moving first to the US, then to Canada. Her memories of war-torn Vietnam and integration into North American life have inspired her two novels: *Palawan Story* (DVP 2014) and *That Summer in Provincetown* (an unpublished manuscript).

A passionate traveller, Vu's travel stories of exotic destinations have been published in Doctor's Review - Medicine on the Move. She has also published stories and articles in the Medical Post, the Toronto Star, the Montreal Gazette, the Geneva Times and the Tico Times (Costa Rica). Like the main characters in her novels, Caroline is a physician and currently works in Montreal.

Deux Voiliers Publishing

Organized as a writers-plus collective, Deux Voiliers Publishing is a new generation publisher. We focus on high quality works of fiction by emerging Canadian writers. The art of creating new works of fiction is our driving force. We are proud to have published Palawan Story by Caroline Vu.

Other Works of Fiction published by Deux Voiliers Publishing

Soldier, Lily, Peace and Pearls by Con Cú (Literary Fiction 2012)

Kirk's Landing by Mike Young (Crime/Adventure 2014)

Sumer Lovin' by Nicole Chardenet (Humour/Fantasy 2013)

Last of the Ninth by Stephen Lorne Bennett (Historical Fiction 2012)

Marching to Byzantium by Brendan Ray (Historical Fiction 2012)

Tales of Other Worlds by Chris Turner (Fantasy/Science Ficiton 2012)

Romulus by Fernand Hibbert and translated by Matthew Robertshaw (Historical Fiction/English Translation 2014)

Bidong by Paul Duong (Literary Fiction 2012)

Zaidie and Ferdele by Carol Katz (Illustrated Children's Fiction 2012)

Cycling to Asylum by Su J. Sokol (Interstitial Fiction 2014)

Please visit our website for ordering information.
www.deuxvoilierspublishing.com

29894940R00140